76 51425 KT-452-908

The Bride of Alderburn

Katharine Beaton believes herself alone in the world—her father unknown, her mother dead. A chance meeting leads to the offer of a temporary refuge in the Scottish highlands, which the friendless girl accepts. At Allt-nam-Fearna she experiences that strange sense of familiarity, almost of 'coming home', yet while some of the family make her welcome, others seem to resent her presence, and always there is the feeling that they know more about her than she does herself.

An old friend of Katharine's mother had laid out her future with the Tarot cards, and the symbols of the Lightning Struck Tower, and of danger associated with crossing the ocean, obsess her. So, too, do the legends associated with the MacRaith family: the forlorn young bride who could not face her future, the girl who vanished with her lover, the deadly rivalry of two brothers. Gradually Katharine becomes aware that her past and her future are irrevocably entangled with Allt-nam-Fearna: aware also that her dilemmas cannot be resolved until she has ventured across the Border between past and present.

The influences of the everyday world and that ghostly other-world of psychic manifestations and dimly understood warnings, blend together in this haunting novel of an earlier generation, by the author of *The Dark Path*.

Also by Marguerite Neilson
MY ONLY LOVE, MY ONLY HATE
THE DARK PATH

The Bride of Alderburn

MARGUERITE NEILSON

ALLAN WINGATE

LONDON

EDINBURGH
LIBRARIES

First published in Great Britain
by Allan Wingate (Publishers) Ltd
14 Gloucester Road, London SW7
in 1976
A Howard & Wyndham Company

Copyright © Marguerite Neilson 1976

For Jean,
Who first pointed me in the right direction
With my love and gratitude.

SBN 85523 075 4

Set in Linotype Baskerville by
Richard Clay (The Chaucer Press) Ltd, Bungay, Suffolk,
and printed in Great Britain by
Fletcher & Son Ltd, Norwich

CHAPTER ONE

ONLY WHEN the train, with agonising slowness, drifted past the familiar name board, past the tiny booking hall, waiting room, and luggage office, and when the last lamp was no more than a far pinpoint in the darkness, did I allow myself to relax and sink back into the corner of the carriage, thankfully free from any other passenger. There had been sharp surges of apprehension as I watched the barrier, and a moment of panic when the face of the ticket collector-cum-porter had swum up to the window like some enquiring fish. But he had given me no more than a cursory glance as he tried the door for security before stepping back to wave the train on its way. It picked up speed, and carried me through the darkness to the blessed anonymity and safety of London, where no one would notice the girl in the shapeless hat and drab cloak. Though I later realised that my disguise, hastily snatched from the rack in the corridor outside the Servants' Hall, would not have deceived anyone observant enough to scrutinise my shoes, or the fine gaberdine of my skirt, even though it was damp and mud-stained from that terrifying journey across the fields to the station. But even if Mugford, the ticket clerk, had recognised me, he would surely see no reason to report as much to the Hall. In any case, this was the last train to London—I had checked it. Tonight no one could follow me, and by morning I could be submerged in the human tide of the great city.

For the time being, then, I was safe from pursuit; and

5

because I was deadly weary from grief and anxiety and near despair, I slept.

'Come along, Miss.' A cheerful cockney voice broke into my confused dreams. 'Don't go no further, we don't. 'Ave ter walk the rest, you will.'

I opened my eyes, and gradually realised where I was. I thanked the man, and stumbled to my feet, out on to the platform into the bleakness of London in the early dawn. I was stiff, cold and hungry, and had I been making for any place but Aunt Zen's, I would have hesitated to knock on the door at such an unearthly hour. But Aunt Zen's house was an ever-open sanctuary, and I hurried towards it like a hunted runaway. And that was, in effect, exactly what I was.

Aunt Zen didn't waste time on questions. She bundled me into bed with a hotwater-bottle, and before I could slide into waiting oblivion, made me drink hot milk with a more than generous fortification of whisky. To ward off a cold, she informed me when I protested, and she stood over me while I drank it.

'What am I going to do, Aunt Zen? Please tell me,' I pleaded. 'I can't go back there. *I can't*. And as for marrying that—that——' I choked at the remembered horror.

'No one's going to make you, dearie. Not while I'm alive.' Aunt Zen's plump, florid face was set and determined. Her eyes were still puffy from weeping, and as tears brimmed over, she dabbed them away impatiently.

'What am I thinking of?' she said, almost to herself. 'It's not me that should be crying.' She leaned across the table and refilled my teacup. Then, leaning back in her chair, she sighed, shaking her head, as if still unable to credit the news I had brought.

'I still can't believe it,' she whispered. 'Your poor dear

6

mother—so full of life, and so beautiful. It seems wicked that she should be taken.'

'I can't believe it, either,' I said. 'I'm waiting to wake up from a bad dream, and then I'll hear her singing, as she always did when she was learning a part, and I shall be playing the accompaniment for her, and——' Misery flooded over me again, and I had to fight for composure.

'Have a good cry, dearie,' Aunt Zen urged. 'Do you good, it will.'

I shook my head. 'I've cried all I can,' I said. 'I've got to get used to it, and to think about it without dissolving into tears every time anyone mentions her. I've got to get used to living without her. Oh, God! If only I'd gone with her that day. They wanted me to, but sailing boats always make me dreadfully sick, so they left me behind. And she never came back. A freak storm, they said. It drove them on to the rocks and splintered the boat like matchwood. They *did* try to save her, Aunt Zen. I really do believe that. But it was hopeless.' I stared at her through the tears I couldn't hold any longer. 'She's gone. *Really* gone. They never found her. She's down in that grey darkness, all alone. If I'd gone with her, at least we'd have been together.'

'You weren't meant to go, dearie. There's a time for all of us, and yours isn't yet.' Aunt Zen spoke with a curious authority, and that dignity which I knew so well, which could hold an audience in thrall, seemed to clothe her like a royal garment, so that one was no longer aware that she was a rather fat, ageing woman with crimped hair dyed an incredible red, with pinchbeck hoops in her ears, and fake diamonds on her plump fingers.

'Come to my room,' she said. 'We'll see what the cards tell us.'

I followed her upstairs, to the little closed-in room,

7

smelling faintly of incense and hung with black velvet on which were embossed strange signs in vivid colours. A fire burned in the small barred grate, and before she sat down Aunt Zen took à piece of charcoal from a box on the mantelpiece and set it in a shallow bowl of sand. She lit a taper in the flame of the fire, and held it to the charcoal till it smouldered and glowed red. From a smaller bowl on the mantelpiece she took some opaque, yellowish grains and dropped them on the charcoal. As they melted, a fine spiral of smoke rose and dispersed in a fragrant drift, pungent, evocative.

I sat quietly, and watched as she laid out the cards. I had shuffled and cut them, and now she dealt out my fate. And though I had seen her do it a hundred times, both in this room and on the stage, where 'Madame Zenobia the World-Famous Seeress' had dazzled the gullible and sceptic alike, I was yet again caught in the spell. I knew that in spite of the near-trickery of the stage act, she did have this odd power—not to be called on when she willed, for the amusement of the multitude, though even in that sphere there had been uncanny flashes which had evoked a startled reception from the querent.

'Strange. Strange country, strange people, and a castle.' She pointed. 'The Lightning Struck Tower. Doesn't always mean a building, in the literal sense, though that's there. I can see it—not in the cards, but here.' She raised her fingers to her temples. 'A castle. Old, grey, almost a ruin, but the stones soaked with all that has gone before. You'll live there.' Aunt Zen raised her head, and stared at me. 'Live there, and maybe die there.' She continued to stare at me, almost as if she were puzzled. 'Yes, you'll die there,' she repeated. 'But not in this life. Some other time.' She shook her head. 'It's not clear. It's you, and yet it isn't you. But there was death. And you will take the same

8

path.' Aunt Zen shrugged her plump shoulders. 'They don't always tell you clearly. But there are people around you—people you haven't met yet. But they are *your* people. Wherever it is, you belong there.'

You belong there ... they are your people ... Aunt Zen voiced the dearest wish of my heart. This was something I *must* know, and I stifled my rising impatience and the desire to interrupt her. For I sensed that there was more which she must tell me—for my own good. For my safety, even.

'The same path,' she repeated. 'But *you* will return. Only you must take careful note of the way back. Remember that, always.' She looked up, and again stared at me intently. 'But I shall be there, to guard you, and to guide you back.'

'Back to what, Aunt Zen? Where am I going?'

'A long way, dearie. A long way in distance, and in time. It's a journey you have to make, but there will be danger—danger over the water. Not just a river, or even the sea, but the great waters of the ocean.'

'But, Aunt Zen,' I objected. 'Where on earth do I start? I have no people, have I? No family. At least, not as far as I know. So how do I start looking for them? Because until I know who they are, and where they live, I can't go there, can I?'

She pointed to the spread of cards. 'It's all there,' she said. 'The people, the place, the danger. But you've got to be patient. No use scurrying round looking for things. You must wait, but it will come, you'll see.' Again she spoke with complete authority.

I knew she was right. But it would be hard, because by nature I was not patient, and I wanted to know—now. I felt I could not just sit, composed and expectant, until my future flowed up to me. It was all so frustrating and puzzling, and not a little frightening.

'Tell me,' I said, pointing to the cards. 'Who are they, these people? Let me see whether I can interpret the cards.' To my surprise, Aunt Zen did not demur, but turned the lightweight card table so that the spread faced me.

I gazed down at the cards, with their strange, symbolic pictures, and an indescribable feeling seemed to take hold of me, as if a current flowed through me from Aunt Zen's hand resting lightly on my shoulder.

Half scared, I turned my head and looked up at her.

'Don't be frightened, dearie,' she said. 'Just look at the cards, and let your own intuition tell you what their message is—perhaps something different from mine.' She shrugged. 'Who knows?' She moved away towards the mantelpiece, and dropped another piece of the resin crystal on the still glowing charcoal. And now, after many years, I never catch the aromatic drift of incense without reviving the imprint of that day.

It was as if Aunt Zen's touch had passed on to me some of her power, or even that it had stirred some latent power of my own, so that my inner senses all seemed sharpened into awareness. I looked intently at the spread. I did not know the traditional meaning of each individual card, but it was as if a picture, superimposed, built up. I was there, yet I was not there. Afterwards, I was to understand this awareness of being present in some other place, though I neither slept nor dreamed.

Now I could make out people. There were five of them —three men and two women, and I knew that they were all linked together by birth, and that between them and me a link also existed. These were—and for some strange reason an old song came to me—'My Ain Folk'. I seemed to hear again the nostalgic air which my mother had sung to me, so long ago. I knew, too, that the men represented three generations. A young man, about my own age; an older man, yet not so old that he was my senior by so many years; and a patriarchal figure, bearded, impressive, and with an overriding authority to which the others deferred.

Of the women, one could have been my own age, and the other, of my mother's generation.

The whole picture was clear, yet obscured in places as by drifting mist. I could not make out the features of any of the figures, or their style of dress, though at the same time I received no impression of the fashions of another era, and the men, I thought, were kilted.

The setting had an unfamiliar kind of ruggedness. Wall and ceiling seemed to merge in one great arc of rough stonework. Skin rugs were scattered on the floor, and the furniture had none of the spindly, fretted character of the present day.

One thing stood out with amazing clearness. Over the wide hearth, where huge logs made a glowing cavern, crossed swords were surmounted by a great round shield of hide, darkened by time, slashed but never pierced by attacking blades, the brazen studs dinted by blows while yet withstanding the worst an enemy could do.

Then it was all gone. The smoke from the charcoal died down, and Aunt Zen was gathering up the cards.

'You saw it, too?' I whispered.

'Yes, dearie. That is where you will go. Those are the people you will live amongst.'

Together we went downstairs, and the everyday world flowed back. We talked, Aunt Zen and I, when we were alone, about the days when I was a child, and she told me all she knew of my mother.

'Such a lovely girl, she was. Slim as a willow, hair like

silk, and so fair that it was almost silver, and of course that voice. Pure gold it was, and she sang her way into the hearts of every audience she faced.' Aunt Zen sighed. 'Those *were* the days,' she said. 'I was at my best then, and we shared top billing, your mother and me.'

'But who *was* she, Aunt Zen?' Reluctantly I broke in, because her reminiscences always fascinated me. But I had to dig deeper. The world of the theatre was almost a closed one to me. I had never been permitted to snatch more than a brief glimpse from behind the curtains of a box, after which I was hustled home and, when I was old enough, back to school and the cloistered existence which had now come to such an abrupt and terrifying end, throwing me out into an unfamiliar world, alone and defenceless like a crab without a shell.

'Ah, that's something I can't tell you, dearie, because I don't know. I met her when I was touring up North. We had to share a dressing-room. Not that I usually shared, mind you, because I was a top attraction then, and had the star's dressing-room, which was bigger, so that's why I was asked if I'd mind sharing with this young singer, because one of the other dressing-rooms was being painted. That was a lucky meeting—fated, I think it must have been. Somehow I felt, even before I saw her, that her life and mine would be linked, and when she stood there, with you in her arms—eighteen months old, you were—well, I just *knew*. Katherine Beaton, she was billed as, and I believe that was her own name, though she never said, and I never asked her.'

'Aunt Zen,' I said slowly, 'you've got—well, *powers*. I mean, you *know* things, without being told. Can't you—I mean, didn't you ever read the cards for her, or anything?'

'Yes, I read the cards for her, more than once. And it was true, what I told her. But it doesn't work like that—not

12

the way *you* want it. I can't *use* it. It isn't right. It's only meant to help and guide, not to find out things before you're meant to know them. I know what you want to know—you want to find out who your dad was, and what his people, and your mother's people, were like, and where you really belong.'

'Yes, oh, yes, Aunt Zen,' I broke in eagerly. 'Help me, please. Tell me——'

'I can't, dearie,' she repeated. 'But when it's right for you to know, you'll be shown. All I can do is to pass on what I see. I saw that your mother would become a great star, and that men would cluster to her like bees on a flower. But what she'd left behind her—well, she'd closed the door on that, and it wasn't for me to open it. I knew that she was a widow, and that she was still grieving desperately, and I did what I could to comfort her.' She leaned over and took my hand. We were sitting in the conservatory, and through the open door the breeze was warm, and I could see daffodils nodding their promise that winter had gone. 'I gave her hope,' Aunt Zen said. 'Hope that she would see him again, and that they would be together. So don't grieve that you didn't go with her, my love, because she's not alone now.'

'I wonder who she really was,' I said, 'and who my father was.'

'He was a gentleman, dearie, just as your mother was a lady. That stood out a mile, same as it does with you.'

'But that still tells me nothing,' I exclaimed. 'I've been through her papers, and they were few enough. There's nothing, absolutely nothing. At the very least I'd have expected to find her marriage certificate and my birth certificate, but even those are missing—perhaps they were in that little leather case she always had in her bag. But it was as if she wanted to be nobody except who she was now, if you see what I mean.'

'I do see,' Aunt Zen answered. 'And that's how it always was. She cut herself off completely from the past, and at first, you know, she was afraid of something. I don't quite know what, but once, not long after we met, she had pneumonia—only slight, and she soon got over it. But she was a bit rambling, and all she wanted was that I should take care of you and not let *them*—whoever they were—take you away from her. You were her whole world, and whatever she did, she did for you, to make your future safe.'

'Then why, why, *why* did she leave me in that man's charge?'

It had come to the surface at last. The horror I had been pushing down for the last days, ever since that flight across the fields and the furtive journey through the night to the sanctuary of Aunt Zen's house.

She listened without comment while I stumbled through the tale which still made me sick with revulsion. A revulsion which was greater because it was tinged with guilt. When my mother had arrived back from a tour of the Continent, bringing with her a new husband almost ten years her junior, the gap of years between Gerald Foliott and myself was not wide enough to prevent the romantic longings of a fifteen-year-old leaping to disturbing life. Now, I prayed fervently that my mother had never suspected my feelings. Feelings which had changed to disgust when, after her death, Gerald had announced that he was fully aware of my infatuation for him, and that there was now nothing to prevent our marrying.

'But that's obscene!' I had exclaimed. 'You loved my mother. She's dead, and you can offer this monstrous insult to me, of all people.'

'Yes, I loved your mother,' he said. 'Deeply and devotedly. Perhaps that's why I want you—so like her, except

14

that your hair is bronze where hers was silver.' Before I could move out of reach he had swiftly pulled the tortoise-shell pins from my hair, so that it cascaded down my back. I jerked away as he picked up a strand and held it in his hands. 'I want you,' he repeated, 'and I mean to have you.'

And his arms were round me, pinioning me so that I was helpless while his mouth found mine. Something inspired me not to struggle, but to let myself go so limp that I was a dead weight and he could no longer hold me. I scrambled to my feet and backed away from him.

'Don't touch me! Don't ever touch me. If you do, I'll kill you.'

'I believe you would.' His smile mocked. 'Don't worry, my dear. I'm not going to play Sir Jasper. Force doesn't appeal to me, and I don't want an unwilling bride. But you *will* come to me, and of your own accord.' His confidence frightened me, finding as it did an echo in my own response to his kisses. My disgust was less for Gerald than for myself, at the upsurge of emotion for which I was totally unprepared. In that moment I knew I had to get away.

'Katharine, I'm sorry, truly I am.' Perhaps he was sincere, but I clung to my repugnance.

'Maybe you are,' I said. 'Maybe you forgot yourself—I think that is the accepted phrase. Give me my hairpins, please.'

Silently he handed them to me, and I twisted my hair inexpertly, since it was so recently 'put up' after my school days. I jabbed the hairpins in almost viciously, and hoped my hair would stay securely fixed.

'Even if I wanted to marry you,' I said, 'you must see that it's quite impossible. It's not even legal.'

Gerald had not answered me, and into my mind suspicion crept like a dark serpent.

15

'It *is* impossible, isn't it?' I insisted, silently beseeching contradiction of the unvoiced, unacceptable misgiving.

'No, my dear. It's not impossible.' He had taken my hand. 'No, don't shy away, Katharine. I won't repeat the performance, but I would like to explain.'

I shook off his hand. 'What is there to explain?' I demanded. 'You're trying to tell me that my mother was a loose woman—your mistress, not your wife. And now you want me to take her place. Well, I won't. You can afford to go and buy yourself another *whore*. And I will never forgive you for what you have done. Not to me, but to her.'

'Sit down, Katharine, and listen.' I had turned to go, but Gerald caught me by the arm and half threw me into a chair. 'By God, you *shall* listen to me, you little vixen. I told you I loved your mother, truly, deeply, and faithfully. And she loved me. We had four wonderful years together.'

'Then why didn't you do her the honour of making her your wife?' My voice had been cold, and I knew from his face that the words had cut like steel.

'Because until six months ago, I *had* a wife. A sick, helpless wife who had lain for five years in a hospital bed, unable to move even her head. Don't condemn me, Katharine. Your mother didn't. She took me, and loved me, and healed me, when I was at the end of my tether. And I was only human. I loved her in return, even though I still loved that poor creature. I had done all I could for her. I had nursed her myself until the doctors took her away from me, and for the few terrible years which remained, she wanted for nothing, because there was nothing she wanted, except the one thing denied her—a return to health.' His voice had dropped to a whisper, and because I knew what loss was, I could have wept. Gerald's face

16

was set, haggard, as he went on.

'They told me from the beginning that there was nothing anyone on earth could do, except ease her days and nights. So when she died, she went gladly, and no one could wish her back.'

'Least of all you.'

'By God, Katharine, you're hard.'

I have to be, because you move me to pity, and pity's akin to love, and to allow myself to love you, I would have to live with an unendurable self-hate.

'Six months, you said? Ample time in which to get a Special Licence, I should have thought.'

He flushed angrily. 'You may recall,' he said quietly, 'that your mother was on tour abroad until just before Christmas. And you may like to know that we had planned to marry at Easter.'

I stood up. 'Well, I don't propose to be party to a switch of brides. And now, if you will excuse me, I will go to my room. This has been a most upsetting and distasteful scene.'

'One more point, Katharine. I am not putting this as a threat. I'm merely acquainting you of a fact. Until you are twenty-one, I am your legal guardian.'

'Prove it,' I flashed. He shrugged. 'Easily. It is expressly stated in your mother's will.'

The mention of my mother brought an upsurge of emotion that threatened to destroy my composure, and I took refuge in defiance.

'Guardian you may be,' I retorted. 'But short of locking me up with bread and water, I think you'll find that you have no real control over my life.'

'So you see, Aunt Zen, I couldn't stay there, could I?'

Her gaze was shrewd. 'And you had to run away, dearie.

17

From him, or from yourself?'

I flushed. 'From myself, I suppose, if I'm honest,' I answered in a low voice. 'But now I wonder if he's regretting being such a gentleman, and he'll try to find me and take me back. I didn't tell you this, but yesterday, when I took Dog Tray for his walk in the Fields, I'm sure someone followed me.'

'Aren't you going in for a bit of melodrama, dearie?' Aunt Zen's commonsense brought me back to earth. 'After all, what can he do? Can't drag you off by the hair. He can't even stop your allowance, because your mother's trustees wouldn't have any hanky-panky like that.' Again she patted my hand comfortingly. 'No, dearie. You stay here as long as you like, and it'll come right, you'll see.'

'I suppose you're right,' I said. 'But I could go to Somerset House, couldn't I, and get my birth certificate. That might help.'

'It might, and it might not.' Aunt Zen was cryptic. 'Still, a day's shopping wouldn't come amiss, seeing that you came tearing up here without so much as a toothbrush.'

So it was, at a casual word from Aunt Zen, that I set out on the journey which was to change my life. Afterwards I wondered whether there is, in fact, anything at all in life which can truly be labelled casual, since in the analysis every move we make seems to lead us to an inevitable destiny.

I finished my shopping and gave instructions for the delivery of my purchases, then walked by way of the Strand to Somerset House.

An hour—two hours—later, for I'd lost all sense of time, I stood again on the crowded pavement. In the gathering dusk people hurried by me, and overhead a million starlings swooped and wheeled. The people all knew who they were, and where they were going. The starlings were all tiny furies, deriding me.

I alone, in all London, was—*nobody*.

Or so it seemed to me. For I could not trace my mother's marriage, and worse, I could not find any record of my birth having been registered. According to the records, I did not exist.

The days which followed dragged by in a grey mist of despair. I wonder that Aunt Zen did not lose patience with the apathetic creature who wandered from room to room, from house to garden, and who allowed herself to be drawn, unseeing, along the paths of the Fields by the eager, friendly little dog who required daily walks. And on one of these walks I tripped, literally, into the next chapter of my life.

Since my failure to trace my own identity, part of the stress with which I had to contend had been the strange dreams which haunted me. The actual components, though juggled about in each successive dream, were always the same. A rugged, bleak castle exterior. That, I told myself, could be accounted for by the dream recollection of Aunt Zen's reading of the cards, and the half-vision I had had. But that did not explain the clear impression of the long gallery, lined with portraits and show cases, and having a polished wooden floor of such a distinctive pattern; and the woman, tall, elegant, not unfriendly. There was the feeling that she was one of the group I had seen in that vision.

I had slept so badly that I woke with a headache, and it did not need much prompting from Aunt Zen for me to go in search of the keen, bracing air which always seemed to blow across the Fields—straight from the North Pole, or so it felt on the colder days. So with Tray pulling eagerly at his lead, I walked between banks of shrubs along a path which stretched for some distance, and at a point where the path was joined by another fork, a man stood. Almost before he turned his head, I knew he was the man who, I was certain, had followed me on more than one of these dog-walking expeditions. Unreasoning panic surged through me. Though there was nothing tangible to confirm my suspicion—after all, he could have been, like myself, a regular dog-walker—I swung round sharply, meaning to retrace my steps. Then Tray, his doggy mind apparently interpreting this as some new game, barked and dashed right across my path, so that as I made to take a step, my foot caught in his lead, and I fell headlong. Bruised and winded, I lay helpless, until hurrying footsteps galvanised me into action. A hand under my elbow helped and at the same time restrained me, and still dazed from the fall, I allowed myself to be guided to one of the wooden seats which stood at intervals along the path.

'Are you all right, Miss Beaton—it *is* Miss Beaton, isn't it? I've seen you several times, and very much wanted to speak to you.'

'How do you know my name?' I stared up at the man. I was still breathless, and very conscious that I must look muddy and dishevelled. One of my gloves had split, and gravel had scored my palm. Tray's lead, looped round my wrist, restrained him, but he was tugging and barking.

'Tray, *down*. Be quiet,' I commanded. I looked at the man. He was ordinary enough, quietly dressed, youngish, and by no means a menacing type. But he had obviously taken the trouble to find out who I was, and I could think of only one person who could instigate such an enquiry.

'I don't know who you are, and I don't want to know you,' I exclaimed vehemently. 'Please leave me alone.'

'But Miss Beaton—you *are* Miss Beaton, aren't you? At

20

least let me see you home—you've had a nasty fall. Besides, I've information for you——'

'I don't want to hear it,' I interrupted. 'Go back to your employer and tell him I want nothing further to do with him.'

'But Miss Beàton,' he protested. 'You're mistaken——'

I stood up, brushing the dust and twigs from my skirt.

'Go away,' I repeated. 'Go away before I call a policeman and give you in charge for pestering me.'

'Is this man annoying you, my dear?' I turned to look at the speaker, whose approach I had not heard. Through a whirling mist I seemed to see the woman of my dreams. Then blackness came down on me.

The first thing I heard, even before I opened my eyes, was Tray's whining, as if he were anxious for my safety. I heard the same voice, gentle and concerned.

'My dear, that fall must have shaken you badly. Stay still awhile, then I'll call a cab for you—you can't walk home in this state.'

'You're very kind,' I managed to whisper. 'That man—has he gone?'

'I sent him about his business,' she reassured me. 'Now, tell me where you live, and I'll help you to the park gate.'

'Oh, please,' I protested. 'I'm quite all right, really. And I couldn't put you to so much trouble.'

'But it isn't a trouble, my dear. Now do as I say,' she insisted gently, and I had the odd feeling I was being bidden by someone to whose authority I was subject. Docilely I allowed her to support me as far as the road, where she hailed a cruising taxi-cab.

'What is your address, my dear?' I told her, and she repeated it to the driver, at the same time handing him sufficient coins to cover the fare and, I suspected, a generous tip. When I protested, she smiled.

'We shall meet again,' she said.

It was with no surprise that I answered the door, a few days later, and again faced the woman who had stepped from my dreams into reality. It seemed the most natural thing in the world to invite her in, settle her in Aunt Zen's drawing-room, and talk with her over afternoon tea, as if I had known her for years. After that, we met regularly in the Fields on fine days. Soon, it seemed, she knew all about me, though I learned little enough about her beyond the fact that her name was MacRaith, Agnes MacRaith, and that she was staying in London on an indefinite visit. She wore a wedding ring, but whether or not her husband lived, she never said, and probing would have seemed an impertinence on my part. I judged her age to be about fifty, though she retained the figure and movements of a much younger woman. She was always elegantly and fashionably dressed, though without any ostentation. In conversation she was cultured, well read—and completely unrevealing. Her name hinted at connections north of the Border, though, of course, a married woman's surname need not be indicative of her origins.

I imagined that she took some pleasure in my company, as I did in hers, and I was dismayed when she announced that she was leaving London.

'I shall miss you,' I said. 'You've been so kind, and your friendship has helped me so much.'

'That pleases me greatly,' she said. 'Tell me, Katharine, what plans have you made for the summer?'

'None, really,' I answered. 'I'm living in a kind of limbo, and it's difficult to make plans. I know that I can stay with Aunt Zen for as long as I need a home. But I live from day to day, and until I settle on a career I'm drifting, with no set purpose.' I had told her about my fruitless search for my family, and my own identity. 'I feel as if my life will never have any sort of direction,' I went on. 'Can you advise me?' I turned to her impulsively.

'What about your mother's lawyers, and your trustees?' she asked. 'Have you consulted them?'

I shrugged. 'In the essentials, they know as little as I do,' I said. 'So far as they are concerned, my mother's life began when she consulted them in the matter of a trust fund to take care of my education, and to provide me with a small income in the event of her death. But of course, that was something she didn't really take seriously—I would always have a secure home with her—until I married.'

'Which, since you are such an enchantingly pretty girl, is inevitable.' I blushed at the compliment, and she went on, 'I don't wish to appear unduly inquisitive, but is there any likelihood of your marriage in the foreseeable future?'

'No. None whatever. I do not wish to marry.'

She did not comment on my vehemence, but merely continued with a question.

'What kind of career were you considering?'

'I had thought of nursing,' I replied. 'I've taken no positive steps yet, and I know it's a hard life, but that wouldn't put me off.'

'It's a very noble calling, and I don't think you're the kind of girl to have romantic illusions, nor would you shun hard work. But I wonder, before you finally decide your future, would you like to come with me when I return to Scotland? It's so lovely at this time of year, and I think a holiday and a change of scene would benefit you.'

'You're very kind,' I said.

'But of course,' she went on, 'you must consider the matter before you make up your mind, and talk it over with your guardian.' She meant Aunt Zen, and here I felt terribly guilty because I had been less than frank with her, and had not contradicted her when she had assumed that it was Aunt Zen who was my guardian. Gerald I had not mentioned at all, and the opportunity to leave London for a destination so far away and so unlikely, appealed strongly to me.

'Yes, I would like to discuss it with Aunt Zen,' I said. 'Though I imagine she won't raise any objection.'

That evening, in the little velvet-lined room, Aunt Zen laid out the cards for the second time. For some reason of her own she had never met Mrs MacRaith, though I had asked her often enough to join us over the tea table.

Now she explained. 'I had to keep the scene clear,' she said. 'I had to be certain in my own mind that this was the right path for you, my love, and it is. I'm sure of that now.'

Again she lit the charcoal, and burned the aromatic crystals, and again she dealt out my fate.

'There it is—the Tower,' she pointed. 'And the people you saw, they're here, and I can see them more clearly now.' She drew me to her side, and pointed, and the card which I knew as the Empress seemed, in some strange way, to be a portrait of Mrs MacRaith. But hers was the only face which was clear. The others were still in the mists of the future.

CHAPTER TWO

I was far too excited to sleep. The whirl of shopping and preparation that had filled my days after my final acceptance of Mrs MacRaith's invitation had left me like a taut spring, and now as I lay in the comfortable sleeper, swiftly carried through the night, the whole scene played before my eyes like a *camera obscura* with its ever-changing colours and people. Since I knew so little of what I might expect, I had willingly accepted Mrs MacRaith's guidance in the purchase of my new wardrobe. The time had come when I might properly graduate from the rather juvenile styles proper to a young girl, and tactfully steered by her, I had selected an extensive range of clothes suitable for whatever occasion might arise. And I thought with joyful anticipation of the pleasure of wearing such gowns.

Some of the items suggested had surprised me a little, and I must have betrayed myself, since she commented with some amusement.

'It's not all snow and Scotch mist, you know,' she laughed, as the head of the department paraded dinner and evening gowns for my choice. I had spent freely, but after all it was the first time I had ever had control over my own finances. I had expected some opposition from my trustees, particularly in the matter of the necessary advance, but no objections had been raised and here I was, by now many miles from London, heading for an unknown destination (though I did have an address to leave with Aunt Zen, but it might have been anywhere at all, as I had no idea where it really was).

For the first time, with opportunity to relax and consider, I wondered just how wise I was in entrusting myself to this unknown woman, travelling to this unknown place, to an unknown destiny. Then my confidence in Aunt Zen reasserted itself, and I knew that outrageous as it might seem, this *was* my destiny—that in some way I could not understand I was being guided along the right path.

Gradually the motion of the train and the rhythm of the wheels lulled me to a doze. Then, suddenly, I was wide awake, my heart beating with the shock of being sharply roused. Holding my breath, I listened, waiting for a repetition of the sound which had awakened me. But apart from the train noises to which I had become accustomed, there was nothing, and I told myself that it must have been the extra clatter of the train passing over points. The beating of my heart slowed gradually, and I settled myself to sleep again, when I heard the tapping, as if fingernails drummed on the door of the compartment.

'Who is it?' I called, and waited. There was no reply, only the faint tapping, repeated with more urgency. 'Is anyone there? Who is it?' I repeated. 'And what do you want?' Again silence. Then it occurred to me that Mrs MacRaith might be unwell and wanting me, and I struggled into my dressing-gown. Apprehensively I unlatched the door, opened it and peered down the corridor. Taking a few steps, I listened at the door of Mrs MacRaith's compartment, but there was no sound, and I realised that if she really had been unwell she would not only have repeated her summons, but would have rung for the attendant.

I turned to go back to my own compartment, and as the train lurched round a bend, I was thrown against the panelling and the motion sent my hand tapping on the woodwork. So that was the solution—someone passing down the corridor, unwittingly knocking as they were thrown slightly off balance.

I climbed back into the bunk, but sleep had fled, so I switched on the light and reached for a magazine. I also looked at my watch. It was about half-past two. I tried to read, but the printed words made no impression, and I became aware of a strange feeling, almost of emotion, as if I came nearer with every mile to a welcome. As if arms stretched out with love. As if I were coming home. And again in my mind I heard the sentimental old song. Was I at last going to find 'my ain folk'? Lulled with the glow of the thought, I slept.

Then the knocking came again. Decisively, insistently, and with it an urgent whisper: 'Katharine', and once more I was jerked into wakefulness, startled and choked with the beating of my heart.

'Yes, I'm coming,' I called, and reproached myself for having ignored the earlier summons. I pulled on my dressing-gown and flung open the door, to see the figure of a woman moving away from me down the corridor. In the dim light it could have been Mrs MacRaith, and I hurried to help her, imagining she must be really unwell. But as I moved towards her, the corridor seemed to stretch out like an endless, narrowing tunnel, leading into darkness from which wreaths of mist billowed and drifted. The figure of the woman became a part of the mist, but before her form completely merged into the greyness, she turned and smiled at me, and I seemed to see a face that was my own, yet not my own.

Sick and trembling, I leaned against the panelling, and stumbled like an old woman back to the compartment, to sit on the bed, shivering as if with an ague. For a moment I considered asking Mrs MacRaith if I might spend the rest of the night in her compartment, but dismissed the idea of disturbing her. And after all, what could she do? She could not do battle with the figments of my own imagination, for that was the explanation. I must be firm with myself, and not allow these baseless imaginings to sap my nerve. I called Aunt Zen to mind—dear Aunt Zen, who had loved me and cared for me and who had sent me on this journey into the unknown. Aunt Zen would never have allowed me to go in the first place had there been danger, either physical or emotional. The only real danger, I recalled, lay across the great ocean, whither I had no intention of voyaging.

So, gradually, I calmed myself, and at last slept again. When I woke, it was to the light of early dawn. I pulled up the blind and stared at the unfamiliar landscape, blurred and colourless. Trees, small buildings, glimpses of water, cattle, waking birds, glided by, and once a face came to the window and was gone—some early traveller standing on the platform of a wayside halt? Or my own face reflected in the window? Resolutely I dropped the blind, and made my morning toilet, so that when the train wound its slow way through the outskirts of the city to the terminus, I was ready to answer Mrs MacRaith's summons.

'The baggage is all taken care of, my dear. We will have breakfast at the Terminus Hotel, then we take the local train, and I promise you some of the loveliest scenery in Scotland.'

It was obvious by the respectful attention which she received at the hotel that Mrs MacRaith was a valued client, and by virtue of this very service, conversation over breakfast was confined to trivia. So by the time we were settled in the train which was to take us on the next stage of the journey, I had dismissed the events of the night as being no more than 'daggers of the mind' conjured up by fatigue and the excitement and stresses of the last few days. I was glad that I had not voiced my fears. I did not want Mrs MacRaith to think she had a guest subject to neurotic spells and liable to prove an embarrassment or even a nuisance. But I had counted without her sharp eyes and acute awareness, for over breakfast she had remarked on my obvious pallor.

'Did you have a disturbed night, child?'

'Well, yes.' I flushed. 'But then, I've never made a night journey like that, so it was hardly surprising that I did not sleep as soundly as I do at home.'

She accepted the excuse, and laughed. 'You shall have an early night tonight, my dear. You'll soon become a seasoned traveller, when you've made the journey a few more times.' She leaned across and patted my hand. 'This won't be your first and only visit to Scotland, you know. You'll return many times,' she told me confidently. And I had the feeling that she was right. Here was a place I would love as long as life was in me, and wherever I travelled, here was where my heart would return.

There was one other odd little incident over breakfast —in fact, a sort of double-barrelled incident.

At my own request, I had been served with a lightly boiled egg, which I had eaten, and then, from force of habit so strong that it overrode manners, I had driven my spoon through the empty shell. I looked up, to see Mrs MacRaith smiling indulgently.

'Now tell me, child, why did you do that?'

'Oh, dear, what a baby you must think me,' I laughed ruefully. 'To tell you the truth I don't really know why I do it—a left-over from childhood, I suppose. I mean, I've always done it, as long as I can remember, and I do it quite without thinking. My mother always did the same thing—don't ask me why. Something about saving a

29

sailor's life, though I can't honestly imagine what that has got to do with it.'

'Then you don't know the legend?'

'What legend? No, I don't. Please tell me.'

'Witches use empty egg-shells for boats. They sail the waves, and call up storms so that the ships break and sink and the sailors are all drowned.'

In spite of myself, I shivered. Coming so close upon the strange events of the night, the picture of the bobbing egg-shells, each carrying its weird, malevolent passenger, had an uncanny pertinence. I recognised my amused riposte for what it was—whistling in the dark.

'But surely people don't believe that sort of thing *now*. I mean, this *is* the twentieth century,' I protested. 'I thought those old superstitions died when they stopped burning witches.' To my surprise, Mrs MacRaith did not share my amusement.

'Witches were hanged as recently as the eighteenth century,' she said. 'And in the Highlands many old legends are still given credence. You subscribed to one without even knowing why.'

'Force of habit, I suppose. I'm not really superstitious.'

'No?' Mrs MacRaith smiled. 'I wonder how many of us can say that with absolute truth. I think most people have a hidden, personal taboo.'

That would have been the time, I reflected later, to have told her of the strange night fantasy, but I allowed the moment to pass without further elaboration. She herself concluded the conversation with another comment.

'You're left-handed, Katharine.' It was a statement, not a query, and I could not deny it, though I sought mostly to conceal it. I nodded, silent.

'Was your mother left-handed?' she asked.

I shook my head. 'No. But I believe my father was—I

mean, I remember her saying, when I was little, that I must have inherited it from him. Of course, at school they tried to stop me, but one of the teachers was left-handed, and she used to stand up for me, and in the end they left me alone.'

'Very wise,' Mrs MacRaith said. 'In any case, you won't be the odd one out at Allt-nam-Fearna. My nephew Iain —you'll met him later—is left-handed, too, and believe me, that caused some heartburning; up here it's supposed to be unlucky. However, I'm glad you don't let it worry you.'

I laughed ruefully. 'Not much use worrying is it, when it's second nature!'

The next part of the journey was, as Mrs MacRaith had promised, incredibly beautiful, and I stared from side to side of the carriage, like a child dazzled by a first glimpse of an enchanted land. The initial sight of any new scene has its own peculiar impact, which must always differ in an unaccountable way from a subsequent viewing. It was my great good fortune to have this lovely panorama unrolled before my eyes in bright spring sunshine; the colour and the grandeur robbed me of speech, and the variety would have seemed unbelievable had it been recounted and not witnessed. The train wound in turn through wide, rolling valleys—straths, as I afterwards learned—carpeted with vivid green turf, then plunged into narrow glens with steep, tree-lined sides, to emerge on to moorland so desolate that the appearance of Macbeth's Weird Sisters would hardly have been out of place. The last stretch was perhaps the most beautiful, and certainly unlike any other train journey I had ever made. The line ran for miles along the side of a loch akin to the fjords of Norway. On the far side great bare mountains trailed their pine-bordered skirts in the deep, still waters which reflected their peaks outlined against the clear sky; the track on which we travelled clung with determination to precipitous slopes, now descending right to the edge of the loch and sometimes carried on viaducts across boulder-strewn gorges washed by hurtling waters fed by melting snows on the summits. One could almost touch the bare cliff from which the rock had been blasted to make way for the consequential little engine and its retinue; yet on the other side of the compartment a sheer precipice, covered with stunted, indomitable trees, dropped hundreds of feet to the dark waters which seemed to wait, and wait, and wait —until a land-slip should pour into their depths the sacrifice of these interlopers. I was fascinated and terrified, and enslaved.

Reluctantly I tore myself from the windows, and shared with Mrs MacRaith the luncheon basket she had ordered at the terminus. But I still watched the unfolding scene. Gradually the line snaked down to the edge of the loch, and at last the train drew slowly into the station which seemed to stand at the very end of the land, defying the winds which blew from the great ocean itself.

A final decisive jerk indicated that the train would go no further. The door of the compartment was opened, and a man stood silhouetted against the light. He held out a hand and assisted Mrs MacRaith to the platform, then turned back to offer me a like courtesy. The proffered hand was firm, warm, and steady, and held mine for a long moment while eyes of an unusual, topaz colour looked down into mine. But the eyes did not smile a welcome, and the mouth was almost sardonic.

'So,' he said. 'You are Katharine Beaton.'

'Katharine, this is my nephew, Alasdair MacRaith.'

I smiled, and mumbled something conventional, and

wondered at the drumming of my heart.

Abruptly he dropped my hand, and swung away towards a large elegant motor car standing some distance away. Mrs MacRaith took me by the elbow and gently steered me in the same direction. A uniformed chauffeur held open the door, and I stood aside for Mrs MacRaith to take her seat. She moved over to the far side and I took the seat she indicated. The driving seat was occupied by Alasdair MacRaith, and the chauffeur took the passenger seat at his side.

'Well, my dear, we're nearly home. You must be fatigued; it has been a long journey.'

'No longer for me than for you,' I said.

'Ah, but I'm used to it. I've made the journey many, many times.' Mrs MacRaith turned her head to stare intently through the window, as if searching for a familiar landmark. 'And do you know, my dear, no matter how many times I return, it's always with a feeling of homecoming.'

'I think I can understand that,' I said. 'You'll think it fanciful but I woke in the night, and it was almost as if I could sense a welcome.'

'What time was that?' she asked.

'I don't really know—some time between two and three, I think. Why?'

'Probably as we crossed the Border,' she answered. 'I think you may be sensitive to atmosphere, Katharine. It will be interesting to see how Allt-nam-Fearna affects you.'

The last leg of the journey was, if possible, more impressive than ever. Alasdair MacRaith drove competently; the car, with the minimum of vibration or jolting, bore us swiftly onwards, and if what I had already seen was astonishing, the road we now took was breathtaking. For a few miles the road ran close to the waters of the loch, and at times it seemed that the phalanx of trees must march forward to drive us into the water. The trees, too, had had their battles, and in places huge swathes of forest had been smashed like matchwood as if the fury of an idiot giant had wrought senseless havoc.

'That was what the storms did earlier this year,' Mrs MacRaith told me. 'It was quite terrifying, and we were cut off by road and by sea.'

In the clear spring sunshine it seemed hardly possible that Nature could behave with such savagery, but that was something I soon had to learn. Today, the land smiled. The road had shrugged off its cloak of trees, and we were moving up a steep, bare hillside. To the right, a high, rugged cliff was interlaced with a myriad rivulets, some of which spilled across the road and continued their headlong course down the terrifying drop that fell away to the left, a drop so steep that I hardly dared to look. Yet it had a fascination, and I stared down into the valley, which lay in a huge cleft in the mountain. I had the same queasy sensation as when I sat in the high balcony at a theatre and nerved myself to look across at the top of the proscenium. On the far side, the road was no more than a thread, only identifiable by a toy-sized cart drawn upwards by a miniature horse. At the head of the valley the walls of the mountain closed in until they were close enough to be spanned by a bridge over a gorge down which a glistening torrent of water hurled itself.

'The Maiden's Tresses,' said Mrs MacRaith, and the water did indeed resemble a cascade of silver hair, while the bridge heightened the illusion by its resemblance to a metal clasp, incredibly magnified, holding in place the flowing hair of some primeval titaness.

'Oh, how wonderful,' I breathed. 'I've never seen any-thing so—so awe-inspiring. I could gaze for hours. I must

34

try to get it down on paper, though I could never do it justice.'

'You shall have the opportunity,' she promised. 'We'll have a picnic here. But you must promise me never to venture alone up the path to the head of the Falls. It can be very treacherous, and if you missed your footing you'd go headlong into the gorge.'

'I promise. Indeed, I doubt whether I'd ever be tempted to venture,' I said. 'It looks daunting. I'm quite content to look from a safe distance.'

By now we were approaching the bridge, and the thunder of the falling water was deafening. I turned my head sharply.

'You spoke to me, Mrs MacRaith?'

'No, my dear.' I could hardly hear her for the noise of the Falls. 'Did you think I called your attention to something?'

'I must have imagined it,' I said. 'I could have declared that someone called my name.'

'It must have been a nixie,' she laughed. 'It's been said that they try to lure people up the path to the Falls, and call them to jump into the Devil's Pool.'

'Well, it won't lure me,' I said. 'I can't swim.' But for all my joking, I suppressed a shiver. For someone *had* called to me.

The road still climbed, and then, when we were out on the open moor, I learned just how capricious the weather could be. Like a grey wall, the mist rolled towards us across the wide, bleak moor. I had the impression of dull green turf, close cropped by sheep of a breed quite different from any I had seen in England. They moved indifferently aside as we passed, sometimes trotting off into the swirling mist, their black spindly legs and long fleeces giving the impression of ballet dancers dancing off-stage.

Despite the mist, Alasdair MacRaith drove with confidence, as if he knew the road well and had assessed the possibility of obstruction. Of course, I told myself, this was not the Strand. This was an open moor where the only hazards were sheep.

The road dropped from the moor, and the mist thinned. I could hear water chattering over stones, and on either side were trees which I later learned were the alders from which Allt-nam-Fearna took its name. For a mile or so more the road followed the river, which was wider and deeper than the little rivulets which made the water noises. In the distance I could see a bridge, of rugged grey stone, rising in one graceful curve over a perfect inner arch which made a circle with its own reflection in the still dark water. And beyond the bridge, looming stern and forbidding out of the mist, I saw the huge, irregular mass of walls and turrets which was Allt-nam-Fearna itself.

Through a haze of weariness I was aware that we had passed under a moss-grown archway into a large cobbled courtyard, across one corner of which stood great oak double doors, heavily banded with wrought iron, and looking as if they could withstand a battering ram. At the base of a circular tower was a smaller door, and it was towards this that Mrs MacRaith steered me. Alasdair MacRaith had waited no longer than it took us to alight from the car, then had driven it in the direction of some outbuildings. I did not see him again that day.

The small door stood open, and silhouetted against the darkness of a small vestibule was a fresh-faced girl who smiled at us and then turned to call over her shoulder, so that as we reached the door there was a quick tattoo of steps and another girl appeared. She was small and fair, with the same topaz-coloured eyes as Alasdair MacRaith.

'Aunt Agnes—oh, how lovely to have you back!' The girl flung herself into Mrs MacRaith's arms and kissed her warmly. 'Oh, you don't know how I've missed you, and it's simply ages since you went traipsing off to London——'

'Ishbel, my dear! Now let me get my breath back, and let me introduce our visitor.' She turned to me. 'Katharine, this is Ishbel. Ishbel, this is Katharine Beaton.' The girl turned to me and took my hand. For the fraction of a minute she scrutinised me, then said, 'How nice to meet you at last, Miss Beaton. My aunt wrote about you, and you're very welcome. Let me take you to your room. You must be fatigued after your journey. I'll send Kirsteen to unpack for you, and perhaps you will join us for tea when you have washed the dust of travel off. Ring for Kirsteen and she'll guide you through the maze—else you'll get completely lost.' She turned to Mrs MacRaith. 'Your trunks have arrived—and Miss Beaton's, too. I'm simply dying to see all the latest fashions from London.'

'What a child you are, my dear.' Mrs MacRaith spoke indulgently. 'But I've brought you something which will please you—you'll have to wait for it until I can remember which trunk I put it in.'

'Don't tease, Aunt Agnes. You know exactly which trunk it's in. Now, Miss Beaton, follow me.'

By now we were in a kind of dining hall, the walls of which rose in a sweeping curve to meet the ceiling, the whole of rough-hewn stone devoid of plaster. And at the far end, over a huge fireplace where logs as big as trees flamed and smouldered, I saw the crossed swords and shield of my vision. My head swam and I felt almost faint.

'Miss Beaton.' Slowly I turned, and the present flowed back.

'I do beg your pardon,' I said. 'You must forgive me, I'm very tired.'

'Of course, my dear. Now, Ishbel, take Katharine to her room.'

I was too dazed with fatigue and wonder to take note of the route we followed, and I knew I would never find my way back without guidance. And yet, without being told, I knew instinctively that from the window of my room I would look down into a walled garden, in the far corner of which was a little garden-house of red brick.

Ishbel was flitting round the room, setting to rights things which were already in place, and I sensed that she was prolonging her visit from curiosity, and something deeper. In some way I was being assessed. Did she, I wondered, regard me as a potential rival in the affections of someone I had yet to meet? She was interrupted by the arrival of the maid, Kirsteen, with a can of hot water which she carried over to the wash-hand stand and poured for me. My toilet things were already set out, and now Ishbel could hardly linger any longer without appearing discourteous.

'Ring when you're ready, Katharine, and Kirsteen will come and bring you down.'

I made my toilet and, refreshed, took stock of the room. I wondered which floor it was on, since I dimly remembered climbing what seemed an infinity of narrow, winding stairs, a spiral which had added dizziness to weariness. Now, looking from the window, I could see that it was probably only two storeys, though I was to learn that with the conglomeration of buildings which formed the castle, the multiplicity of levels was a perpetual bewilderment.

The garden was so familiar as to be uncanny. I could have described, with closed eyes, the close-cut turf and the tiny box hedges which bordered the gravel paths and the garden beds. In the centre was a sundial around which were set four stone benches; behind each one, triangular beds formed a square, and in each bed the box had been trained to depict, in alternate corners, a thistle and a Tudor Rose. To the left, in the far corner, almost concealed by an enormous, twisted laurel bush, I could make out a door in the wall, leading into a brick-built gardenhouse. Beyond, the ocean, and nothing else, for thousands of miles. Of something else I was certain, without being told. Outside the wall, the cliff fell sheer to the water on one side, and on the other, steps cut into the rock led down to a jetty.

I could hear Ishbel moving around in the room next to mine, and assumed that she herself might forestall Kirsteen as an escort, but when the girl knocked at the door, all was quiet in the neighbouring room.

As she guided me through the intricacies of the castle, the girl did not speak, even when I spoke to her. She merely smiled, and indicated the direction, and I wondered whether she was in fact a little simple. Later, I learned that she spoke only Gaelic, and I thought it a trifle odd that she should have been allocated to my service, though in all justice I had to admit that she was expert in carrying out my wishes and direct communication seldom seemed necessary.

Tea was taken in the hall where we had entered, and I learned that this was always referred to as the Guardroom, for such it had been in the old days when a castle was a fortress.

'You'll meet the rest of the family later, my dear.' Mrs MacRaith poured tea for Ishbel and myself, and then her own. 'After tea, I suggest you rest until it is time for Kirsteen to help you dress for dinner—I ought to have warned you that she has no English, though she does understand a little. I'm sure you'll find her a very efficient maid.'

'Katharine, I'm so glad you've come to stay,' Ishbel burst in. 'There's so much for me to show you—you ride, of course?'

'Oh, yes. I love riding. I had my own horse at——' Too late I realised that I had almost given away the very thing I wished to keep secret. 'At one house where I stayed,' I finished lamely.

'That's good.' She did not take me up. 'Then I can show you the country, and mostly that's only possible on horseback—unless, of course, you're one of these dedicated people who must tramp everywhere on their own two feet.'

'I don't mind walking, in moderation,' I said cautiously. A few miles was my limit and I did not wish to commit myself to a trek of twenty or thirty miles.

'I hate walking,' Ishbel admitted frankly. 'Thank goodness for the man who invented motor cars; one of these days I'll have one of my very own—women do drive cars, I believe.' She turned to me again. 'Katharine, can you drive?' Again caution was called for. Gerald had, in fact, given me some driving lessons, but I did not wish to face an inquisition, so I hedged. 'I hardly know anything about cars,' I said. 'Though I suppose that one day they will supplant the horse.'

'Not on these roads,' Mrs MacRaith commented wryly. 'Though I must admit that I found today's journey considerably shortened, and quite enjoyable, in Alasdair's new toy. But I think Katharine will be happier on one of the horses—they don't break down or get punctures or run out of oil or whatever it is these new-fangled things function on.' She refilled my cup, and the rest of the meal passed in a discussion of plans for future excursions.

Ishbel piloted me back to my room after tea. 'Dinner's

at seven-thirty,' she said. 'Informal, unless there are guests. Kirsteen will bring you hot water and help you to dress—about six o'clock?'

'Yes, thank you, that will suit me admirably.'

She did not make to enter but said merely, 'I'm quite near you, so if there's anything you need, come and call me.' I had moved inside the room, so I did not see in which direction she went, though I took it for granted she was in the next room, and I was not surprised to hear her moving about. It was comforting to know that in this strange place I had the support of close proximity to a companion of my own age and sex.

Since I had ample time before dinner, both to rest and to explore, I continued with the latter. My besetting sin, my teachers had always insisted, was the innate curiosity of a cat, stemming not from the inquisitiveness which must pry into the affairs of others, but from an interest in and an awareness of my surroundings. Again, I was drawn to the window, set in a deep embrasure indicative of the great thickness of the walls. This spot was to become for me more and more of a focal point as the days passed.

The window itself was not very large, which was not surprising, since in the early days of such a fortress, glass would have been virtually unknown as a means of protection from the elements. Folding wooden shutters, each leaf made in two sections, afforded what was now no more than token protection within the later addition of diamond-lattice casements. From the window, the walls sloped away to form an alcove that could be screened off by the heavy velvet curtains now drawn back and secured by broad bands of embroidery in a design formed by continuing loops of colour. The same design was also picked up in the borders of the curtains, and repeated on the long gros-point cushion that covered the box seat along one wall of the alcove. I sat down, and traced with an idle finger the interlacing pattern which wound along one border to the corner, down the short edge, then back again to where I sat, conscious of a sense of continuity flowing from my own present-day being, back into the past. I felt an affinity with the woman who had laboured long hours to stitch the glowing wools, the never-ending design, and I had then an impulse to take up again a craft which had always interested me. When I returned to London, I would buy canvas and wools and work my own testament for the future. Perhaps, I thought, it is the very resistance to time which makes the working of a sampler or a picture such a satisfying exercise, as if one is creating a small artistic legacy for those who come after. And how many of these beautiful pieces, I thought, must have been worked by the women whom life had passed by; women who would bear no children to whom they could hand on their skills, but who could yet leave something of their own being to enhance a time they would never see.

I shook myself out of my reverie, and wondered where such thoughts had come from. I was too young, I hoped, to sit melancholy on the roadside, watching the panoply of life passing me by. I continued with my examination of the other interesting pieces in the room. Opposite me, within reach should I wish to use it, was a little writing table, with two small side drawers and a larger one in the centre. On it rested a clean blotter, and an ink-stand, with ink gleaming black like fluid ebony. The sight of these reminded me that I should write to Aunt Zen. I must remember to get paper when I had the opportunity to visit a shop—I blithely assumed that we were within walking distance of a village.

'You will find writing paper and envelopes in the middle drawer.'

Startled, I swung round, thinking that Ishbel had entered unheard and had somehow read my thoughts. But there was no one there, and I knew that the words had only been spoken in my own mind. But the drawer was such an obvious place in which to keep writing materials that my momentary astonishment died. I had merely been making a predictable surmise, and I was not surprised, on pulling open the centre drawer, to find a neat stack of writing paper embossed with a crest, and the matching envelopes.

I had paper and ink, but no pen, and instinctively I pulled the left hand drawer, which resisted as if something were jammed, then came suddenly open. All the drawer contained was a quill pen, yellowed and worn. I picked it up and drew the shaft through my fingers, smoothing and straightening the ruffled barbels; and I knew, in that instant, that in another age, in another life, I had held this pen, and smoothed it and dipped it in the ink, as I now did, and had scribbled idly. What I had written on the blotter made no sense to me, being a meaningless jumble of letters. Automatically, as one inevitably does, I wrote my name, then stared in amazement, for instead of 'Katharine', I had written 'Catriona'.

As if it had burned my fingers, I dropped the pen, and the present flowed back. But the name scrawled on the blotter remained, and I wondered who she was, this Catriona whose personality was so strong that it could reach across the years and dictate what I should write. The quill lay where I had dropped it, a gout of ink hanging from the nib. Gingerly I picked it up, wiped it clean, and replaced it in the drawer, and again I was conscious of this 'otherness'. If I wanted to write my own words, I must find another pen, and I opened the right hand drawer, and saw, to my relief, a selection of penholders and nibs. But I knew curiosity would lead me back to explore the scene that the quill pen had conjured up. I must tell Aunt Zen, I thought, and take note of her advice.

A light knock on the door, and I called, 'Come in', imagining it might be Ishbel. However, it was Kirsteen who entered, and since conversation was not possible, I could do no more than smile, though I did say 'Thank you', and her answering smile indicated that she understood. She carried a can of hot water across to the wash-stand that stood in the recess on the far side of the room, set it down, then moved to the alcove to close the window.

I swung round, hearing her gasp of horror, and saw her standing rigid, one hand still grasping the edge of the curtain. She was staring down at the blotter, and had the message written there come from hell itself, she could not have been more petrified with terror. I moved towards her, meaning to try to reassure her, but with a swift movement, she raised her hand in a strange sign, then almost ran from the room. She did not return, and I made my evening toilette myself, though this was no hardship, since I was not dependent upon the services of a personal maid—life in a boarding school has no such trappings.

Finding my way to the dining-room was, however, quite another matter, and I was grateful when Ishbel arrived. I said nothing to her of Kirsteen's odd behaviour, of which she was apparently unaware since she made no mention of it, but the whole episode had intrigued me, and I determined to find out what had, in fact, been written on the blotter. The probable explanation, I told myself, was that the words meant something faintly shocking, if indeed, they had any significance at all. It could be that the name 'Catriona' meant something disturbing to Kirsteen. I had

44

rather unformulated ideas on the subject of ghosts, atmosphere and the like, in spite of my long association with Aunt Zen. Up till now, I had never regarded myself as being in the least sensitive or psychic, but the prevision resulting from the Tarot reading had shaken my convictions a little, and the odd sensation of being 'taken over' when I picked up the quill pen had added its contribution. This, I felt, was going to be a very interesting holiday.

Dinner was a quiet, simple meal, at which only Ishbel and Mrs MacRaith were present. I was conscious of a small stab of disappointment at Alasdair MacRaith's absence, and also would have expected that Iain, whom I assumed to be Ishbel's brother, would have dined with his aunt on her return. But I was so fatigued that I was really relieved not to have to make conversation with people I did not know.

'You look weary, child. Didn't you rest as I told you? Well, it's an early night for you.' And with this gentle command I was in no mood to disagree. Fatigue has the odd effect of reducing me almost to tears, though I am not normally given to crying, and I imagine that Mrs MacRaith's perception was keen enough to mark this fact, for when we had finished our coffee, she rang for Kirsteen and gave her an instruction in Gaelic. The girl nodded respectfully, disappeared for a space, then returned, bearing a small lighted lamp.

'Kirsteen will take you to your room,' Mrs MacRaith said. 'Sleep well, my dear.'

CHAPTER THREE

A BRIGHT fire now burned in the grate, and I was cheered by its warmth and by the dancing flames. Kirsteen put the lamp on the mantelpiece, then set about helping me to undress, and to prepare for bed. I found her attentions pleasantly relaxing, and when she released my hair from the pins to which I was still barely accustomed, the gentle, measured strokes of the brush soothed and dispersed the tension which had brought me to near to tears.

'Thank you, Kirsteen,' I said. 'That will be all. I'll put out the lamp myself.' It was a little odd, conversing with someone who could not answer, but she seemed to understand, and made to go, but I called her back. Mention of the lamp had reminded me that nowhere in the room had I seen matches, I was reduced to making signs as to what I required, but again, she seemed to have no difficulty in catching my meaning. Moving across to the hearth, she picked up a small carved pot which held twisted paper spills, then pointed to the fire. And with that I had to be content, though even in that instant I wondered how I should manage if I woke in the night and the fire had died. Here was another item for my imaginary shopping list.

Once in bed, weariness must have taken over immediately, and I slept even before I could turn out the lamp.

It seemed only minutes before I was awake, with the startled, heart-pounding awareness of a sudden arousal.

The room was in complete darkness. I lay rigid in the stifling blackness.

Then I heard the door close softly.

The remnant of a childhood superstition brought faint comfort—so long as I stay curled under the bed-clothes, I was safe. I stared into the nothingness, irrationally looking for the sound of whoever or whatever was in the room. There was nothing. Nothing but black silence. I held my breath, waiting, watching, listening for I knew not what, until commonsense took over. I heard nothing, because there was nothing to hear. The lamp had burned out because of my swift surrender to sleep. The closing door could have been anywhere in the corridor where my room lay—possibly Ishbel, in the adjacent room. I had no idea of the time, and no means of making light since the embers of the fire no longer glowed.

At last the beating of my heart slowed to normal, and I slept again, until an indefinable sound jerked me awake once more. It had been part of the fabric of my dream, the actual remembrance of which escaped me for the time being, but I knew it was the cry of a child, and it carried over into my waking, so that I knew it was a reality. It was neither the discontented wail that demanded attention nor the irritable screaming of a tantrum, but rather an echo of my own feelings; the sharp cry of alarm from a child wakened by a nightmare, calling to the night in vain for comfort and reassurance.

Again, I 'looked' for the sound; again I held my breath, waiting for a repetition which never came. The darkness and the silence were almost tangible. Even my own breathing was shallow and inaudible, so that I was able to hear quite distinctly the swish of a skirt over a wooden floor.

Perhaps in broad daylight, with the everyday bustle of

people moving about, unseen but audible, since people don't creep when going about their normal tasks, the sound would have made no impact on me. Now, my strength still drained by fatigue and my nerves taut with apprehension, I huddled deeper into the bed-clothes, trembling with an irrational fear which in my normal senses I should have derided. Would that cry come again? Would I hear again that soft dragging sound? The beating of my heart nearly choked me and my breath came in shuddering gasps as if I had run and run and run. I did not know which was worse—to lie in complete darkness, or to see the lurking shadows made by a lamp.

At last, exhaustion brought merciful oblivion and I slept, though it was only that shallow slumber which leaves one with the leaden feeling of not having slept at all, while the mind roamed wildly through a misty half-world of dreams. Unfamiliar faces swam into my consciousness; faces so ordinary that I felt, in my waking recollection, that somewhere in the world they must exist as real people. Even the disconnected snatches of conversation I seemed to hear, had a ring of authenticity.

Until one figure seemed to draw the gaze of the milling crowd which parted to allow her to approach as if from a great distance. Slowly she came towards me, moving with the unearthly glide of a wraith, and as she came, she grew taller, taller, taller, until she towered above me to the bright sky, the light from which dazzled my unwillingly opened eyes. I stared in terror at Mrs MacRaith.

'My dear child, you really did have a good long sleep.' The commonplace phrase, in a familiar voice, swept away the mists of my illusory fears. Bright sun poured through the window; fragrant pine logs crackled and snapped, and the tinkle of china indicated the utter normality of my surroundings.

'Mrs MacRaith, I do apologise. I didn't mean to sleep so late.' I struggled to sit up, reaching for my dressing-gown.

'Never mind, child. You were utterly worn out—we let you sleep on. You slept for nearly ten hours; when Kirsteen brought you a hot drink last thing, you were sound asleep, so she just put the lamp out and left you.'

So *that* was the softly closing door.

And the cry in the night? Probably nothing more alarming than the night call of an animal.

That left the swishing of a skirt. Maybe it had been simply that. Ishbel or Kirsteen, passing along the corridor. Except that both wore skirts of a practical length reaching no lower than the ankle. Resolutely I pushed the thought aside. There would be a rational explanation, even if it were not immediately apparent.

Mrs MacRaith was speaking again. 'Normally, of course, breakfast is from eight o'clock onwards. Kirsteen will call you about seven-fifteen and bring your early tea, then hot water. Now, just settle yourself in this morning, and we'll meet at luncheon in the Old Guardroom—Kirsteen will guide you.'

For a reason which I was unable to define, I had the impression of being given veiled orders, and I was at a loss to understand this odd feeling that I must do as I was told. Normally my reactions to other people were spirited enough and I found this sense of defensive subjection quite unfamiliar. Yet I could not escape an impression that this assumption of authority was entirely proper in my personal relationship, and I was utterly mystified.

Then Ishbel arrived, bubbling with plans, and like a fresh morning breeze dissipated my imaginings. I pushed all my fears to the back of my mind; but one resolution remained. I must write to Aunt Zen, firstly to let her know of my safe arrival, and then to tell her of the strange

49

events of the night. She would allay my fears and advise me on how to combat these unformulated terrors.

'May I come and help you arrange your things?' Ishbel asked.

'Of course. Do you know, I don't really know myself what's in my trunks. It all happened in such a hurry that I'm still in rather a whirl, but your aunt was so helpful. I'd never have been able to manage without her guidance. She seemed to know exactly what I would need.'

'So long as you didn't find her *too* managing,' Ishbel remarked drily.

'Why, no,' I replied. 'It was odd, really. I had the feeling that she had a perfect right to tell me—in the nicest possible way, of course—just what I ought to order.'

'Now I wonder why you should feel like that,' Ishbel said slowly. She stood up and crossed to the door. 'I must let you finish your breakfast and get dressed, then I'll come back, if I may. I know, we'll have our morning coffee here, shall we? About eleven o'clock?'

'Lovely,' I said. 'There's just one letter I must write this morning, then perhaps we can walk to the village this afternoon and get some stamps and one or two things I've contrived to forget.'

Ishbel's laughter pealed. 'Oh, Katharine,' she gasped. 'That would be a jolly long walk—it's about twelve miles to the nearest shop. But there, how were you to know?'

'Oh dear.' I must have looked dejected because she continued: 'It isn't so bad, really—we can ride, as soon as we've chosen a horse for you. And if it's letters you're worried about, they will be lifted daily from the box in the Guardroom and Murdo or Kirsteen takes them to the post.'

'But I've no stamps,' I objected.

'You'll always find stamps in the little box,' she told me.

'Take what you need and put a token coin in the box—it's counted as unlucky not to pay for stamps, you know.'

I finished my breakfast and Kirsteen removed the tray and left a large can of hot water. When I had washed and dressed, I sat down at the table in the window, meaning to write my letter.

And I saw that the blotter was quite clear of any writing. But of course, I thought, Kirsteen would have removed the scribbled-on sheet when she came to prepare the room for me while I was at dinner. But now I would never know what the message was. Unless——

Almost furtively I took out the quill pen, dipped it in the ink, and sat with it in my hand, and this time I first took from the drawer a piece of writing paper. I sat quietly, the pen poised, as if I were about to write 'Dear—' To whom was Catriona writing, on that day long ago?

Then I realised something else. Catriona, too, was left-handed, for the sharpened quill had a slant, and was it for my convenience that the table was placed so that the light from the window fell from the right?

But though I relaxed and consciously emptied my mind, the pen made no movement whatever. There was only a strange vibration which seemed to flow into my hand. I realised that this was something which could not be commanded. I must wait patiently for whatever message I might receive, and at the appointed time. Carefully I replaced the pen in the drawer, then set about writing to Aunt Zen.

I was so engrossed in my narrative that I did not hear the light tap at the door which announced Ishbel and morning coffee, but she must have taken as read my permission to enter, for it was with a start that I suddenly realised that I was being watched intently.

'Oh, Ishbel, it's you. Just a minute and I'll finish this

51

letter, then it can go in the box when we go down to lunch.'

She sat down, still watching me, but did not speak until I had scribbled a few more lines, signed my name, read through and folded the bulky letter, and put it in an envelope which I then sealed and addressed.

'That's some letter,' she commented. 'You must have written a novel, by the look of it. Is it to your fiancé?'

'My fiancé?' I stared at her. 'Who said I had a fiancé?'

'Well, haven't you?' Ishbel countered. 'Surely anyone as attractive as you must have a string of admirers, and there *must* be one special one, like the old song. Do you know it?' She hummed a few bars of 'Coming through the rye' and I took it up, knowing well the lines she meant.

'"Among the train there is a swain I dearly love mysel'"!'

She clapped her hands in delight. 'Why, you know it! Finish the verse, then,' she commanded.

'"But what his name and whaur his hame, I dinna care to tell!" Well, I'm sorry to disappoint you, but there isn't any swain.'

'No?' Ishbel tilted her head quizzically. 'Not even a *secret* love? You disappoint me—or rather, the gallant swains of London Town do. They must be a laggard lot.'

'Ah, well,' I laughed, 'up here you're used to the Lochinvar type, aren't you? Well, so far no one has come riding out of the west to sweep me off my feet.' Ishbel's question had been artless enough, but I could not rid myself of the impression that there was an element of probing. Not in any sense of idle curiosity or inquisitiveness, but rather because in some way it was of considerable importance to her to know whether I was a rival, though in what field I had yet to learn.

But the ingenuous catechism continued.

52

'Fancy your knowing the words of a Scottish song. And about Young Lochinvar, too. Where did you learn that?'

'At school. We had a song book with all the traditional songs. We also learned reams of poetry, and Lochinvar was one of them. I rather liked that one. It was gay, and dashing, and I used to imagine that my father must have been rather like that, because——' I pulled myself up sharply. I had no wish to be drawn into relating my family history. But Ishbel was not easily deflected.

'Because what. Go on, Katharine. Did he gallop off with your mother?'

'I don't really know,' I answered. 'I never saw him, I was only a baby when he died. But from something my mother once said, I got the idea that it was a runaway match.'

'How romantic! Did they elope to Gretna Green and get married over the anvil?'

'I don't think so,' I laughed. 'I don't really know where they were married.' *Or even if they were married.* I remembered with a sinking heart that dreadful day when I had searched in vain amongst the records. For most of the time I could forget, and take life as it came, but there must always be times when some chance remark would bring the whole scene vividly before me. Would I ever be *someone*, I wondered. Someone with a name, and rights, and an entity of my own?

Fortunately Ishbel's rather butterfly mind had flitted away on another ploy, and she was outlining the plans for the afternoon, provided the weather stayed kind.

'What's that?' I said sharply. 'That cry. Are there children in the castle.' The cry came again, and Ishbel laughed.

'That's nothing but a whaup—a curlew. You'll hear plenty of those.' She looked at me curiously. 'Did you

53

think you'd heard it before, and that it was a child?' she asked.

'I thought I heard a child cry in the night,' I admitted. 'At least, it seemed as if it were in the middle of the night but perhaps it was very early in the morning. With the curtains drawn, it was pitch dark, and I really don't know what time it was, so you were probably right, it was—what you said it was.'

'A whaup. Yes, it could have been.' But she was still eyeing me almost speculatively.

When a moment later Kirsteen came to collect the coffee tray, Ishbel said something to her in Gaelic, and the girl answered. Ishbel turned to me.

'You'll have to excuse me, Katharine. Aunt Agnes wants me. Lunch will be in about half an hour and Kirsteen will come and fetch you.' She hurried from the room, followed by Kirsteen, on whose face I caught a look of puzzlement. I wondered what Ishbel had said to her, and whether the girl had really told her that Mrs MacRaith required her.

When, about twenty minutes later, Kirsteen came to fetch me, I followed her through the labyrinth of corridors and stairs, the latter winding downwards in the thickness of the walls, in a dizzying spiral to which it took me some time to get accustomed. Kirsteen descended featly, with easy familiarity, but I picked my way more slowly, my hand on the stone newel as I set each foot carefully on the wedge-shaped steps, worn hollow by the many feet which had trodden up and down them over the centuries. I paused, just before the last turn, running my hand over the ashlar of the wall, because stone always gives me a sense of contact and continuity with the past. I sought in my mind's eye to visualise some of the people who had passed this way and long since gone on the long journey into time, but no specific picture emerged, only a sense of excitement and urgency, as if someone went to a tryst.

And because I had paused and not come down into the Guardroom immediately behind Kirsteen, I was an unwilling eavesdropper. Ishbel seemed to be arguing.

'Then why have you brought her here? I tell you, she heard the bairn greet, and you know what that means.'

'I know your obsession with these old legends.' It was Mrs MacRaith who answered, and her voice was cold and incisive. 'Now let there be an end to this nonsense. How many times do I have to tell you that such a marriage is not possible.'

Because I had no wish to cause embarrassment by allowing it to be known that this exchange had been overheard, I waited until at least another minute had gone by before I picked my way carefully down the remaining steps and rounded the last curve down into the Guardroom.

'Ah, there you are, child. Come to the table.' Mrs MacRaith indicated a place and I moved forward, then froze, and stared into the dim far corner of the room, where a tall figure stood looking fixedly at me. Ishbel, from the window embrasure, followed my gaze, and laughed.

'It's all right, Katharine. That's only the Redcoat—he's always there, but you'll get accustomed to him in time. He's quite harmless.' I did not answer. Not because I feared the apparition, but because a far memory was stirring. Somewhere in time I had known the Redcoat.

'Ishbel, you are not to tease Katharine.' Mrs MacRaith spoke sharply. She took my hand and piloted me to my place at the table. I sat down, shaken, but my eyes were still drawn to the still figure in the corner. Then I saw that it was indeed quite solid and material—a dummy, in fact, complete in every feature, and dressed in the uniform of an English soldier of the time, I imagined, of one of the Georges.

'Why, of course, how silly of me! But you know, to be a genuine old castle, you must surely have a ghost somewhere?' I spoke with deliberate lightness, and I think I would have been relieved by a denial that such things might be.

'Any building as ancient as this one must, I suppose, retain some imprint of the past,' Mrs MacRaith answered. 'But I don't want you to be worried and apprehensive, my dear. And don't place too much credence on Ishbel's old tales.' Her smile took the sting out of the words, but I wondered, nevertheless, whether there was a veiled warning to Ishbel.

'The Redcoat has been here for nearly two hundred years,' she went on. 'Not that actual figure, of course. That is modern, but the uniform dates back to The Fifteen, when the castle was occupied by the English.'

Ishbel was quiet during lunch, and I wondered whether the little encounter I had overheard was the cause of her near-sulk. I had been puzzled by her phraseology, too. Whereas I would have expected her to ask, why I had been *invited*, the expression '*brought her here*' implied deliberation on the part of her aunt, and this I found wholly unaccountable. Why should anyone wish to bring me to Allt-nam-Fearna? And why, a new thought insinuated, was I attended by a maid who spoke no English? Was it to preclude questions about the family or the castle, or—what? With a mental shrug, I shelved the problem. Aunt Zen would know the answer, and my letter would fill in the background for her. But I knew, with an implicit trust, that she would never have permitted me to stray into a situation of real danger, and I must simply await her reply and meanwhile, I would enjoy my holiday in this very lovely country.

'Now why don't you take Katharine to the Waterfall this afternoon?' Mrs MacRaith's suggestion was a covert command. 'You'll need your walking shoes, my dear,' she told me. 'Oh, don't be alarmed, it isn't a lengthy trek, just a couple of miles along a fairly easy path. But that is one point I must impress on you from the beginning, Katharine. Don't ever go beyond the policies by yourself.'

'I beg your pardon?' My bewilderment was patent and both my companions smiled apologetically. 'You'll get used to our quaint terms in time—what you'd probably call park land round the castle, we call the policies. And as I said, it's better that you don't venture too far alone. It's fatally easy to lose your bearings out on the moor, and mists come down so suddenly, so please——'

'I won't stray, I promise you, Mrs MacRaith. I'm not the venturous type at all, and mist terrifies me.' Now why had I said that? I had the ordinary, normal dislike of fog, with which I was only too familiar in London, but suddenly, as if a mist had seeped into the very room, I was afraid, and in some strange way the Redcoat in the corner was one of the strands in that web of fear. I was glad when I was able to leave the table and return to my room.

Once there, commonsense reasserted itself. After all, it was not surprising that the Guardroom should have a sinister atmosphere. How many strange and possibly horrifying events had stamped themselves into the stones, each successive impression imposing itself like a palimpsest over the previous one. Suppose, I mused, one could summon all those who through the centuries had passed through those doors. What a fascinating assortment would then be revealed. I wished Aunt Zen could bring her sensitivity to bear on what lay behind the everyday activities of this place.

Thinking of her, I remembered the letter I had written, and when I had finished tying my shoelaces I crossed the room to the table by the window. As I picked up the letter, I glanced down into the garden and saw Ishbel standing by the sundial. I wondered, in passing, how she had changed her dress so quickly. Then she turned her head and looked directly up at my window, and I saw that it was not, after all, Ishbel, so I concluded it must be another of the maids. As I turned away, she hurried across the garden and through the door in the wall which apparently led to the little brick garden-house. She seemed to be carrying something in her arms. A white bundle that could have been a bundle of washing, or a baby.

Carefully ticking off mentally the landmarks on the way, I found my way back to the Guardroom. As Ishbel had said, on a side table was a wooden box with a slit in the lid. Beside it was a small box in which I found stamps, for which I put in the necessary coin. As I dropped my letter into the box, I said a small message to Aunt Zen. A message of love and thanks.

CHAPTER FOUR

'WHAT A charming garden,' I exclaimed. 'These tiny box hedges round the flowerbeds—I want to pat them. How beautifully kept. You must have a very good gardener. But then, the Scots are noted gardeners, aren't they? I remember there was one at——' Almost too late I remembered, and to cover my lapse, went on hurriedly. 'This is like the garden I can see from my bedroom, isn't it?'

Ishbel stared at me. 'This *is* the garden you can see from your room, Katharine. I suppose it does look a bit different from another level, but I assure you this is the only one like this at Allt-nam-Fearna. It's always called Catriona's Garden, so I expect that's why you like it so much—did you know that Catriona is the Scottish form of Katharine?' She went on talking but somehow I only half heard her, though I must have made the correct replies. *Catriona*. Who was she, the woman whose name I had been impelled to write?

The garden *did* look different. I would have stood up in a Court of Law and asserted on oath that in the centre was a sundial—where now I saw a large clipped bush in the shape of a bird.

'That's Murdo's pride and joy. It's supposed to represent a phoenix, symbolising Allt-nam-Fearna rising from the flames.'

'Was the castle burned down, then?' I asked.

'More or less. The English garrison after The Fifteen fired the interior and what wouldn't burn they pounded with cannon. You can still see the marks. But they didn't

59

succeed in battering down the main walls. They'd stand till Doomsday!'

We walked round the garden, and Ishbel pointed out its various features, and all the time I wanted to ask about the sundial. Above all, I wanted to know who Catriona was, and why a garden where I felt so much at home should be named for her.

'Who was Catriona?' I asked, and as an afterthought, added: 'May we go and look at the garden-house, please?'

Ishbel stopped abruptly, almost as if she had walked into a brick wall.

'What garden-house?' she demanded.

'The one I can see from my room. Over there, behind that big bush.'

Ishbel continued to stare at me, and the question about Catriona went unanswered.

'There is no garden-house,' she said flatly. 'There hasn't been one for two hundred years. That was the first thing to be destroyed. They bombarded it from a ship anchored out in the Sound. Katharine, are you psychic, or something? It's a bit uncanny that you should know about something that was destroyed so long ago. Unless, of course, you've seen pictures in an old book.' She laughed out of relief. 'That must be it. This place has been written about quite a lot, because so many famous—and infamous—people have stayed here. It's simply crawling with legend, you know.'

'You must tell me some,' I said, and allowed her explanation to stand. But I knew that I'd never seen any picture in any book.

She led the way to a gate in the wall near the one where we had come from the castle. The path we took skirted the main curtain wall, then curved away across park land to where the ground became more rugged, sloping upwards until it cut the skyline in a straight sharp ridge. From a deep cleft in this ridge a waterfall spilled over and hurled itself in a tumult of white foam into a dark pool which in turn drained away into a small ravine, boulder-strewn and lined with tormented, stunted little trees clinging with fierce determination to the steep sides.

'That's the Allt-nam-Fearna that gives the castle its name. Those are alders, so I suppose you could call that the Burn of the Alders.'

'Alderburn,' I said immediately. 'That was the name of a house where we once lived when I was quite small. What a coincidence.'

Slowly and carefully we picked our way up the gorge, scrambling over the stones which could have sprained an ankle. At last we reached the edge of the pool, and sat down to rest.

'That's as far as we can go, from this side, at any rate,' Ishbel said. 'It's too steep to climb to the very top, unless you go through the wood over there and take the Shepherd's Path.' She looked at me critically. 'Was it too much of a climb for you? Don't say anything to Aunt Agnes, will you? She'll give me a telling off for tiring you out.'

'Oh, I'm not that exhausted,' I protested. 'But it's so lovely here, and I'm quite content to look at the view, and listen to the water. I love the sound of it, and it looks so clear and cold. Can one drink it?'

'If you like. Try it.'

I picked my way gingerly to the edge of the burn, and stooped to catch the water in my cupped hands. It spilled between two small boulders and made a tiny cascade, one of many in the descent from the main fall. It was so icy that it seemed to burn, and as I put my lips to my hands, the drops which spilled seemed like splashes of fire. I took a mouthful, and swallowed, and choked with distaste.

I looked up, Ishbel was watching me intently, as if she had been waiting for a reaction. I said nothing, merely fished in my pocket for a handkerchief. I wiped my mouth and hands, and climbed back to the little turfed platform where she sat.

'Well?' She waited for my comment.

'It has a strange taste,' I said guardedly. 'There must be some kind of mineral content, though it looks clear enough.'

'What kind of taste?' And I had the feeling that she knew without being told, that to me, the water had the taste of blood. I shuddered, and was silent.

'What kind of taste?' she repeated. 'Like blood?'

'Well, yes. But that's absurd. How can a clear mountain stream taste like blood?'

'Do you know what they call these falls?' she asked softly. 'No, of course, how could you?' She stared up at the tumbling waters, and said something in Gaelic, then translated for me.

'The Falls of Blood.'

'Oh, *no*!' I whispered.

Suddenly the day was cold. Sinister. A cloud had covered the sun, and away out of sight a curlew called like a lost soul.

'Did the name come from the taste?' I asked.

'In a way, yes. But it isn't anything in the water, you know. It's the Curse of Gruagach, and it isn't everyone that can taste it, only those who are——'

'Only those who are what?' I demanded.

Ishbel shook her head. 'Don't ask me,' she said. 'You'll know—in time.'

The cloud moved away and the sun shone again, and Ishbel's mysterious hints took on the nature of a joke.

'You're teasing me, Ishbel! Making up stories to scare

the Sassenachs, all Celtic Twilight and that sort of thing. Own up, now.'

'You can laugh, Katharine. I suppose it does seem a lot of superstitious nonsense to you, coming from London to the wilds of Scotland. But odd things do happen up here, you know.'

And even odder things, did you but know it, in a rather ordinary London suburb, I thought.

'There's a pretty grim story attached to the Falls,' she went on. 'Ages ago—oh, back in the pre-history days, almost, the chieftain of these lands had three sons named——' The Gaelic names she used were utterly incomprehensible to me, and my bewilderment must have been obvious, because she translated for me.

'Alasdair the Black, the eldest. Black of hair and black of heart, the legend says. The middle one, Malcolm. He doesn't seem to have had any kind of nickname, and always appears as a rather shadowy character. Then the youngest son, Iain Ban. That means white, fair-haired, like his mother who was a Viking princess. Well, he and Alasdair both loved the same woman, and *she* loved Iain, and wouldn't have anything to do with Alasdair.' Ishbel shrugged. 'Just like today, isn't it, and it has been the same for centuries, one man wanting another man's woman.'

'And vice versa, sometimes,' I said, drily. She looked startled.

'How did you know?' she demanded.

'Know what?' I said. 'I didn't mean anything in particular. Just an observation. Please go on with the story.'

'Well, it was all very predictable, really. Alasdair wanted her—her name was Gruagach—and he just took her, and carried her off to his stronghold and forced her into marriage, and he ill-used her to such an extent that her first

63

child, a daughter, was born prematurely, only seven months after the marriage.'

'What about Iain?' I asked. 'Didn't he try to rescue her?' Ishbel nodded.

'Yes, of course. But it wasn't easy. All the land round here, and all the fighting men, owed allegiance to Alasdair, and of course, even those who didn't were much too scared to join any sort of foray against him. So Iain had to rescue Gruagach by stealth. He got Alasdair out of the way by a false summons from the overlord, and then he and Gruagach contrived to get out of the castle at dead of night.' Ishbel's voice dropped to a dramatic whisper.

'Can't you imagine them, Katharine, stealing away across the moor, with no cover but the heather, down the steep path to the loch-side where the horses were waiting. And then, when they reached the burn——' She paused, and I was rigid with suspense. 'When they reached the burn, Alasdair and his men were waiting in an ambush. Malcolm had betrayed his brother, telling Alasdair that the summons was a false one.'

'So the fleeing lovers were captured, and brother killed brother, and all lived unhappily ever after——' My almost flippant interruption was a reaction to an unbearable horror; the giggle at the climax of the ghost story. For I was *there*. My heart still pounded with the terror of that stealthy journey through the heather, and I knew the choking despair of realising that it was in vain, and that henceforth my life would be an unutterable torment till death should bring the ultimate freedom.

Ishbel shook her head. 'Not immediately. He was an extraordinary man, with his own standards of justice. He dismissed his followers, and made Iain and Gruagach and Malcolm ride with him to the crest there——' She pointed upwards, to the edge of the moor where the tumbling waters hurled themselves down to the pool. And in a dream I could see the strange procession, the riders like black shadows against the pale sky of dawn. I watched as they dismounted, and as Ishbel's voice continued her narration, I watched the grim drama. On the edge of the ridge, the quartette divided, two and two. Iain and Gruagach faced Alasdair and Malcolm, and I tensed as Iain braced himself for the dual attack. But instead Alasdair turned to Malcolm.

'... then Alasdair turned swiftly, and plunged his *sgian dubh* into Malcolm's heart. "You betrayed my brother. When it serves your turn you will betray me. So I will put an end to your treachery." And he hurled Malcolm's body over the cliff, and it lay there till the corbies had picked the bones clean. And because he was denied burial, Malcolm still walks.'

'Oh, how horrible.' And I could not laugh in disbelief, because I had seen it happen, and I knew that the end of the story was even more gruesome.

'Then Alasdair drew his claymore, as did Iain, and the brothers fought till the sun rose, red and baleful, and because its rays dazzled Iain, his brother, with one sweeping blow, severed his sword arm at the wrist.'

'Then killed him?'

'No, that would have been too easy. Alasdair had to prolong the torture. He picked up Iain's claymore, prised open the fingers of the severed hand, and tossed the weapon to his brother. "You still have a hand to lose, and a stump will serve to hold your targe before your body." And so the fight went on, till Iain, his life-blood draining away, sank to the ground, never to rise again.'

Ishbel spoke as if in a trance, repeating words and phrases hallowed by tradition. Heavy clouds now veiled the sun, as if in mourning, and across our line of vision two birds flew. They were almost as large as ravens, but their backs were a dark grey. Their harsh calls held sinister derision, and I hardly needed Ishbel's identification as she glanced upwards.

'Corbies,' she whispered. 'Hoodie crows.'

'What was the end of the story?' I asked.

'Alasdair dragged his brother to the edge of the burn, at the point where it spilled over the falls, and left him lying on that rock, with his life-blood streaming from his body into the water. And so that Gruagach should be spared nothing of his death, he tied her to the alder tree, using her own long plaits of hair, so that she could not move or turn her head away, and even though she closed her eyes she could still hear his agonised moans. And she watched all day, and when the setting sun turned the water of the falls to red blood, and Iain's last breath was sighing away, Alasdair cut her free. She dragged herself on to the rock, and cradled the dying man in her arms, and she cursed Alasdair and his line for all time.

'Then she told him that the daughter she had borne was no child of his, but Iain's, already carried by her when Alasdair had abducted her. "No matter," he cried. "You shall yet bear *me* a son." Then he took her, there on the rock, before Iain's eyes.'

I was too sick with horror to speak. I looked around me and it seemed unbelievable that the now sunlit little glen could have been the setting for such villainy. But Ishbel seemed determined to spare me nothing.

'And when her child was born, it was a son, black as Alasdair, and as evil. Gruagach contrived to send her baby daughter away with an old nurse, who promised to care for her and bring her up away from Black Alasdair. And a year and a day after Iain's death, Gruagach took her son, and climbed to Iain's Craig, and leaped to her death, taking the child with her. The pool is so deep that their bodies were never found.'

'They were barbarous days. It doesn't seem possible that men could be so vile.'

'Black Alasdair could. He tracked down the old woman and dragged her back to the castle and tortured her till she was nearly dead. Then he flung her out in the snow, and she crawled a league, to get to the child. He followed her tracks, and found the child. She was brought back to the castle, and kept in seclusion till she was of marriageable age, when he took her by force. After he'd made sure she was with child, he made her go through a form of marriage. She gave birth to twin sons, but for the rest of her life she was completely insane, and had to be confined to that tower room.' Ishbel pointed to the castle, to where a small, circular turret jutted from the main wall. Beneath a 'candle-snuffer' roof, I could just see a tiny slit of a window, from which a poor mad creature had gazed at the sky and at the falling waters where her father and mother had died.

'And from those twin sons,' Ishbel concluded dramatically, 'the two lines can be traced, unbroken, until the present day.'

'Two lines?' I queried. But my curiosity was not to be satisfied that day. For with the inconsequent change of mood which was almost childlike, Ishbel jumped up, shook the twigs and leaves from her skirt and said: 'That's enough of those old tales for today. Come,' she held out her hand. I took it and she pulled me to my feet. Together we hurried back to the castle, and joined Mrs MacRaith for her tea in her own sitting-room.

And after tea, confident now in my ability to find my way back to my room, I took what I thought was the stairway

67

that would bring me there, only to find myself in a completely different part of the castle. Different, yet the same, since all the walls seemed to have the same wood panelling and doors, so that it was not until I opened the door at the head of the staircase that I saw that I was not in my own room.

Bewildered, I stood in the doorway, then something seemed to draw me—no, it was something stronger than that—*something* welcomed me into the room. Not *someone*, since I was not conscious of any presence there, only a general sense of fitness and belonging.

It was a homely, unpretentious room, the furniture old and with a comfortable shabbiness, though not dilapidated, and its age gave the impression of antiquity, of an era many decades back. Straight-backed, solid oak chairs, dark with time, stood round a refectory-type table, and I knew that the scratches on the footrest, and the carefully gouged initials, had been made by boys and girls who had long ago taken the road into the sunset. I moved nearer, and traced with my finger the initials at one end of the table. Two children had sat side by side, each industriously scoring a record for those who came after. Together they had wrought an intricate little escutcheon, within which they had engraved their initials—'A.MacR' and 'I.MacR', in the top left and bottom right corners respectively, and slanting downwards from left to right, the date, '1701'. So it was over two hundred years since the two brothers—I pulled myself up short. Why was I so certain that they had been brothers? The conjecture that they were boys was obvious enough; carving initials was a mainly male field, and the necessary penknife was not usually a ladylike possession. But I could almost see the two heads bent over the task on which they lavished considerably more concentration than on lessons. One dark, one fair, and their ages, some ten or eleven years—or were they twins? The impression faded, and the dream children receded into the past.

I skirted the table, passing the end of a high-backed settle, and saw that the worked cushion on its seat matched that on the window seat in my own room. Instinctively I looked for an embroidery frame, and there it was, standing by the window, beside a work table which I knew would hold the coloured wools to complete the stretched canvas on the frame. And though the room was obviously long unused, as evidenced by the thin film of dust which dulled the polished surfaces, the colours of the settle cushion and of the partly worked canvas were undimmed. It could have been only minutes ago that the still threaded needle had been left stuck through the canvas as though the work had been suddenly interrupted.

I bent down to study the design. It was about twenty inches square, marked for a chair seat. In the centre, worked in the finest petit-point, was a full heraldic achievement; the background was filled in with gros-point. It was the most exquisite piece of work of its kind that I had ever seen, and must have accounted for many hours of meticulous stitching. Beneath the centrepiece, also in petit-point, I read the initials 'C.MacR', on each side of which two figures, '17' and '19' indicated the year. Catriona, who had walked in the walled garden? The garden visible from this window, as from my own. I stared downwards in unbelieving panic, because again, instead of the clipped bush, I could see a sundial. And in the far corner, behind the laurel bush, the roof of the garden-house.

What power was there, in this place to which I had come all unaware, to make me feel that I knew what *had* been, so many years ago? What presence now urged me to sit down, take up the needle, and complete that unfinished stitch. Little of the canvas remained to be worked, only a small corner of the background, executed in gros-point tent stitch. I continued to set the stitches, evenly and carefully, and so fresh were the colours that the line I had worked was all of a piece with the original stitches that had stood untouched for almost two centuries. What, I wondered, had taken Catriona from her work so urgently and finally?

One other point gave me thought. The way the frame was set, and the position of the chair relative to the light from the window, confirmed that Catriona had indeed been left-handed. Now, the rapidly passing time hindered my continuing to sit in that other world, to which I knew I would return, secretly, guiltily, but inevitably. I knew that I ought to quit the room by the same door by which I had entered, but first, I had to know what lay beyond the other two doors.

The one in the far right hand corner led to a bedroom. A child's bedroom, or more correctly, a room which its owner had used from infancy to adolescence. An old wooden cradle pressed into service as a container for logs; a wooden rocking horse in the corner, and a doll sprawled on a shelf. But in front of the window, a quite adult dressing table, and alongside, a single bed with faded chintz hangings.

I picked up the doll. Her waxen face smiled vapidly at me, as if she were showing off her finery—her fashionable sacque dress, its taffeta ruches brittle and split, and the lace yellow with age. Her body, legs and arms were made of fine kid. She was not even yesterday's doll still treasured by a young lady just leaving girlhood. No, this doll belonged to the day *before* yesterday. I smoothed her skirts and almost tenderly, as if she were a possession which I personally valued, I laid her back on the shelf.

I returned to the room I had mentally named The Schoolroom, and crossed to the other door. I turned the handle, but the door resisted, and I saw that the key was still in the lock. The temptation to turn it, to see what was the other side of that door, was overwhelming. I stifled my guilty sense of prying, turned the key, and opened the door—into my own room.

Footsteps in the corridor warned me of the approach of either Ishbel or Kirsteen, and I moved quickly into my room. Behind me I heard a click, as if the door had swung shut behind me, and when I turned, only a flush run of panelling faced me. There was absolutely no indication that any door existed in that wall. Puzzled, I fingered the key in my pocket. Somehow I must find my way back to that other room and return the key, locking the door as I did so, but Kirsteen's arrival with a can of hot water prevented me for the moment. When she had gone, I dropped the key into the drawer of the lowboy, and when Ishbel knocked, I had almost completed my toilette.

'What are you wearing?' she asked. She herself was dressed almost as if for a dinner party, and it occurred to me that there might be more than just Mrs MacRaith and perhaps Alasdair at dinner.

'What do you suggest?' I asked. 'I mean, is it a formal dinner party?'

'Not exactly,' she answered. 'Just the family, but rather special. You see, Grandfather will be dining with us.' I must have looked puzzled, because she went on to explain.

'He's very old. Mostly he stays in his room, because the doctor says he must harbour his strength. But he wishes to meet you—in fact, it's quite an honour, because he doesn't bother with everyone. But then, you *are* rather special, aren't you?' The tone of her voice brought me round

71

smartly and I was unable to account for the blend of admiration and bitterness. Did she see in me some threat to her happiness? I could see no reason why she should, since I had no inclination to supplant her in anyone's affections, even if I *knew*.

'What do you mean by special?' I asked guardedly. 'Because I'm English?'

'Oh, no. Look, Katharine, forget what I said. I was just blethering.'

'I see.' But I didn't. Why on earth should I be regarded as 'special' by anyone. Who was I, anyway? The old bitterness surged up, but I fought it down. I must never let my personal problems intrude. So I applied myself to the more immediate matter of selecting a suitable dress.

'This one,' Ishbel said. I looked at her in some surprise. 'But that's almost the same as the one you're wearing. Mrs MacRaith chose it for me, and I do like it, but surely you won't want us to look like twins?' I spoke lightly as if to make a jest, but Ishbel nodded seriously.

'It's the correct wear,' she said. I shrugged. 'If you say so.'

'I do. Wait now, and I'll fetch you a sash, unless you already have one.'

She returned five minutes later, carrying a silk tartan sash similar to the one which she already wore. She waited while Kirsteen finished dealing with the fastenings of my dress.

'You need a brooch,' she said. 'Preferably a silver one.'

'You'll find one in my jewel case,' I said. 'The one with the stag's head.' She found the brooch, and stood with it in her palm, staring with an expression of utter disbelief.

'Where did you get this?' she demanded, her voice low and tense.

'It's rather nice, isn't it?' I said, quite casually. 'I don't know where it came from. It was with my mother's things,

72

and of course, they all came to me when she—when she died.'

'Oh, Katharine, I'm sorry. I shouldn't have asked, if it makes you unhappy. But I didn't know.' She arranged the scarf and fastened it. 'There.' She stood back and admired. 'Turn round and look at yourself. A real bonny lassie.'

I hope I'm not unduly vain, but my reflection in the long mirror was not displeasing. The simple white gown made the vivid colours of the tartan glow with life, and for no reason that I could explain, I felt a lifting of my spirits, almost a sense of anticipation, as though I had walked a dreary road which now turned a corner and brought promise of a brighter scene. I turned to Ishbel and took her by the hand, drawing her to my side so that we stood together, reflected in the mirror.

'*Two* bonny lassies,' I said. And on impulse I kissed her. 'Dear Ishbel. Thank you for helping me, and for lending me this beautiful scarf.'

'It's yours,' she said. 'Keep it, please, as a "Welcome" gift.' She moved towards the door. 'I'll go and tell Aunt Agnes we're ready,' she said. 'Kirsteen will bring you down.'

While I was at school, I had acted in many of the plays we had staged. Now, as I waited, I had the same tightening of nerves that I'd always had just before the curtain went up; a mixture of apprehension and exhilaration which often heightened the performance one eventually projected.

The previous hour's exploration of the adjoining rooms still remained in my mind, exciting and intriguing. And one small, odd thing which would take some explaining. In the instant when I had stood the other side of the concealed door, looking down at the floor, I had seen in the film of dust a clear swathe, as if a trailing skirt had swept over the long undisturbed grains. Who had walked across the room, in the dark of the night, and stood listening? Kirsteen's arrival interrupted my thoughts, and I followed her from the room, and by another route, to where an archway gave access to a gallery, broken midway by a broad staircase.

Kirsteen stood aside and I passed through the archway, as if from the wings on to a lighted stage, and the whole scene had the unreality of a play, like the dreams I had often had in which I found myself staring across the foot-lights, knowing that I was playing the lead, and having not the faintest recollections of my lines.

And when I took in the scene below me, I knew it was the same as my prevision, the night Aunt Zen had read the cards for me.

CHAPTER FIVE

I STOOD at the head of the stairs looking down at a group
of people who could have been figures in a waxworks
tableau, so still were they, and silent. The pause could
have been no more than fractional, yet it was as if we were
all held in a trance, while they watched me, and I watched
them. I saw two women, whom I already knew—Mrs Mac-
Raith and Ishbel. One man, Alasdair, whom I had already
met fleetingly, and two men half recognized from my
vision, and now seen clearly for the first time. The younger
of the two was personable enough, though with no out-
standing impact; the elder, straight as a ramrod, and over
six feet tall, was the handsomest old man I had ever seen.
He seemed to dominate the company, overshadowing even
Alasdair, who now moved to the foot of the stairs and held
out his hand to me.

Carefully, as if making a planned entrance, I stepped
slowly down the first short flight to the half-landing, and
paused, still dazed. Alasdair mounted the half dozen or so
steps of the lower flight, reached up and took my hand,
unresisting in his firm grip. I allowed him to lead me
down the stairs and across the hall. Again the feeling
swept over me that this man would change the whole
course of my life, but somehow I was aware of a strange
confidence and strength transmitted from his hand. In a
low voice he said, 'Don't be frightened, little Katharine.
He's not as fearsome as he appears.' As if he were present-
ing me to royalty, he led me to where the old man stood
before the great stone fireplace.

'Grandfather, may I present Miss Katharine Beaton.' He turned to me. 'Miss Beaton, this is my grandfather, Duncan MacRaith.'

'I am honoured, sir.' He took my outstretched hand in both his, and I did something which I had never done before, save in the presence of royalty.

I curtsied. And as I stood up, my hand still resting between his, Duncan MacRaith carried it to his lips.

'My dear Miss Beaton, it is I who am honoured. I bid you welcome to Allt-nam-Fearna, and I wish you all happiness and content within these walls.'

It was a strange greeting, carrying as it did the implication that I might almost be coming to stay at Allt-nam-Fearna for some considerable time. In her original invitation, Mrs MacRaith had set no term to my visit, but from my own experience of house parties during my mother's lifetime, I imagined that about a month at the outside was implicit, and while it would be discourteous to raise the matter so soon after my arrival, I must nevertheless take care not to outstay my welcome.

'And allow me to present my grandson, Iain.' Duncan MacRaith turned to the younger man, who bowed, and said: 'Let me add my welcome, Miss Beaton. We are all happy to have the pleasure of your company.'

Did that greeting, I wondered, find an echo in the mind of Alasdair? I was to ask myself that question many times in the days that followed, and it would be a far distant day which would bring me the answer, after many intervening days when the thought would be a torment that that answer might never be the one I so wanted to hear.

And what had been the meaning of the overheard snatch of conversation between Mrs MacRaith and Ishbel, who so far had shown no overt resentment, yet whose words had been the reverse of welcoming?

I should, of course, have been prepared for what happened next, knowing where I was, but the unearthly wail which suddenly sounded took me completely by surprise and I spun round as if a banshee had swept through the open door, instead of a piper, marching down the hall. I had, of course, heard the bagpipes played at military parades and the like, but never before at such close quarters, and the sound swelled and echoed to the very rafters. Yet as my initial shock subsided, my blood seemed to stir to the wild air.

Alasdair's laugh was sardonic. 'That is a sound, Miss Beaton, to which you must become accustomed. I'm sorry if you were startled. Maybe you should have been forewarned. May we hope that you do not find it unendurably barbaric?'

Mrs MacRaith spoke for the first time. 'Don't tease Miss Beaton, Alasdair. That noise is enough to scare anyone at first hearing.'

'I beg your pardon, Miss Beaton.' His bow was ironic. 'I should have remembered that the *English* take their meals quietly.'

I tilted my chin and met his eyes squarely. 'I believe the pipes are meant to strike fear into the heart of the enemy, Mr MacRaith. Remind me to be suitably impressed. You may be surprised to learn that some Southerners even *like* pipe music. In fact, *I* do.'

'That doesn't surprise me, Miss Beaton. Looking at you, I find it hard to believe in your Sassenach ancestry.'

'And that, I take it, is the highest compliment you can bestow. Thank you, sir.' I curtsied, this time in mockery.

Alasdair's riposte was cut short by a stir at the other end of the hall, as the double doors opened and a little clutch of some half dozen people made their entrance. Mrs Mac-

77

Raith went forward to greet them, and introductions were made.

Ever afterwards, that evening remained stamped in my mind with the imprint of a stage performance. The chief characters already on stage, *Enter Right, various Guests*, and James Ridley, who stood out in complete contrast to the other men, since he was the only one not wearing the kilt.

The effect of theatricality was heightened because I knew nothing of the backgrounds of the various protagonists, and like the spectator, I would have to watch the play unfold before I could sort out the plot. Pressing the image still further, this was the Grand Transformation Scene, and the only reality became the painted gauze behind which, in the utter darkness, lay my previous life. I acknowledged each person introduced to me, but at the end of the evening, only one had made any lasting impact, and that was James Ridley. But that scene came later, at the end of the Act, so to speak.

One of the guests, a shortish, rather tubby, sandy-haired little man of middle age, detached himself and came up to Duncan MacRaith.

'And how is the Auld Laird tonight?' Behind the jocularity lay a shrewd concern, and the reply confirmed my suspicion.

'Well enough, young Laidlaw, to dispense with your physic and fuss. And well enough to take my dram, and to enjoy the company of a bonny lassie.'

With that he turned to me, extending his arm. 'I shall be honoured, Miss Beaton.'

Flushed with pleasure, I rested my hand lightly in the crook of his arm, and I felt like a princess as we passed into the dining-room. As was fitting, the Auld Laird took his place at the head of the table. I sat on his right, and on my right was the young man who had been introduced to me as Iain. Mrs MacRaith presided at the other end of the table, with the rest of the company ranged on either side. Immediately facing me a smiling little grey-haired lady kept a watchful eye on the Auld Laird, and I afterwards learned that her name was Euphemia (Phemie for short) Wishart. The next time I saw her, she was back in her nurse's uniform. On her left, facing me, James Ridley seemingly could not take his eyes from me, and his scrutiny at first embarrassed and puzzled me, then, unaccountably, I accepted as my due this look which held an element almost of recognition.

Conversation became divided between the Auld Laird and Iain, with whom I established an immediate bond in our mutual left-handedness.

'My dear Miss Beaton, you don't know what a relief it is to have a left-handed companion! You can't imagine what complications I usually have to cope with at dinner parties.'

'I can,' I said drily. 'I know what I went through at school. They just won't leave you alone, will they?'

'They will when you make your point with a straight left,' he laughed. 'But then, you could hardly take such unladylike action, could you. Are there others in your family?'

The casual enquiry lifted the edge of the gauze momentarily. Were there others? How was I to know? My mother was not left-handed. My father I barely remembered. And the normal family entourage of aunts and uncles, cousins, grandparents—where were they? I closed the conversation with a flat 'No', and changed the subject, turning to talk to the Auld Laird. This was no mere empty courtesy. I was genuinely drawn to Duncan MacRaith. I would have been proud had he been *my* grandfather. I have said that he was handsome, but it was something more than that. With his mane of flowing white hair, his piercing eyes and firm mouth, he was the image of all the patriarchs and saints. There was dignity, authority, and above all, a spiritual strength which seemed to flow from him. It was hard to assess his age. There was none of the softening which extreme age often brings, with its veil of sexlessness that makes a face neither male nor female. He had passed his looks down through the generations, for both Alasdair and Iain could have sprung from no other stock, and even Ishbel, in a gentler mould, showed the same features.

'Well, Miss Beaton, how do you like this part of the kingdom?'

'It's difficult to express how I feel,' I said. 'I find it at once beautiful and frightening, but above all, I feel at home here, but I can't really account for that, because'—I pulled myself up in time, and continued—'this is my very first visit to Scotland.'

'Then we must hope that it will not be your last.' He smiled, and raised his glass to me. 'To Catriona.'

'Thank you,' I said. 'That sounds so much more beautiful than Katharine, I think. No one would dare to shorten that, would they? I used to hate it at school, when I was called Kitty, or Kate.'

'Catriona it shall be, then, from now on,' he said. 'Between us twain.'

I don't know what drew my gaze, just at that moment, to the part of the staircase just visible through the wide-flung double doors, but I felt the compulsion which springs from being watched.

At the head of the stairs a woman stood. She wore a white dress, and a stole-like scarf of black lace, cobweb fine, so that the satin of her gown gleamed through it. Even as I looked, she turned and moved out of sight, into the darkness of the archway.

A movement from the other end of the table indicated that the ladies were about to withdraw. Mrs MacRaith said, 'Such a beautiful evening. It would be pleasant on the terrace, don't you think?' We followed her, and disposed ourselves on various seats, and listened to the piper who had played all through dinner. I sat gazing across the green park land, with its smooth turf patterned by the long shadows of the trees. In the distance I could see the cascade which fell continuously from the moor, and the combination of the strange, wild music, and the turbulent water, and the distant mountains brought a choking melancholy. It was so beautiful that I could have wept.

'You look pensive, Miss Beaton. Not sad thoughts, I hope?'

'Mr Ridley!' I swung round, startled.

'Oh, I do apologise. How clumsy of me to intrude into your reverie.' James Ridley stood looking down at me, and because his back was to the westering sun, I could not read his expression, or know whether he mocked. So I smiled and said: 'No matter. My thoughts are unimportant.'

'I can't believe that.' He made no move to leave my side, so I had to make the obvious gesture and invite him to sit in the vacant chair alongside my own.

'We have much in common, you and I, Miss Beaton. Strangers in a strange land.'

'A very beautiful land, though,' I answered. 'And one where I could happily spend the rest of my life, if fate so decreed.'

'You must dree your ain weird, Miss Beaton.' Alasdair's voice broke in, and I saw that I was now placed between two men whose mutual antagonism was almost tangible. 'You must excuse me, Ridley.' The apology was perfunctory. 'Miss Beaton, the time has come for you to be initiated into our outlandish rituals. Will you do me the honour of partnering me, please?'

Behind him, on the flagged terrace, Ishbel, Iain, Dr Laidlaw and the others were forming a set.

'But I know nothing of Highland dancing,' I protested.

'You'll learn.' He took me by the wrist and I rose to my feet.

He swung me into position, facing the Auld Laird, for whom a great carved oak chair like a throne had been placed on the threshold of the open casement; I saw that the piper had now exchanged his bagpipes for a fiddle, and as he gave us the opening chord, the ladies curtsied and the men bowed, then each of us turned to face our partner, whom we similarly honoured.

And then came the first of those inexplicable happenings for which I am still, after many years, unable to find a word which truly describes them. The nearest I can achieve is 'invasion', as if my whole personality, even my mind and memory, were at the disposal of another being, while I still had control of my own body, so that no one else appeared to notice anything different. As I had told Alasdair, I knew nothing of Scottish dancing. I did have, as some kind of background, a knowledge of English Country Dancing, from my school days, so that I was conversant with some of the terms. But this did not explain the ease with which Alasdair was able to guide me through the movements of a figure which I had never known.

'So you know nothing of Highland dancing, Katharine Beaton?' His whisper, as he took my hands and swung me in a kind of balancing movement, was ironic and incredulous. 'Well, then, let's see how you get on with "The MacRaith's Rant." ' He signalled to the fiddler, and the measure changed from a fairly slow beat to a rapid, wild dance which left me breathless and exhilarated and, when I had pause to think, astonished at the familiarity with which I moved through a maze of quite intricate figures. So that when the dance ended, and Ishbel came up to me, there was a strange look of reluctant admiration on her face, and I wondered what explanation I would be able to give her. The need was forestalled by Alasdair's hand beneath my elbow, steering me firmly back to my place at James Ridley's side. 'Oblige me, Katharine Beaton,' he said, in low voice inaudible to anyone else, 'by entertaining Captain Ridley.'

'*Captain* Ridley?' The pitch of my voice matched his.

'Yes. And I've reason to think he has other interests—which do not at the moment concern you. Just do as I ask, and don't ask questions.'

I felt my temper rising. 'Mr MacRaith, this is only the second time you have condescended even to acknowledge that I *exist*. Just what right does that give you to issue orders to me? I understood that I was a guest in this house, not an employee or a servant.'

He halted, and manoeuvred in such a way as to face me, as if engaging me in casual conversation.

'So, Katharine Beaton, you have spirit—and temper.' He stared down at me, half in mockery, yet tinged with something I was at a loss to identify; pleading, supplication, I couldn't name it, and then I had it. An appeal for my co-operation, as if we shared a secret. And I knew I would do as he asked, without question.

'There, Ridley, I am returning your charming companion. May I hope that you will appreciate and remember my generosity.' He bowed, and left us. James Ridley turned to me. 'Now just what does he mean by that, Miss Beaton? Believe me, I am delighted, but there are times when MacRaith leaves me puzzled.'

'Shall we charitably assume that it's a Scottish quirk?' I laughed lightly, determined to play the scene as comedy. 'Maybe we Sassenachs should band together. They say there's unity in strength, and it looks as though you are saddled with my company for the rest of the evening.'

'A charming burden and one of which I would never willingly be relieved.' He replied in the same vein, and I sensed that it would not be difficult to keep him at my side. Without staring too openly, I contrived to study him, and I liked what I saw. James Ridley, even in conventional evening dress, still looked what he was—a soldier. He was fair, without being strikingly blond, and his thick, straight hair lay sleek and neat to his well-shaped head. His features were almost aquiline, but without the ultimate fierceness the word implies. He lacked Alasdair's height by nearly a couple of inches, but his upright slenderness made him look taller than he was. Although there was no hint of foppishness about him, the adjective which to me summed up his appearance was *elegant*.

'You find this a great contrast to London, Miss Beaton?'

That ripped a hole in the gauze, and I was at once on my guard.

'You know I come from London, Captain Ridley?'

He smiled and shrugged. 'I suppose I jumped to a conclusion, Miss Beaton.'

'I see. Do I take it, then, that you too are from London. You said earlier that we have much in common.'

'Surrey. But near enough to get lumped in with London, which seems to be spreading out tentacles like an octopus.' He was regarding me with no attempt to disguise the scrutiny. 'You know, Miss Beaton, in spite of your English voice, you fit in here to the manner born. I suppose it's the dress, and a similarity in colouring, but you and Miss Ishbel could pass for sisters. And you danced

84

as if you had known those steps since childhood.'

'Oh, well, I was carefully piloted through the figures, you know, and if one watches the other dancers, it helps considerably.' Here was a Heaven-sent topic to steer him away from my real background. 'I find it a wonderfully exciting kind of dancing. Rather like a greatly speeded up quadrille, and it's really great fun—you must learn it if you're staying North of the Border.'

'I should be more at home doing the Lancers,' he answered drily. 'I feel that the kilt is part of the attraction.'

Somewhere in the distance a clock chimed, and he broke off, counting the strokes.

'Eleven o'clock already. And still not dark. I'd no idea it was so late. If you'll forgive me, Miss Beaton, I must leave you. I've an engagement.'

'At this time of night, Captain Ridley?' I raised my eyebrows and smiled with unashamed coquetry. 'Oh, come, surely you mean an assignation?'

He flushed crimson. 'Miss Beaton, please believe me, I have no wish to leave you and seek other company, but——'

'I believe you, Captain Ridley. I only teased. But look——' I indicated the four men now coming through the open casement, each carrying a sword. 'You can't leave just yet. They must be going to do a sword dance. We must see it.'

Alasdair, Iain, Dr Laidlaw and the other man whose name I learned afterwards was MacGilvray, stood four-square, facing inwards, and each saluted with his sword, which he then placed on the ground, the four points meeting in the centre. The gillie, Murdo, had laid aside the fiddle and had taken up the bagpipe. The tunes he played were the wildest yet, and I watched, fascinated, as the dancers sprang from side to side over the gleaming blades, with a precision and neatness that was incredible.

The strain died to a wail, then surged upwards again as the tune changed. It was a gay, impudent tune, that mocked and derided. And as the dancers stepped and whirled, they were smiling, as if at some shared ribaldry. I heard the man at my side draw in a sharp breath. I turned to look, and met a glance of such frustrated rage that I could only wonder whether it was something I had said which might have given rise to such fury.

The dance finished, and with only the most perfunctory 'Good night, Miss Beaton,' Captain Ridley was striding across the terrace towards the house. I saw Alasdair move unobtrusively to block his progress, and as if suddenly mindful of his manners, the captain veered and crossed to where the Auld Laird still sat.

'Sir, I have to thank you for a most pleasant evening. But if you will excuse me——'

The Auld Laird inclined his head. 'Captain Ridley. A pleasure indeed. But you'll not be leaving us so early, surely.'

'Captain Ridley doubtless has—*duties*, Grandfather.' Alasdair spoke. 'But you'll take at least a dram before you go, Captain. We had hoped that you might stay long enough to hear some music—even, perhaps, add your own contribution. Miss Beaton,' he turned in appeal to me. 'Persuade our gallant captain that the night is young, too young to drag himself away.' The words were bantering, but the message was deadly serious. Why, I wondered, when his antipathy to Captain Ridley was abundantly clear, was Alasdair so insistent that he should remain? I met his eyes defiantly.

'Why should you imagine that *my* wishes carry any weight, Mr MacRaith? If Captain Ridley wishes to leave us——' I shrugged. 'Surely that is a matter for him to decide. Nevertheless,' and I turned to the captain with what I hoped was a beguiling glance, '—I do hope that you *will* stay a little longer—just to please me?'

He stared down at me, almost grimly.

'You leave me with no alternative, Miss Beaton. There has never been a time when your wishes would not weigh with me.'

I was conscious of a surge of triumph. Here was a power of which I had never dreamed. And in that instant, I knew that it was not really mine, but that of the entity which had invaded me, and I was afraid, because I was helpless. Tomorrow, I would write to Aunt Zen and seek her guidance. For tonight, I was alone, and must rely upon myself.

I followed Mrs MacRaith into the hall, and across to another double door that led into a most charming salon, at one end of which stood a grand piano. Ishbel was already seated on the long stool, running her fingers over the keys. She played a selection of airs, some Scottish, some operatic, and for me, I supposed, some traditional English ballads. It was Iain who first drifted across, to lean on the piano, and sing, in a pleasing light tenor voice. It was an odd choice, I thought, and seemingly directed at Ishbel herself, this plaintive little ballad of frustrated love and parting, with 'ae fond kiss'. And was the sadness on Ishbel's face more than just my imagination?

She twisted round and called across to Dr Laidlaw. 'Now, Doctor, come and liven us up with one of your cheerful ditties. What will it be, now?'

The little doctor crossed the room with a jaunty jigging step.

'What better than "The De'il's awa' ",' he said.

Ishbel's fingers danced over the keys, and the doctor sang, if you could call it singing. He had no voice, but a cheerful, raucous delivery that chased solemnity out of the window. Most of the words were in such broad Scottish dialect that I barely understood them, but the gist of the song was that the Devil had danced away with the Exciseman. And I recognised the air, gay, impudent, and mocking.

Alasdair, Iain and the doctor semed to be sharing some private joke. The Auld Laird sat in his high chair, brought in from the terrace by the piper and another gillie. He sat with his eyes closed, but for all that, he was not dozing. The smile on his lips gave the lie to that, and I knew that he, too, shared the joke, whatever it was. So did the whole company, but for two—myself because I knew nothing, and James Ridley, to whom the song had some peculiar significance. This time his anger was carefully suppressed, but it was there. When the doctor had finished, James Ridley rose to his feet and crossed to Alasdair.

'MacRaith, you really must excuse me. It's past midnight and I must be on my way.'

'Then I'll not detain you, Ridley. Thank you for honouring us with your company for so long. I trust the evening was not—unendurable.' He glanced across at me.

James Ridley flushed at the irony. 'It has been a delightful evening, with charming company. But it must end some time, you know. I will pay my respects to the ladies and to your grandfather, and take myself off.'

The anticlimax must have been doubly humiliating. James Ridley took his leave and within a quarter of an hour, was back, flushed with exasperation.

'My car has let me down again. I can't get her to start.'

'Capricious as a woman!' The doctor's jocularity seemed a little misplaced, but he did offer assistance. 'Never mind, Ridley. Wait and I'll drive you back to the inn. Unreliable, these mechanical innovations. I'll stick to my mare. She'll get me up mountains that would rip the guts out of that fire-breathing chariot of yours.' But the doctor seemed in no hurry to leave. And for some strange reason, the urgency of James Ridley's departure had faded. With a glance at his watch, and a sigh of resignation, he sat down again, accepted another drink, and resumed his place at my side.

'Come, now, Katharine,' Ishbel called across to me. 'It's your turn now.'

'My turn? Whatever for?' She was gathering up her music, but still standing at the piano.

'Why, to let us hear *your* party piece, of course.'

'But I haven't one,' I protested. 'I don't sing, or play the piano, or anything. I've no accomplishments, I assure you.'

'I find that hard to believe, Miss Beaton,' James Ridley said. 'I thought all you young ladies were tutored in these arts.'

'Well, here's one who was not,' I said firmly. 'I've no intention of making an exhibition of myself, especially after such a standard as we've heard this evening.'

I prayed silently that Ishbel would not press me further. I had only to sing or play the piano to betray myself utterly, since, without conceit, I knew I had inherited my mother's voice and talents, and hidden in my papers were certificates to prove it. James Ridley came from London. He could not fail to know of my mother's fame, and it would not take long for him to connect Katharine Beaton at Allt-nam-Fearna with the Katharine Beaton of Daly's and the Alhambra. Was it my fancy, or did he regard me with some speculation, as if wondering whether he had indeed seen me before? That, of course, was impossible, but the chances were that he had seen my mother perform, and he could not know that the last thing I wanted was to be identified as Katharine Beaton's daughter. Of what use then my refuge, in this remote place? For I still feared that Gerald would exert pressure, and there were moments when it seemed that I had escaped far too easily. I still held firmly to the opinion that the man who had dogged me in the park had, in reality, been hired by Gerald to trace me and engineer my return to Fordingham.

I was saved from further embarrassment by the arrival of the tea tray, with accompaniments, for the ladies, and drinks for the men. James Ridley made it his business to wait on me, and it seemed to me that he had contrived so to position his chair that we were almost screened from the rest.

'Miss Beaton, I find this a little difficult to say, and I trust you will forgive my presumption, but have I your permission, when you return to London, to resume our acquaintance? It would give me the greatest of pleasure.'

It was a stilted little speech, outmoded in its phraseology, but I knew it masked a far stronger sentiment, and I was at once pleased and frightened. To command admiration was always pleasant, but I had to tread cautiously. To gain time, I temporised.

'That would be nice,' I said. 'My plans at present are a little uncertain, but if you will give me your London address, perhaps we might arrange a meeting.' James Ridley brought out a card case and selected one. 'And if I might pay my respects to your parents?' he queried.

'My parents are dead,' I said quietly. 'I have only a guardian.'

'I am sorry, Miss Beaton. Forgive my clumsiness.'

Once again, to my intense relief, further conversation was interrupted; this time by Ishbel resuming her place at the piano, to accompany Alasdair in one more of the strange, yearning Scottish airs which seemed to carry the sadness of the ages. Unwillingly, I looked up, aware once more that I was being watched. This time it was Alasdair's glance that caught and held mine, and I looked away quickly, because I knew that my own face would reflect the emotion I felt. But I could not shut out the words, and they went straight to my heart, sending a surge of joy through me.

> 'Bonny wee thing, canny wee thing,
> 'Lovely wee thing, wert thou mine,
> 'I would wear thee in my bosom,
> 'Lest my jewel it should tine.'

The song ended, and there was a general stirring among the company. The Auld Laird, leaning on Alasdair's arm, made a stately progress from guest to guest, and then stood at the foot of the stairs bidding each farewell. I was aware that Captain Ridley had taken my hand and was speaking to me. I must have made the appropriate replies, because he made his way to the door, then turned to look back at me. *And in that instant, I felt that unaccountable splitting of my being, because I can find no other description. It was as though half of me stood in the great hall, while the other half drifted silently up the staircase and along the gallery, and so great was the draining of my spirit that I feared I might faint. And to shut out the image of that strange 'double', I closed my eyes. When I opened them, the captain had gone, and with his going, I was myself again, whole, and unwearied in spite of the long evening.*

'You look tired, Katharine Beaton. You should be away to your bed.'

Alasdair stood before me, and I stiffened at the implied

command. The gentleness that had veiled his eyes as he sang was gone, and I wondered, now whether it had ever been there, or whether it was my imagination. I stared up at him defiantly. I would not be dismissed, like an obedient child who had finished the task she had been given.

'That, surely, is for me to judge, Mr MacRaith.'

He shrugged. 'As you please.' He turned from me and swung across the hall to give an order to the gillie who now stepped forward to assist the Auld Laird. On an impulse, I ran to him and placed my hand in his. The old man smiled, and leaned down, to brush my cheek with his lips.

'Such a bonny lassie,' he said. 'Stay, Catriona, now that you're home once more.'

I could not sleep. Too many odd little happenings disturbed me. What was the link between me and Captain Ridley, and what was the meaning of his words: '... never been a time when your wishes would not weigh with me ...'

What, too, was the reason for the antagonism between James Ridley and Alasdair? I did not dare flatter myself that it was on my account. In spite of the message in the song, I must not allow hope to govern reason.

Questions whirled in my mind, like an endless procession of people whose acquaintance I had to make. One above all puzzled me; the Auld Laird had treated me as if I were a member of the family, long absent and now returned. I was no more than a guest, I told myself firmly. My presence here was entirely fortuitous, depending on a kindly impulse on the part of Mrs MacRaith. Or was there some deeper reason for my presence here? Alasdair had said I must dree my ain weird. I took that to mean that I must endure what Fate had in store for me. I shivered, in spite of the warm summer night. Aunt Zen's words came back to me, and I wished for her counsel and guidance. Tomorrow I would write to tell of all that had passed.

Sleep still eluded me. I wished I had some means of lighting the lamp, so that I could read. But the fire was by now quite dead. It seemed odd to me, coming from the south, that even in the height of summer, the chill of the thick walls made this little log fire welcome. The crackle of the wood and the sharp aroma of the burning pine would always be with me, as a reminder, to carry me immediately to this far place where I seemed to belong though I did not know why. Now, lying in the half-dark, I knew I would not sleep again, and one thing bothered me. A prosaic enough thing—thirst, brought on by the highly seasoned dishes at dinner, no doubt. Carefully I groped for the carafe that always stood on the bedside table. I found it, and the glass; and because I was worried in case I spilled it, I got out of bed and padded across to the alcove, to draw the curtains in the hope that the window would afford at least a lightening, so that I could fill the glass.

The carafe felt curiously light, and as I gently shook it I realised with dismay that it was empty.

What had at first been no more than an irritation now became almost a torment. The 'Want a drink of water' of childhood was enhanced into a clamouring demand that would not be appeased. Of course I ought to have realised the utter stupidity of wandering round an unfamiliar house in the dark; but all I could think of was that long, cool draught of water. I would go down to the dining-room. Surely there must be water in a jug on the side-board. Even soda water would be better than nothing.

I had not bothered to put on slippers, and the stone stairs were cold to my feet, but I did not care. I reached the dining-room, and such had been my obsession with my need that the eeriness of the deserted hall made no impact on me. I cautiously turned the handle and stole like a thief towards the huge carved oak sideboard, which held an array of decanters, but not one carafe of water. Not even a syphon of soda water. I could have wept with the misery of my thirst. Still clutching the glass, I wandered back to the hall, and the full strangeness of my surroundings overwhelmed me in a flood of terror. What lurked in the dark shadow of the enormous open hearth, wide enough and high enough for a man to stand concealed? At one end, moonlight streamed coldly through the long windows, and even as I looked, it seemed that a shadow moved stealthily. Reason told me that it was nothing but a drifting cloud, but was it? And now I must climb the wide staircase; from the walls, the old Mac-Raiths stared down on me with cold malevolence. Their faces were no more than white blurs in the dim light, but I *felt* their enmity for this southern intruder.

My composure broke, and I ran wildly up the stairs, along the gallery and through the archway to the stone steps. I stumbled over each worn slab and still running, reached thankfully for the handle of the door. But now I found myself in another gallery-like room, with windows at each end. To the left, only the slightest lightening of the blackness, pierced by faint stars, indicated windows; to the right, the same cold arrows of moonlight as in the hall picked out the portrait of a woman, full length and life sized, on the wall facing me. Unwillingly, I was impelled forward, to stare at a likeness which almost gave the impression of looking in a mirror. One is generally credited with not recognising one's own image in another, but this was inescapable. The colouring was mine, the features, and the expression—what my school companions had always referred to as my 'you-be-damned' look, and the teachers had called dumb insolence.

Fascinated, I could not drag my eyes from her. Who was she? What had called forth that mutinous, defiant look which the artist had caught so admirably. It was a look which nevertheless had an element of humour and courage, and I hoped I might in time acquire such qualities myself. And even now, I felt that my fear had drained away. Here, in this long, bare room, I was at home. In the past, I knew, there had been furniture here —chairs, tables, and, most certainly, a spinning-wheel, and I was not surprised that in the corner, quite near the portrait, one did indeed stand, silent and still these many decades.

Once more a cloud veiled the moon, and I shivered. I must return to my own room for what remained of the night, though the greying of the far window meant that day was waiting. I turned to look once more at the portrait which seemed to glow white in the gloom. I had again that odd feeling of 'invasion', and it was with absolute confidence, as if I were quite familiar with the layout of the castle, that I quietly closed the door behind me, walked unfalteringly along a corridor, and opened a door. The door to the room I had found earlier. I crossed to the communicating door and opened it, passing through the adjoining room which I was certain had been Catriona's bedroom. On the night table beside the bed was a carafe of water. I filled the glass which I still carried, and drank deeply.

The water tasted of blood.

Sick with horror, I flung glass and carafe to the ground, and because there was not, as I would have expected, a splintering crash and the splash of water on my bare feet, I found myself whispering to myself, 'I must be dreaming.

This is a dream, a nightmare. I will wake up, I must wake up, I must ...'

But I found that I could not move. I was so weary that even to lift my arm would have required a strength I did not possess. At last I compelled myself to walk slowly towards the door which I knew led to my own room. I had not locked that door. That much I remembered. I fumbled for the handle, and with all my energy, pushed until I could just force my way through the gap. Again, the door closed behind me with a click.

I stumbled across the room towards the bed, and my foot must have caught in the trailing hem of my dressing-gown. I was falling, falling, down and down, into a deeper blackness than before, and I flung out my arm in an attempt to save myself from the shock of the crash I knew must come when my body hit the ground. As I fell, I saw the flash of gunfire, followed by the reverberation of the explosion.

CHAPTER SIX

THE CANNONADE went on. Blinding flashes, followed immediately by explosions which shook even the impregnable stonework of the castle. I could hear the rataplan of the fragments of shattered stones as they rained down ...

I opened my eyes. The din continued. Gusts of wind hurled a fusillade of rain against the windows and the lightning and thunder were virtually simultaneous. One earsplitting crash sent me diving under the bed-clothes in a childishly spontaneous reaction, and when I did pull back the sheet, I nearly screamed with fright. In the half light, a white figure stood beside my bed.

'Katharine! What a storm. I came to see if you were all right—that last crash was awful, wasn't it?'

I sat up and pushed the damp wisps of hair from my forehead.

'Ishbel! I thought for a second you were a ghost.' I let out my breath in a great sigh. 'What a night. It just doesn't seem possible after such a lovely evening.'

'It happens up here.' Ishbel perched on the edge of the bed. 'These sudden changes. I expect it was the climax of all that hot weather.' She got up and wandered over to the window. 'It doesn't look as if it will clear much today. We shall have to find something else to do with ourselves. I'd planned to take you riding, but that can wait.'

So that was how we came to be making a detailed tour of the castle. For myself, I did not mind at all. It was all new and interesting, and I could happily have spent many hours wandering from room to room, and along the panelled corridors, and up and down the winding stone stairs.

Ishbel was a competent and knowledgeable guide, and because she so obviously loved Allt-nam-Fearna, she made its history alive and interesting, without any of the dry repetition of the professional guide.

'How old is the castle?' I asked.

'Older than history. They say that there was a Pictish fort on this site before the Romans came. The castle itself was built somewhere in the twelve hundreds and it lasted for over five hundred years—until the English battered it to rubble in 1719.' She looked sideways at me. 'It was little more than a heap of ruins,' she went on, 'until about a hundred years ago, when Grandfather's grandfather re-built it. Where we are now—the Old Guardroom—is the oldest part. And the wing where you are, that's part of the original castle.'

I stared round the room curiously. It was strange, yet familiar, and as I laid my hand on the rough stone wall, I seemed to drift back down the ages. I shivered a little.

'Dreadful things happened here,' I whispered. 'Here in this room—hate, and death, torture, murder. But love, too. Love that was—no, *is*—stronger than death, and still has power.'

'How do you know?' Ishbel demanded. 'What can you know? You're right, though. Did you read the story somewhere?'

I shook my head. 'I'd never even heard of Allt-nam-Fearna before your aunt invited me to stay. But I suppose every old castle has seen some pretty horrible deeds within its walls. There's the Tower of London as example.'

It was Ishbel's turn to shiver. 'There were grim things done there,' she agreed. ' "Man's inhumanity to man." Why are men so cruel, Katharine?' I shook my head helplessly. 'That's something we'll never understand,' I said.

'What did you mean, just now, when you said something about love that still has power? Do you really believe that?'

'In a way, yes. It's hard to explain what I *did* mean, but in some odd way I know that here, in this room, something still has to be resolved.'

I walked over to the figure of the soldier in the red uniform. 'Who was this?' I asked. 'Does he come into it somewhere?'

'That's quite possible,' Ishbel said. 'One of the more grim relics, in fact.' She came and stood beside me, and pointed. 'He's said to have shot himself. If you look closely, you can see a splash of blood on the red.'

'He had nothing to live for,' I said. 'Everything he cared about was gone, wasn't it?'

'We don't know.' Ishbel looked bewildered. 'How do you know, anyway? I mean, we don't even know who he was, just that he was one of the occupying garrison—a captain—whose body was found here after the bombardment.' She looked around to see if anyone was listening. 'Some say he walks, but I've never seen him.'

I touched the arm of the figure and it was almost as though the sleeve contained a flesh-and-blood arm rather than a wooden one. 'I wonder what his name was, and what connection he had with this room.'

Ishbel shrugged. 'I don't suppose we'll ever know. Most of the records were destroyed in the fire.'

'We shall know. Not yet, but eventually. We shall know,' I said with conviction.

'Katharine, you frighten me. Are you sure you're not

psychic or something? I mean, you do really say the oddest things, and you seem to know about Allt-nam-Fearna when you couldn't possibly know, if you see what I mean.' She took my arm. 'Let's go and look at the rest of the castle. There are times, particularly on a dull day like this, with the rain drumming, when this room gives me the creeps. This is where the prisoners waited, before they took them out and shot them. Sometimes the rain sounds like the drum roll.'

The tramp of feet in the stone corridor could have heralded the arrival of a 'Prisoners Escort' but proved to be nothing so fearsome. Alasdair came in, stamping and shaking raindrops from his cape, and tossed a bundle of newspapers on the table.

'There you are, ladies. All the latest fashion, gossip, scandal and crime, all the way from England. And while we were in Kyle, I collected the post.' He sorted through a bundle of letters, laid some on a side table, retained a couple, and handed a small bundle to Ishbel. 'Take those to Aunt Agnes, will you, please. I rather think it's the invitations to the ball at Dunkillan.'

Perhaps I stood looking a bit like Oliver Twist, because he smiled at me with a touch of irony. 'No, Miss Beaton. I'm sorry—nothing.'

I felt unaccountably desolate, then told myself that I could hardly expect letters so soon after my arrival. My own letter to Aunt Zen could barely have reached her, let alone received an answer. Ishbel sensed my disappointment, and linked her arm through mine. 'Come with me to Aunt Agnes's room and we'll have our coffee with her, then I'll show you the rest of the castle.'

Alasdair looked up from the letter he was reading.

'You'll find it interesting, Miss Beaton. Although we can't compete with Glamis in the matter of dark secrets known only to the heir, we still have our own brand of horrors, as Ishbel has doubtless told you. I understand you have already visited the Falls of Blood. I trust you enjoyed taking the waters?' He was watching me carefully, and I determined to give him no satisfaction.

'Yes,' I answered. 'A beautiful spot, and a water supply that must have been a blessing to the dwellers here in former times.'

'You drank some?' he persisted. 'How did you find it?'

'Why, like water, of course. What else?' I said lightly. I felt Ishbel's grasp tighten on my forearm, and wondered what the little exchange meant. But she drew me towards the stairs, and together we made our way to Mrs MacRaith's charming little sitting-room.

She was not alone. Standing in the window alcove, staring out at the dripping trees, was Iain, and the expression on his face could scarcely be described as amiable.

Coffee had already been brought, and Mrs MacRaith waved us to chairs.

'Just at the right time,' she said. 'Katharine, I know you take yours white.' She filled a cup and handed it to Iain. 'For Miss Beaton, Iain.' He took it with patently bad grace, handed it to me, then made for the door.

'Don't go, Iain. Stay and take coffee with us. It's hardly courteous to our guest to hurry away.' She poured his coffee. 'Black for you, and white for Ishbel.'

Without appearing boorish, Iain could not escape, and since the only seat was at my side on the little chaise-longue, he sat down. I caught the glance that flashed between him and Ishbel, a blend of mutiny and resignation.

'Now tell me, what have you girls been doing with yourselves?'

'Ishbel is showing me round the castle, Mrs MacRaith. Such a wealth of history, quite fascinating. When we have finished coffee, perhaps you will excuse us—there's still so much to see, and we don't wish to hinder you.'

She glanced through the window. 'What a pity there is such a change of weather; and the rain makes it all the more dreary. But you must not judge our climate by this one day, Katharine. You will see that it will change just as quickly, and you will be able to resume your excursions.' She turned to Iain.

'I leave it to you, Iain, to see that Katharine is suitably mounted—nothing too fiery, please. Have a word with Alasdair, and naturally, you must consult Katharine herself.'

'Yes, Aunt Agnes.'

'And of course,' she continued, 'you will ride with Katharine. I don't care for her to risk losing her way.' And again, that exchange of looks with Ishbel.

'Ah, there's something else.' Mrs MacRaith indicated the letters which Ishbel had brought with her. 'The Dunkillan invitations—you will, of course, accompany us as our guest, Katharine. Iain will partner you.'

I heard Ishbel draw in her breath sharply, but she said nothing.

'I will accept on your behalf, Katharine. I am sure you will have a most enjoyable evening, and we must select a costume for you—maybe Ishbel did not mention that it is a masked costume ball?'

'No. But we hardly had time to discuss it. Thank you very much and I shall look forward to it. What costume do you suggest I wear?'

'Oh, I leave that to you girls to decide.' She smiled. 'I'm sure whatever you choose will be attractive. Then we'll have little Miss Mackenzie in to do the work. She sews for us, you know, and she's really very obliging.'

The chime of the elegant little ormolu clock on the

mantelpiece reminded us of passing time. Iain stood up and held the door open for us. I smiled and passed through it, but as Ishbel followed, Mrs MacRaith called her back.

'Ishbel, dear, I shall need your help with my letters this morning. Iain can take your place and escort Katharine round the castle.'

'But Aunt Agnes——' Both exploded with the same protest, then each waited for the other. Ishbel, looking resigned, pursued the matter no further, and obediently sat down at the writing desk. Iain, however, was more determined.

'I'm afraid Miss Beaton will have to excuse me, Aunt Agnes. I've an appointment with Alasdair to ride over to the Mains.'

'I understood that that was not until after lunch, Iain,' Mrs MacRaith said smoothly. 'You will oblige me by doing as I ask.'

I stood in the doorway, feeling thoroughly uncomfortable. The tension was unmistakable, as was the determination of each of the trio, though for what reason, I could not possibly know. Mrs MacRaith's attempt to throw me into Iain's company was verging on blatant; it had begun with her placing us together at dinner the previous night, and later in the evening I had been fleetingly aware of her veiled displeasure that I had danced, not with Iain, but with Alasdair, and later had been monopolised by Captain Ridley. Could it possibly be that she had selected me as a likely bride for Iain? I felt my mouth set involuntarily. I would not be manoeuvred into any marriage which did not spring from my own wishes and desires; further, I would have no respect for a man who allowed himself to be so used.

Iain looked desperately uncomfortable. To continue to

defy his aunt laid him open to a charge of discourtesy towards me. For my part, I disliked being put in a position where I felt a thorough nuisance, and I sought in my mind for an excuse which would release both of us, but that again, was elusive, and was finally forestalled by Iain's capitulation.

'Very well, Aunt Agnes. If you will allow me, Miss Beaton.' He closed the door behind him, and led the way along the corridor.

We emerged on the main gallery which led to the great hall, and there I paused. 'Mr MacRaith——'

'Iain, please,' he interrupted me. 'And, if you will allow the liberty, Katharine?'

'Of course—Iain. But please, if I'm being a nuisance, I can just go and wander round the castle by myself. You don't need to escort me, though I'm not denying that it's always more interesting to have a guide.'

'Katharine, I'm delighted. It's just that I feel that Aunt Agnes is at times——' he shrugged. 'Please don't misunderstand me, but because she reared me, and Ishbel, after we lost our parents, she does tend to assume rights of control.'

I smiled. 'Don't they all? My mother was just the same.'

'And your father?'

'I don't know—I mean, I can hardly remember him.'

'Well, I think he would probably have spoiled you outrageously. Who wouldn't, with such a pretty little daughter.'

'Now that is sheer flattery,' I laughed. 'Come, now, and show me all the beauty of Allt-nam-Fearna—tell me first, when did you kiss the Blarney Stone?'

'Never,' he said seriously. 'I'd no need. I spoke but the truth.'

I felt my colour rise, but all the same, such admiration

was not displeasing. 'You're very gallant,' I said softly. 'Even with all these beautiful ladies watching us——' I indicated with a sweep of my hand the portraits which lined the walls.

'Even with the beautiful ladies,' he said gravely. 'And had we a Raeburn or a Reynolds at our command, you could have taken your place without fear.'

One by one he recounted the histories of the various people depicted. But the catalogue came to an abrupt halt early in the eighteenth century, after which there was a gap of about a hundred years.

'The rest of us are in the dining-room and the salon,' he said. 'I won't bother you with them—you'll see enough of them in the next few weeks. Let's go and look at the State Rooms——' He led the way up the other flight from the main staircase.

'This, of course, is where Bonnie Prince Charlie slept?' I gazed in astonishment at the huge fourposter, hung with heavy brocade curtains, and with extraordinary carved urns sprouting ostrich plumes, and my remark must have sounded more flippant than was intended, for Iain answered it seriously.

'By the time Prince Charles Edward came to these parts, Allt-nam-Fearna was hardly in a condition to afford him any shelter. Of course, some of the MacRaiths were out in the Forty-five. Others of that ilk—well, we don't care to talk about them.' I sensed that I had made rather a *faux pas* and was grateful that he ignored it, and continued on another line.

'This room is really rather a sham. Oh, I don't mean that the bed and all the other furnishings are fakes. They're genuine enough, but they're not part of the original contents of the castle. Most of those were destroyed in the fire—I expect Ishbel has told you about that?' I nodded and he went on:

'Then when Great-great-grandfather began the rebuilding at the turn of the century, about 1802, he went searching for suitable pieces, and that was one of them. In fact,
the whole place is a bit of hotch-potch. Great-great-grandfather must have had big ideas, and he got an architect
who humoured him and came up with this pseudo-
Norman-cum-Gothic grafted on to what remained of the
original fortress of the MacRaith's.' He paused, and gave
an embarrassed little laugh. 'Oh Lord, Katharine! I'm
blethering on like a guide-book. You must be utterly bored.'

'I'm not,' I said. 'I mean that. I find it fascinating—this
continuity. It's difficult to explain, but I feel linked with
the past—I suppose we all are, really. But in a setting like
this, the feeling's particularly strong. Please go on,' I
pleaded. 'There's so much I want to know.'

'You're being kind,' he said. 'But you did ask for it!' He
led the way from the main gallery and up another of the
spiral staircases—there seemed so many of them—to a
corridor which seemed familiar, and soon I realised why.
This was where I had wandered in the night. And when
Iain opened a door, we were in the room where I had
seen the spinning-wheel—and the portrait.

'Now this is really genuine—about all that survived,
with the Old Guardroom, of the original fortress. This is
Catriona's Gallery.'

Just in time I stopped myself from saying: 'I know.'
But the portrait drew me like a magnet, and I walked
swiftly across the polished floor which daylight now
showed to be patterned with an inlay of different woods
in a strange design of linked squares, similar to the
tapestry design in my room.

I halted before the portrait, dumb with amazement.
The face which last night had gazed back at me in a

reflection of my own features was now veiled. At first I thought it was a piece of delicate black lace which had been hung from the top of the frame, and put out my hand to draw it aside and look again on that face. Iain's voice stopped me.

'Incredible, isn't it. Everyone thinks it's real.'

'When was it overpainted?' I heard myself ask the betraying question.

'Now how did you know that, Katharine?' Iain countered. He spoke softly, almost accusingly, and I flushed crimson, stammering in my confusion.

'I—I don't know—well, I suppose I read it somewhere. In some book——'

'But it has never been written about, Katharine. This is one of our little family secrets, rather like Glamis. This room isn't generally shown to casual visitors.'

'Then why——'

He shrugged. 'I don't know; I simply felt that you were a fitting person to be admitted. Don't ask me why.' He took my arm and led me over to the deep window embrasure, with its bench seats similarly cushioned to those in my room. I sat down, and from the diamond-paned casement I could see into the walled garden. I worked it out that we were on the same corridor as my bedroom, and it seemed to me that this room must lie on the other side of the rooms into which I had blundered. But I said nothing of this to my companion.

'There's a story about the portrait and most of the contents of this room,' Iain continued. 'That is Catriona. She sat for an unknown painter who might have been staying in the castle to do work on the older pictures. Anyway, this was apparently finished in 1714. She would have been about nineteen, and very lovely, by all accounts. Even beneath that veil, you can see that she had the most glorious hair—almost bronze in colour.' I realised that Iain was staring unashamedly at my hair, and I was aware of the unspoken comparison.

'Please go on,' I said. 'Tell me about the veil.'

'Well, after The Fifteen, the castle was occupied by an English garrison. At first they behaved very well, but then there was that little affair in 1719 at Glen Shiel, and the English shelled Eilean Donan. I suppose they thought that while they had some ammunition handy, they might as well do the same for Allt-nam-Fearna. So they marched the garrison off and cleared the castle, and banged away from the Sound. Most of the castle was destroyed; this bit survived, and so did the portrait, but Catriona vanished. In fact, she rather let the side down. She ran off with a Redcoat.'

'Is that the only portrait of her?'

'The only remaining one. There was a miniature, according to an inventory which came to light during the restoration of the castle. Catriona spent some time in Edinburgh, staying with a distant cousin who was married to an artist, for whom she sat. There's a portfolio of his pencil drawings in the library, and one sheet is noted as being preliminary sketches for a miniature.'

'And he actually did paint it?' I asked.

'Oh, yes. One is ringed, with a further note "completed and presented to Mistress Catriona on her birthday". It isn't dated, but it would have been about the same time as that portrait, or possibly a little earlier.'

I was looking down into the walled garden, now blurred with the fine rain that fell from the dull grey sky. 'I wonder what happened to her?' I said. It would not be difficult to imagine that I saw her moving about the garden, and Iain's words were an echo of my thought.

'She is said to walk. Down there, in the garden, and—here in this room.'

'Have you seen her?' I challenged. 'Do you believe that?'

'Have I seen her? No. Do I believe she walks?' He pointed to the portrait. 'The man who painted that veil saw her. He came from Paisley to work on the restoration. Some of the family portraits were found hidden in the cellars. Others were traced to people who had bought them when the old castle was looted—again by the English, if you'll pardon the insistence.'

'It happened,' I said. 'One isn't always proud of the way in which one's forebears behaved.'

'Well,' he shrugged, 'I suppose one can be grateful to the people who had bought them and handed them down. But some did need cleaning and so on, and this laddie spent hours in this room—until the night that Catriona came and ordered him to paint that veil over her likeness, and told him to give the family a message: that it would be removed when she was restored to her rightful position, but that would not be for two hundred years.'

'Seventeen nineteen. Nineteen nineteen. Seven years from now. I wonder where we shall all be by then.' I looked at Iain and pressed my hands to my lips to prevent myself from crying out. To my horror, I could see right through him, as if he were a ghost. The impression was momentary, but utterly uncanny. If Iain noticed my dismay, he made no comment but went on with his narrative. 'He did as he was told, as you can see, but he left the castle in the morning, utterly distraught, and never even waited to be paid for his work.' He stood up, and held out his hand to me. 'Come along, little Katharine. That's enough for today, and it's nearly lunch time anyway.'

'Then I must go and tidy myself,' I said. 'I might as

well go this way, rather than go down all those stairs and up again to my room.' I walked to the door, and was going to return to my room along the corridor I had taken the previous night—until I recalled that I had only dreamed that I had visited this room. *But did I dream?* It had been so real at the time, but I had to offer myself a rational explanation, even if my mind refused to accept it.

'You can't go that way, Katharine.' Iain spoke almost peremptorily. 'There's no way through to that wing—now.'

'How silly of me,' I laughed to cover my confusion. 'I've lost my bearings completely. Well, you'll just have to guide me, please. And of course, I do thank you for a very interesting morning. It has all been quite absorbing. I wonder what happened to Catriona's diary, though.'

'Who said she kept a diary?' Iain demanded. 'No one's ever found one; it would be in the Library, if it survived the bombardment.' He caught me by the wrist, and swung me round to face him. We were so close that he could have taken me in his arms and kissed me—had he been so inclined.

'Just who are you, Katharine Beaton, and how is it that you know so much about Allt-nam-Fearna?' He spoke in a fierce whisper. 'Above all, why are you here?'

And I could not answer him.

In silence he piloted me back to the main gallery and indicated the way to my room. I found my way without difficulty, washed my hands and tidied my hair, and when the luncheon gong sounded went down to the Guard-room.

The afternoon brought no improvement in the weather, and Ishbel apparently had no inclination to resume her

110

role of guide, so I made my excuses and went up to my room. Over lunch the suggestion had been put forward by Mrs MacRaith that there might be an excursion to Inverness, with some shopping in mind, and I fell in with the idea willingly, since I wished to make arrangements with my bank. Though why I should have need of money, I did not know. Everything was provided at Allt-nam-Fearna, down to postage stamps for which only token payment was expected. Even in the short time I had been there, it became quite plain to me that I was completely dependent for any form of transport upon the family or the servants, who would only act on instructions. Virtually, I was marooned, unless and until Mrs MacRaith gave me some indication that my visit was at an end.

I sat at the lowboy, and took a sheet of paper from the drawer. I selected an ordinary pen, and began to make notes of the purchases, minor enough, which I would make in Inverness. I wished to select some little present to send to Aunt Zen, but this was not an easy choice, since she was no ordinary person, and the run-of-the-mill gifts would hardly appeal to her.

I finished making my list. It was short enough, and for that matter, could have been entrusted to anyone else making the journey. But I felt that I must explore what I later came to regard as my escape route, though why I should have this thought in my mind, I could not explain. Mentally, I went back over the route by which we had come to Allt-nam-Fearna, and recalling that long drive by motor, from the station to the castle, I realised just how cut off I was, and how I had committed myself to a visit which could only be terminated at the will of my hosts. Why should this give rise to alarm, I could not say, except that the very situation gave me the impression of being trapped. But I dismissed such fears as being over-imaginative, and forced my mind back to more everyday matters.

And since I had nothing to do until tea time, I took out my pencils and sketch pad, and started to make rough drawings of the costume I might wear to the ball. I drew first a Plantagenet costume, but I dismissed that idea on account of the flowing drapery of skirt and sleeves, added to the steeple hennin which would prove cumbersome and uncomfortable. I fiddled about with an Elizabethan design but that again I dismissed for the same reason. It would be no easy matter to dance reels and strathspeys while wearing a farthingale. I considered Regency, and the design I produced was pleasing and wearable, and I went on to elaborate it.

Then, incredibly, I saw my hand, quite without direction, pick up the pencil and literally slash a heavy line right across the sketch.

'Now why on earth did I do that?' I was so utterly astonished that I spoke aloud. 'But I suppose there was something wrong with it.' I let my hand rest idly on the pad, the pencil held loosely between my fingers. With my eyes unfocused, I stared into the middle distance, seeing nothing clearly, only a blurred impression of tossing sea merging without horizon into a grey sky veiled by the drifting rain.

At first I was barely aware of the movement of my hand, but it became more definite, and I looked down, to see on the pad the incisive lines of another drawing. Some instinct told me to relax and let this strange power have its way. Fascinated, I watched as my pencil, with no vestige of hesitation, added line after line to the sketch of the dress I knew I would wear to the ball.

It was the dress Catriona wore in the portrait. With a few more sure strokes, the pencil completed the hair style, and deftly added the finishing touches of features.

t was—Catriona's face, behind the veil. Or it was my own.

Still obedient to this compulsion, I opened the drawer nd took out the quill pen. Dipping it in the inkwell, I nked in the drawing which seemed to spring to vivid life. o Catriona could draw, too. My own talent was not in ignificant, or so I had been told at school, and later, when had sometimes entertained my mother's guests at Ford ngham, my flair for catching a likeness had earned praise. But this drawing achieved a standard beyond any to which I aspired, and I realised how careful I must be in uture, not to let anyone know of this strange power. It could not be commanded; it was totally unpredictable, and it would set a standard which I could not always reach. But one person must be told, and that was Aunt Zen.

Carefully I made a copy on a fresh sheet of paper, and even doing that brought home how capricious this con trolling entity was, for the sketch I now made was a characterless imitation. But it would serve, and Aunt Zen would understand. Then I realised that I must, of course, send Aunt Zen the original. Only the copy must be shown to anyone else.

Pushing both sketches to one side, I took another sheet of paper and began my letter. I was so absorbed in the relation of the curious events of the last two days that I was unaware of Kirsteen's knock, and only her gasp of dismay as she waited to set down the tea tray, distracted me from my writing.

The impossibility of carrying on a conversation without a common language is more than a little frustrating. All I could do was gather up both letter and sketches, slip them into the drawer, and make room for the tea tray which the girl set in front of me. I saw that there were two cups, and that meant that either Ishbel or Mrs MacRaith intended to join me.

It was Ishbel who knocked, and as I anticipated, the conversation was all of the coming ball. It would be wise, I thought, to find out first what Ishbel intended to wear. She needed no prompting and produced a book, possibly a novel, with illustrations of Stuart costumes.

'I'm going as Henrietta Maria,' she stated.

'Delightful,' I exclaimed. 'Your hair will look charming, with all those ringlets. What colour gown will you wear?'

'Blue. Turquoise blue, and of course, cream lace—Aunt Agnes has some and she'll lend it to me. And I think an apricot under-skirt.'

I handed her the cup of tea which I had poured for her. She sat down on the window seat facing me. 'I hope you didn't mind,' she said. 'I mean, that I told Kirsteen to bring tea up here.'

'Of course not,' I said. 'I'm glad you came. You can help me with my costume.' I opened the drawer just wide enough to get my hand inside, and drew out the copy of the original sketch. 'How do you like that?' I asked.

She took the paper, and stared at it with very nearly as much dismay as Kirsteen had done.

'Really, Katharine, you're uncanny. How could you possibly know what Catriona looked like without that veil—you saw the portrait?'

'Yes,' I said. 'I liked it so much that I wondered whether anyone would mind if I copied the gown. As for the features—' I shrugged '—I just sketched them in from my imagination. Is that what she looked like, do you think?'

'I know she does. I've looked at that portrait so many times, ever since I was quite small, till I feel I really know

114

what she looked like.' Ishbel set down her cup, stood up and crossed to the dressing table, from which she took my silver-backed hand mirror.

'See for yourself,' she said. 'If you wear that dress, you will *be* Catriona.' And I knew she was right, though she could not know just how true her words were. If I wore that dress, the being who had been Catriona would take command. I shivered a little, and wondered just how much of a risk I was taking. Yet I longed to know more of this woman who had lived so long ago and whose hand reached out to me from the darkness, as if she needed my help.

'Well, that's settled, then.' I deliberately brought myself back to a normal plane, and Ishbel and I continued our discussion.

'What about the men?' I asked. 'Will they condescend to dress up.'

'Of course. That's all part of the fun. Alasdair will have to partner me as Charles the First. And if you go as Catriona, Iain will go as James the Eighth. The Chevalier de Saint Georges. The *"Old Pretender"* to you, Sassenach!' She laughed at my lack of understanding. 'There's a family legend—probably entirely without foundation—that he was once in love with Catriona. They're supposed to have met when she was finishing her education in France.'

She didn't love him, though. Her love wore a red coat, and she knew the torment of a divided loyalty. I did not speak the words aloud, but the conviction remained, and I knew that the time would come when I in my turn would be torn in two directions by love. But that prospect I dismissed. I did not like what I had seen of love. I did not want any part of it.

Why, then, was I conscious of a twinge of jealousy when

Ishbel announced that Alasdair would partner her? A[nd] why, come to think of it, was she in turn slightly annoy[ed] that Iain was to partner me? Nothing overt, just a vei[led] resentment, but I could find no reason.

'When is the ball?' I enquired.

'Oh, not for weeks yet—it opens the grouse season [but] the invitations are always sent out in good time, so t[hat] people can get costumes, and also make arrangeme[nts] with their guests who come for the shooting.'

'But I may not still be here,' I said. 'I can't just du[mp] myself on you indefinitely. I didn't expect to stay for m[ore] than a fortnight or three weeks at the outside.'

'Oh, that's rubbish,' Ishbel exclaimed. 'It's lovely h[av]ing you here, and you can stay for weeks and weeks a[nd] weeks. You simply can't go back to London before [the] season opens, you'll miss all the fun. Besides, Aunt Ag[nes] won't let you go.'

And with that parting shot, which gave me much f[ood] for thought, she was gone.

With the intention of finishing my letter to Aunt Ze[n, I] opened the drawer, or rather, tried to open it. Someth[ing] at the back was making it stick, and I eased my hand in[to] try to dislodge it. I took out the letter and the sketch[es] and felt for the quill pen which again seemed to h[ave] curled itself in such a way as to cause the drawer to jam[. I] felt carefully along the underside of the table, and [my] finger caught a kind of ridge, as if there had been a sli[ght] warping where two pieces of wood joined. The end of [the] quill was wedged under this ridge, and I worked [my] fingernail along it, to release it. It tilted under [the] pressure and something—it felt like a notebook—slid i[nto] my hand.

It was a book. Thin, covered in black leather that w[as] dry and flaking though the embossed initials were s[till] bright as the day the gilder had set them there. 'C.MacR', and the year, 1719. This was Catriona's diary.

I opened it at random. The angular writing was difficult to decipher and the ink had faded to a pale brownish tint. But even if I could have made out the letters, I did not understand the words. I spelled out a word here and there; it was neither French nor German, and then I knew. It was Gaelic.

I would have to let someone into the secret; otherwise I would never know about Catriona, and I had a strong feeling that it was essential that I should know more about her. I turned to the last entry. It was dated 31st October 1719. And into my mind came the lines spoken by Hamlet:

'The rest is silence.'

CHAPTER SEVEN

I DON'T know what prompted me then, but I returned the
diary to its hiding place and said nothing of my discovery.
In the whirl of the next few weeks I had little opportunity
for private conference with anyone, and to some extent
the matter was pushed to the back of my mind, rather as
though Catriona had taken herself to some place beyond
my ken. I had written a full account to Aunt Zen, and her
reply, though brief, was explicit. The gist of it was that
the time was not yet, and that I must be patient. For the
time being I was content to obey her. Life had opened
out into a delight of golden days—golden almost in the
literal sense.

For with the clearing of the rain, there followed long
days when the sun shone, and the three of us—Ishbel, Iain,
and I—rode, and picnicked and painted, or sometimes
just lazed by the side of the burn, chattering or silent as
the mood took us. And for gold, there was the broom and
the gorse—everywhere, like a flood, they spilled over the
mountainsides, and along all the roads, in an incredible
blaze of brilliant yellow. The individual blooms were
so close that not a speck of green could be seen. For the
rest of my life, I thought, I would remember that golden
summer.

I began to think that it was no more than imagination
on my part, that Mrs MacRaith had any matchmaking
intention. My relationship with Ishbel and Iain had de-
veloped into a delightful brother-and-sister situation in
which I was all the more happy because I had never

enjoyed such companionship before. Of Alasdair we saw little, and I still retained the impression that he resented my presence at Allt-nam-Fearna.

'Aren't you bored with all this?' Ishbel's question was emphasised with a sweep of the arm. 'Doesn't it seem terribly dull to you after your gay life in London?' Was there a renewed element of probing? I pushed away the idea and answered truthfully that in my present mood I'd ask nothing better than to let life go on in the same way for as long as the Fates allowed.

'Do you really mean that you would never want to return to England? That you'd be happy to go on living here?' Iain demanded.

I considered the question carefully.

'Yes,' I said. 'I really believe I would.'

Ishbel took up the thread.

'In spite of the isolation, and the weather? It isn't always like this, you know. There are days, weeks, even months on end when it's drear and cold, and the rain falls in an endless curtain, or the mist rolls down from the mountains and blankets everything. And then the snow comes, and all the roads over the moors disappear, and the only way open to the rest of the world is by sea, and even that is sometimes taken from us, when the boats daren't venture.'

'You paint a gloomy picture,' I said. 'Are you trying to drive me away?'

'No,' she said. 'Stay for as long as you will—until you see the swallows gathering, and you want to fly with them.'

Iain was silent, as if waiting for my verdict, and I knew that in some way my answer was important to him.

'I think anywhere, whatever the rigours and hardships, would be a happy place, given the right companions.' I deliberately put the word in the plural, but in spite of myself and in spite of my intention to avoid entanglements of any kind, it was Alasdair who came into my mind. So that when Iain leaned towards me and covered my hand with his, and said quietly: 'Then we must find you a husband who will keep you with us, little Katharine,' I felt a kind of treachery, for I knew that I could not respond to the warmth of his growing attachment. I looked up, to meet Ishbel's eyes, and what I saw shocked me. It was the nearest thing to jealous fury that I had ever encountered, and it was gone before I could even be certain. Ishbel, I thought, would make a very difficult sister-in-law. I wondered, then, if she and Iain were twins, which would account for the very close bond which seemed to exist between them. I knew little of the interrelationships of the MacRaiths, and one does not, when one is a guest, ask for the pedigree of one's hosts. And who was I, to enquire about other peoples' standing when my own was so dubious?

But I forgot neither the conversation, nor Ishbel's attitude, fleeting though it was. But why this implication, this time from Iain, that I should remain at Allt-nam-Fearna?

I took up the unspoken challenge by saying lightly: 'I didn't come to Scotland to find a husband, you know. This is just a very pleasant interlude for me, before I get down to the serious business of life. I can't impose on the very generous hospitality of Allt-nam-Fearna indefinitely. Now that we're on the subject, tell me something. It would look ungracious if I went to your aunt and said I wanted to go home, and it wouldn't be strictly true. But I must really return to London soon, so just when and how do I bring my visit to an end, however reluctantly?'

'Do you really want to leave us, Katharine?' Iain asked.

'What I want is not really relevant,' I said a little impatiently. 'I just want to know how long I should stay.'

'I think you should leave that to Aunt Agnes,' Ishbel said. 'She usually contrives to make her wishes quite clear —in the nicest possible way, of course. So as long as you are happy to be here, I don't think you need worry about protocol.' And with that I had to be content.

To change the subject and to ease the slight tension, I asked, 'When is the ball?' Our costumes were ready, and I began to feel considerable excitement at the prospect, like a child who has been promised a treat. It was as if I knew that that night would be one of the pivotal events of my life.

'It's on the 10th,' Ishbel said. 'They'll all come flocking in with their little guns and bang off at those wretched birds, and they'll begin the celebrations with a grand dance.'

'Ishbel, you're a heretic; how can you sit there, within sight of one of the finest grouse moors, and talk like that.'

'Well, you won't get me out there, I promise you. What about you, Katharine?'

'I've got to admit that it's not really something I'd enjoy.'

'But you'll probably enjoy eating the kill, all the same!' Iain riposted drily.

I flushed. 'Oh, well, aren't we all rather hypocritical, loving animals and birds on the hoof and on the wing, but also on the plate!'

'And a nice haunch of venison as well, I suppose.' Iain laughed.

'Oh, come along, let's stop trying to sort out our motives and go home.' Ishbel sounded impatient. I began to get together my painting things, and in the cool of the late afternoon we all wandered back to the castle.

*

I was very conscious of making an entrance. Deliberately I paused at the half-landing. In one hand I carried my fan, and in the other, the little black satin mask, edged with fine narrow lace. Over my arm was draped the gossamer lace shawl which, until tonight, I had not realised was the very finest wool, hand-knitted in an intricate pattern which Ishbel informed me was traditional.

'This isn't——?' I hesitated to take it.

'The one belonging to Catriona? No. she was probably wearing that when she ran off with her Redcoat. It's the same pattern, though. Do you mind wearing it?'

'No, of course not,' I protested. 'It's very beautiful. I'm most grateful to whoever is lending it to me.'

'It's a family heirloom. Aunt Agnes said you were to wear it.' The slight emphasis on the word 'you' indicated that possibly Ishbel herself had thought to wear the shawl, though it would hardly have been a suitable accessory to her costume.

'Come down when you are ready,' she said, and left me to myself, standing before the mirror. I arranged the shawl over my arm and then, for the sake of effect, I held it before my face. The picture was complete. As to what happened next, I shall never be certain. It could have been just a trick of the light, or a defect in the mirror, which seemed to cause my reflection to waver and ripple; and there seemed to be a double image, as if another figure stood behind me, fractionally to my left. The reflection merged with mine, and the mirror was flawless. But for tonight I *was* Catriona.

This time, as I stood on the half-landing, it was Iain who advanced to take my hand.

'Katharine, you look beautiful. Remember me, won't you, when every man on the ballroom floor is jostling to initial your programme!'

'You shall have the very first dance,' I said lightly. 'And if no one else has claimed your attention—perhaps the last waltz, if that is a tradition up here as it would be in England.'

'I shall keep you to your promise, then.'

In the Powder Room at Dunkillan Ishbel and I surrendered our wraps and adjusted our masks. On entering, I had been conscious of a score of curious glances and a little whispering, but Ishbel fended off questions, made conventional introductions, and shepherded me with the ease of familiarity through corridors even more confusing than those at Allt-nam-Fearna.

We entered the ballroom, and Iain's prophesy was fulfilled, for as we joined the men of the party, there was a definite surge in our direction. Masks made formal introduction unnecessary, and competition to initial our programmes was fierce. I was conscious of a sudden silence within our little group, and looked to see the reason. Alasdair and Iain both appeared to be regarding me intently, but I realised that in fact, their gaze was focused a little beyond, on whoever stood directly behind me. Slowly I turned. Despite the mask, the powdered wig and the costume, I was in no doubt as to the identity. I knew now who the Redcoat was.

'Catriona! You have returned to me at last.' I shall never know whether I truly heard those words spoken aloud, or whether they were just in my mind. All I remember with certainty is that James Ridley took the card which I held in my hand, and pencilled his initials in every vacant space—there were few enough. And he frowned at the sight of Iain's initial's for the first and last dances. Then deliberately, he crossed them out and substituted his own.

Iain flushed with anger. 'Ridley, that's unpardonable!'

'I beg your pardon?' James Ridley raised a hand and tapped his mask, and though his eyes were veiled, his mouth twisted in an ironic smile that was not to be mistaken.

'It would take more than a scrap of black satin to hide your identity, Ridley.' Iain's voice held suppressed fury.

'I think tradition gives me the prior right,' Ridley answered. 'The Old Pretender's connection was, I believe, somewhat apocryphal, was it not?'

'Let it rest, Iain.' Alasdair's voice, incisive and commanding, put an end to the little scene. Ridley extended his arm to me, and bemused, I took it.

Because so many of the guests were English, invited for the shooting, the programme was a judicious blend of dances, and I found myself moving easily and smoothly through the familiar figures of the Lancers.

'What did I tell you?' he whispered to me. 'He'll get his own back when it's a strathspey or an eightsome.'

When he returned with me to my own party, the tension seemed to have eased, and because he was apparently unattached, he accepted Alasdair's invitation to join us.

'I had thought that you were away to London?' Alasdair said.

'Unfinished business.'

'Then let us hope that it will soon be brought to a speedy—and possibly satisfactory—conclusion.'

'That is in the lap of the gods.'

'To which particular god do you offer sacrifice?' Alasdair's tone mocked. 'Neptune, shall we say?'

I—or Catriona—tapped his arm. 'Come sir, you are talking in riddles and neglecting me. That is quite unforgivable and you must pay a forfeit.' He turned to me, unwillingly. 'And that is——'

I frowned in mock severity. 'I don't know—yet. But I have no doubt that I shall think of something suitable. I'll hold it in reserve.'

The evening passed in a kaleidoscope of colour and sound, and I was whirled from partner to partner so rapidly that their names made no impression. Only one was written indelibly, both on my programme and on my mind, and I wondered what part James Ridley would play in my future, and what had been his role in the past, in Catriona's life? Her diary might give me some clue, if I could only get it translated. But intuitively I knew the connection did exist.

In one of the longways dances, I found Ishbel at my side. She leaned towards me and whispered: 'You've made a hit with the captain, Katharine. That's quite a conquest, believe me.'

'I don't think so,' I whispered. 'He's just being polite because he was invited to join our party.'

'Don't you believe it! He's really smitten, and I'm simply delighted for you, Katharine. He's a charming man, and he'll make you an excellent husband.'

You're running on a bit fast, I thought. *Why so anxious to get me settled so soon?*

The dance started up, and I had no further chance for confidences for the time being. But later, when the Redcoat's arm firmly held me in a waltz, I felt my pulse quicken. Or was it Catriona who smiled and flirted with this man whose attention she so obviously desired? In the whirl of the dance I came face to face with Alasdair, and the conflict inside me was so fierce that for a second everything blurred before my eyes.

'Catriona, are you all right?' Ridley's voice was anxious. 'It's very hot in here. Will you walk on the terrace with me? The air will revive you.'

'I'm all right, thank you, Captain Ridley, but I think I would like to rest a little.' He steered me deftly across the floor and when we reached one of the open casements, he swung me neatly away from the dancers and out on to the terrace. Discreetly arranged tables, with lanterns swinging from adjacent trees, made convenient little arbours suitable for private conversations, without being so secluded as to give cause for compromise.

We sat down, and for a space there was silence between us, then he leaned over and took my hand.

'*Catriona, we have so much to say to each other.*'

I turned my head, and smiled. 'Yes, Hamish,' I said.

What had I called him? Not James, though it sounded not dissimilar, but a name I had never known before. Later I was to learn from Ishbel that it was the Gaelic variant, yet now I, a Southerner, used it as naturally and unthinkingly as he had addressed me as Catriona.

'What is happening to us, Catriona? How did you come here, and why? And who are you, really?'

Who was I? That question wrenched me back to reality.

'I don't know how to answer you, Captain Ridley. I think we must both have lost touch with reality in this romantic masquerade. It's easy to imagine that we may have met before, perhaps even in some other time. But the fact remains that you are Captain James Ridley and I am —Katharine Beaton, dressed up as a woman who has been dead these two hundred years.'

'I see,' he said quietly. 'So that is how you feel. Well, I must respect your feelings, but you cannot prevent my wishing to know you better, Miss Beaton, and with your permission, which I trust you will not withdraw, I will still hope to resume our—friendship, if and when you return to London.'

'Captain Ridley, you say *if* and when I return. Is there

any doubt in your mind?' He did not answer immediately, and when he did speak, it was with some hesitancy, as if he searched for words.

'Doubt? I don't know. There's nothing I can put my finger on and say: "That's it." Yet there *is* something odd. Miss Beaton, do you have any family connection at all with the MacRaiths?'

'None whatever. As you surmised, I'm a Londoner.'

'Beaton is a Scottish name. And there's this uncanny resemblance——'

'Oh, come, Captain Ridley. The resemblance is only one of colouring, emphasised by the costume I'm wearing. How can you be so certain, anyway, since I'm masked?'

'You won't believe this, Miss Beaton, but I *know* the face of that woman in the portrait. Veil or no veil, mask or no mask, in looks you *are* Catriona.'

'Then it must be the most astonishing coincidence,' I replied. 'I met Mrs MacRaith in London, quite by chance. We became friendly, and she invited me to spend a holiday at Allt-nam-Fearna. It's as simple as that. And now' —I rose to my feet—'we must go back to the others. They will be wondering where we are.'

'As you wish,' he said quietly. 'In any case, it will soon be time for the Grand Parade and general unmasking.'

Unmasking. That was something I'd left out of my reckoning. There might just be someone from England who would recognise me.

'Then I will be the only one who is not unmasked,' I said lightly. 'I may take *this* off,' and I touched the little eye mask which I still wore. 'To remain in character, I must still retain *this*.' And I lifted the lace veil and draped it over my head and face. James Ridley stopped abruptly and catching my arm, swung me round. 'Just what are you afraid of, Miss Beaton?'

'Afraid? Why should I be afraid, Captain Ridley?' I tossed my head and sailed through the open casement, leaving him staring after me, nonplussed.

When I rejoined my party, I apologised for my absence and explained, excusing myself because of the heat and the excitement. And when the signal for the Grand Parade was given, I took my place beside Iain, with Ishbel and her royal partner, as was fitting, in front of us.

Nor were we the only representatives of the Stuarts in that brilliant assembly. The ill-fated Mary, and Lord Darnley; the Young Chevalier and Flora MacDonald; Charles II and a laughing Nell Gwynne; and like the tail of a comet, a motley retinue of all the fictional characters imaginable. The gay procession swept round three sides of the great ballroom to the music of the pipes, and on a dais at one end sat the host and hostess, with the Auld Laird, Mrs MacRaith, and some half dozen more of the local landowners. Each couple in turn moved up the centre of the floor, and just below the dais halted, and removed their masks. The man bowed and the lady curtsied, and was led away to the supper room. When our turn came, Iain took my hand and whispered, 'Come, Katharine, and unmask the loveliest one of them all.' I felt the blood mount in my cheeks, and my hand shook as I removed my mask, still leaving the veil in place. Then Iain, before I could protest or stop him, gently lifted the veil and let it fall to my shoulders. I heard the sharply indrawn breath of some of the lookers-on, and a little spatter of handclaps. Embarrassed, I dropped the deepest curtsey, and then, my heart pounding, I allowed Iain to lead me through the open double doors to the ante-room. Ishbel danced up to me, took my hands, and kissed me on both cheeks. 'What did I tell you, Katharine? And now I'd stake my next month's pocket money that you will be the one to be presented with the Silver Thistle.'

I was too stunned even to ask what she meant. 'The tribute to the most charming lady of the evening, and the most attractive costume,' she told me.

The ante-room continued to fill, until the press was almost unbearable, making it obviously difficult for the footman to reach Iain with the message which confirmed Ishbel's prophecy.

'Come, my lady,' Iain extended his arm to me. 'Do you know that I am the proudest man here tonight?'

The throng parted to make way for us, so that our return to the ballroom resembled a royal progress, and when Iain led me on to the dais, it was the Auld Laird who placed in my hands the velvet-lined case displaying the most charming brooch, in the shape of a thistle, with stem and leaves of silver, and an amethyst forming the flower head.

'Oh, how beautiful!' I exclaimed.

'Then it is worthy of the beautiful wearer,' he said. 'And since beauty lies with kindness, you will, I hope, give an old man the great happiness of dancing just one measure with the loveliest lassie ever to wear the Thistle.'

'I shall be honoured, sir,' I said, and again I curtsied.

I marvelled at the will-power which gave him the strength to carry him through the figures of the dance without one stumbling step, and with a grace and elegance which many a younger man might have envied. Again, as on the first night when he had taken me in to dinner, I felt like a princess. I saw Dr Laidlaw's anxious glance, but it would have been an insult to suggest that the dance should be brought to an end on his account, and when the Auld Laird piloted me back to a seat on the dais, his step was unfaltering.

A spontaneous burst of applause from the other dancers

brought us both to our feet, to acknowledge with bow and curtsey the warm expression of appreciation.

'Lassie, you give me back my youth.' Duncan MacRaith leaned towards me and took my hand. 'Never leave us, Catriona.' I did not know how to answer him, and all I could do was smile, and press his hand in gratitude. What would I not give, I thought, to do as he asked, and stay.

And then Alasdair mounted the dais. 'With your permission, Grandfather.' He bowed to me. 'You owe me at least one dance, Katharine Beaton.'

'I owe you nothing, sir, so far as I am aware.' I flashed him a smile, taunting and coquettish, and stood up. 'But I *will* bestow,' and I placed my hand in his. And so we whirled through the exhilarating 'MacRaith's Rant' once more; it was not mere imagination on my part that Alasdair's arm tightened as he swung me.

The ball was coming to an end. I could not remember when I had had such a wonderful evening. I would try, in time, to remember all those with whom I had danced, but it was a dazzling procession which left me breathless. And I had danced once again with Captain Ridley, whose accomplishments were more extensive than he professed, since I found myself between him and Alasdair in a spirited 'Dashing White Sergeant', at the end of which Alasdair detached me and whispered a command which roused my temper.

'Just tell me why I should go to any trouble to find out when Captain Ridley is returning to London. Ask him yourself, if you're so anxious to find out,' I flashed. Nevertheless, quite fortuitously, I was given the information.

'One more dance, Miss Beaton?' James Ridley's words were almost a plea.

'Captain Ridley, you have completely upset my card tonight!' I exclaimed. 'What will my partners think of me?'

'This one is an extra, at my request,' he said, and swung me into a schottische. When it ended, he did not immediately take me back to my party.

'Thank you, Miss Beaton—thank you for an evening I will always remember.' He lifted my hand to his lips. 'Think of me a little, won't you? I shall take a very happy memory when I return to London next week. I sincerely hope that our meeting will not be unduly delayed.'

I sighed, embarrassed at being unable to give an honest answer. 'I have your address,' I said, 'and you may, if you wish, write to me care of my bankers. I shall look forward to resuming our acquaintance.' I felt as if I had offered dry crumbs to a starving man, but the future was so vague that I could give no other answer.

I returned to Allt-nam-Fearna in a daze of happy weariness, too tired even to contend with Alasdair.

'Well?' he queried.

'Next week sometime. He didn't say which day, so you'll have to be satisfied with that scrap of information.' For a fraction I forgot my tiredness. 'Why are you so anxious to know?'

'Never you mind, little Katharine. But thank you all the same.' He busied himself with lighting my lamp, then slid a hand under my elbow. 'Come, I'll light you to your room—you're half asleep already.' I made no protest, and at the door of my room he handed my lamp to a drowsy Kirsteen, who helped me to undress. I felt guilty that I had kept her so long from her bed while I enjoyed myself. I fell into bed, and the last thing I remembered was Kirsteen stroking the satin of my gown as she hung it in the closet. I smiled and said, 'Thank you, Kirsteen, and good night. It was a lovely ball.' Perhaps she understood me, for she smiled happily, picked up the lamp and shading it with her hand, blew out the flame. Carefully she set the lamp in the hearth, where embers still glowed. Then I heard the door close softly, and I drifted into deep sleep. When I woke, the sun was pouring through the window, and Kirsteen was setting a tea tray on the table by my bed. I hoped she was not as drowsy from lack of sleep as I now was. I stretched like a cat, and relaxed once more while she poured my tea.

A light knock on my door, and in answer to my 'Come in,' Ishbel and Mrs MacRaith entered.

'Well, my dear, and how did you enjoy your first Scottish ball?'

'Mrs MacRaith, it was simply wonderful. I enjoyed every minute.' I sat up and allowed Kirsteen to drape a shawl round my shoulders, though the air was so warm that it hardly seemed necessary. Bright sun made shining beams where particles danced that were invisible by the ordinary light, and I had the fantastic thought that these beams were of the stuff which could on occasion form themselves into definite images in the likeness of a being long taken from this plane.

Ishbel was doing her usual butterfly flit, and had reached the closet where my last night's gown was still visible through the half closed door. She swung the door wide and for a fleeting second the gown filled out and expanded into a figure, and in the dimness of the closet it was not a dress-hanger, but softly rounded shoulders and a swan-like neck which kept it from collapsing to the ground in a flurry of satin and lace. But the face was hidden.

'Mrs MacRaith, I must thank you for the loan of that lovely shawl. My costume would have been incomplete and undistinguished.' I turned to Ishbel. 'Could you pass it to me, please, Ishbel. It's on the dressing table.' She fetched the shawl and I took it in my hands, smoothing the delicate mesh, so fine that it would have passed through a ring. As if she read my thought, Mrs MacRaith said: 'It can be passed through a wedding ring, you know. In fact, this one is a family heirloom and is a traditional wedding gift. My husband's mother threaded it through the ring which my husband later placed on my finger.' She leaned over and took my hand. 'Such slim fingers. All the same, when you marry, my dear, it will be threaded through your ring before your husband slides it on to your finger.'

'But I've no intention of marrying yet,' I exclaimed. 'And why should you give *me* a family possession. There are others with a better right than I.' I looked across at Ishbel a fraction of a second before she could veil her expression, and I shivered a little at this revelation of the other side of her character.

Carefully I folded up the shawl and handed it to Mrs MacRaith.

'Mrs MacRaith, I could not possibly allow you to make such a generous gift, even if I did intend to marry.'

'My dear,' she said quietly, 'it is for *me* to decide to whom the shawl will pass. I have no son to take a wife, nor a daughter to whom I might bequeath the shawl.' Her voice held an infinite sadness.

'Come, Ishbel,' she rose to her feet. 'Katharine will want to dress.'

'Yes, Aunt Agnes.' The words were spoken with deceptive meekness. She was standing by the dressing table, fingering the discarded accessories of the previous night. She looked across at me. 'Are you keeping your card as a souvenir, Katharine?' The artless question held a tinge of malice. 'Where is it? It isn't here. Did you put it in your bag? May I look—I must see who you danced with.'

'Have a look,' I laughed, 'I really can't remember what I did with it—I danced myself to a standstill.'

Ishbel picked up my satin dorothy bag, slid her fingers into the top and eased it open. 'Nothing here,' she announced.

'Then I must have dropped it—I thought I had it on my wrist.'

'So you did,' she said. 'Look——' she picked up and dangled my long kid glove. 'The cord's still there, and the pencil, but no card—now I wonder just which of those smitten admirers stole it as a keepsake—or did *you* give it to the gallant captain?'

'Ishbel, you are impertinent.' Mrs MacRaith spoke from the doorway. She looked across at me, and her expression was not one of pleased indulgence. 'I hope, Katharine, that you were not indiscreet enough to compromise yourself?'

I bit back the retort that it was no concern of her what I did, and treated the matter lightly.

'I think Ishbel is teasing me, Mrs MacRaith. As I said, I danced with so many people that I hardly remember their faces, let alone their names. Yes, I do remember now, it *was* Captain Ridley who chatted with me on the terrace. You recall how hot it became in the ballroom, of course. And I suppose he and I would have something in common —after all, we're both English, so it's only natural that we should gravitate, isn't it?' *Why should I need to defend my conduct? I'd done nothing of which I was ashamed.*

Mrs MacRaith's face softened. 'Of course, child. You'll think I'm a fussy old hen, but I do feel in some measure responsible for you while you are in my house.' She moved away beyond my field of vision, and Ishbel, with an impish expression on her face, skipped after her.

'All the same,' she threw over her shoulder, 'I still think

he's really smitten—and you might do a lot worse, you know.'

Might I? I wondered, as I completed my toilet. There was a substance of truth in Ishbel's raillery, and I could not deny that the captain was a very handsome man, with great charm. But I would not be deflected from my resolve. Before I could accept any man's offer of marriage—other than Gerald's—I *must* know that my own background held nothing that might later bring shame to either partner. And recollection of Gerald initiated another train of thought. Had he indeed given up the idea of pursuing his fantastic proposition? Perhaps my fears were after all groundless, and that the connection between him and the man who had spoken to me in the Fields was, in fact non-existent, since commonsense told me that it would have been a simple matter for that man to trace me, merely by following me home on some previous occasion. *Too many romantic novels*, a mocking little voice in my mind said. All the same, who *was* he, and why had he addressed me by name? It was a little mystery I might never solve.

So I would put it all from my mind, and enjoy the present, and when I did return to London—well, as Alasdair had put it, I must dree my ain weird, and take whatever path was decreed.

CHAPTER EIGHT

THE AUGUST days unfolded, and Ishbel and I were thrown more and more on to our own devices, since Alasdair and Iain were out with the guns all day, and we had no desire at all to follow. We wandered whither we chose, provided always that we kept clear of that part of the moors now sacrosanct to the sportsmen. It had seemed strange to me that Allt-nam-Fearna housed no visitors, but Iain had explained that the shooting was leased to the castle at Dunkillan.

'Landed we may be,' he had said wryly, 'but the days are gone when we could afford to entertain lavishly. Great-great-grandfather's Folly——' he pointed to the grey mass of Allt-nam-Fearna. 'Every penny he had went into the rebuilding and later, into the furnishings.'

'But it is a very lovely place,' I said. 'Outside, it looks grim, but inside, in spite of——' I cut myself short and continued. 'Inside there are so many lovely things, and there's a kind of welcoming warmth. It's difficult to explain.'

'For all its louring exterior, little Katharine, you feel at home at Allt-nam-Fearna?'

'Yes,' I said, startled by his percipience. 'Yes, I do. Though I don't know why I should. I only know that I shall be very sorry to leave, and if I may, without imposing on your hospitality, I'll return.'

'Oh, I know you will,' he said softly. 'Nothing is surer than that.'

'What's that?' Ishbel demanded, as she joined us. Iain

tapped her gently on the nose. 'Keep that little neb out of other people's business!' he said affectionately. 'Now, where are you two off to today?'

'Calum's Castle,' Ishbel answered him. She turned to me. 'It's an old ruin right high on the cliffs, and the sea-birds are fantastic. Have you ever seen puffins? They're like little old bodies holding meetings and they get together in threes and fours and you'd really think they were having the most solemn conference.'

'You'll not go to Calum's Castle today, Ishbel.' Iain's veto was sharp and authoritative.

'And why will we not?' demanded Ishbel defiantly. 'I'm not a child, you know. And neither is Katharine. I'll not be told what I may and may not do.'

'You'll do as I say,' Iain said quietly. 'Those cliffs are dangerous. When I'm at leisure, I'll take you myself.'

'Oh, well! I suppose you're right.' Ishbel's lower lip jutted sulkily. 'Where *can* we go, then? Or should I say, where *may* we go, with your gracious permission?'

'Preferably inland,' Iain said. 'There's a mist coming in from the sea, and you could easily lose your way.'

A gillie came towards us, leading the horses, and he and Iain helped us to mount. As we rode across the courtyard to the massive gateway, Iain called after us: 'Now mind what I told you, Ishbel. Go inland.'

Ishbel muttered something under her breath. 'What did you say?' I asked. She repeated aloud some utterly incomprehensible words, and then translated for me: 'Keep your breath to cool your porridge! Iain, I meant, not you, Katharine.'

'Well, I understand that,' I said. 'But where are we going, if we can't go to the tower you spoke of?'

Ishbel looked conspiratorial. 'Wait until we're out of sight of the house. Then we'll make a wide sweep through the glen and over the river, and you *shall* see Calum's Tower.' She shrugged. 'Oh, it's only a ruin, hardly more than a square of walls and some heaps of stones. In fact, quite a lot of the stones from the ruins were used in the restoration of Allt-nam-Fearna. It gives me the shivers sometimes, when I think that the slab that is part of the ceiling above me, particularly in the Guardroom, could once have dripped blood from a murdered MacRaith.' She glanced back over her shoulder. 'We can turn off here— they can't see us.'

Bearing in mind what Iain had said, I was dubious, and said as much.

'Och, Katharine, don't worry! I've ridden all round here since I was a wean. I'll not get you lost.' Ishbel laughed at my doubts. 'Iain's a proper "Cassandra" when it comes to predicting sea mist—anything to keep folk from getting down to the caves.'

'Why should he do that?' I asked. 'Is he afraid people will wander in and get lost, or something?' Ishbel looked sideways at me. 'Or something,' she agreed. 'Now just look at the weather today. Do you really believe that there's any danger of getting lost in a fog?'

The path on which we rode followed the contour of the hill. Below us, but not so far as to be out of sight, the river babbled over its rocky bed, making leaps over minia-ture waterfalls, swirling into deep pools where it had eroded the banks. Grotesquely twisted rowans leaned pre-cariously over the water; delicate birches dotted the boulder-strewn slope, and where the path dropped to the water's edge, sturdy alders made a denser growth. And through the leaves of the trees, the sun probed with golden fingers. It was indeed hard to imagine how it would look when the coiling mist insinuated between the trunks, blot-ting out the water, darkening the sky, and blanketing everything in the menacing silence which mist always seems to bring.

On the other side of the path, sparse woodland straggled upwards; between gaps in the trees I could see that beyond lay a stretch of turf dotted with stunted bushes and bare boulders, as if the very bones of the earth had thrust through the scanty soil. Higher still, the undulating ridge of the hill cut into the skyline; a few grazing sheep were silhouetted against the clear blue of the sky, where shreds of cloud trailed lazily. From where we were, it was not possible to see that the near horizon was only the beginning of the undulating moor that swept away to the distant mountains, fold upon fold, seemingly unending, stretching to infinity.

Gradually the wooded scene gave way to the encroaching moor, and the path we were following swept upwards in a wide arc which brought us eventually to the top of bare cliffs which fell so sheer to the sea that one could almost believe that in some far distant age a race of titans had thrust their spades deep into the earth, and into the hole they dug, the greedy ocean had rushed, never again to be drained. And even the outline of the cliffs was jagged, where narrow chasms had been hacked into the land, and the besieging waves still clawed angrily at the last bastions of the earth.

'Don't go to the edge,' Ishbel warned. 'Sometimes there are rock falls, where the weather has eroded the cliff face.'

'Don't worry! I'm not the venturesome type.' I said. 'But it is a fantastic rock formation, isn't it?' From where we stood, as it were at the base of an enormous 'V', we could view each cliff face, cut laterally by row upon row of ledges where seabirds jostled and fought for territory. The air was alive with their plaintive wailing as they planed and wheeled, and it was not difficult to translate the sound into human voices calling for rescue from the hungry sea.

'There it is.' Ishbel pointed to where, at the far end of a narrow isthmus, stood the ruined stronghold which had once defied man from landward and Nature from seaward. 'Do you want to go and look at it?'

'Well, I thought that was what we came for,' I said.

'I've seen it dozens of times,' she shrugged. 'I really only came this way just to spite Iain for being so bossy. I don't really want to traipse all that way just to have another look at a heap of stones. But you go, if you like. It won't take you long, then we can go down to the cove and eat our sandwiches and you can do some sketching, if you want to. There's a good view of Calum's Castle from the other side of the river.' Ishbel sat herself down at the foot of a bent and tormented thorn bush and it was quite evident that she had no intention of going further. The horses cropped contentedly at the short turf, and the sheep came to stare and then moved away because no tit-bits were offered.

I walked along the narrow isthmus towards the castle, and even on this calm day, at this height the wind pulled at my skirts. I took care to keep to the centre of what was hardly more than a causeway where only a handful of men could have marched abreast to storm Calum's impregnable fortress, and where a determined sortie by the defenders could have hurled the invaders into the deep chasms on either side, into the waiting waters.

I reached the outer wall, and saw that Ishbel was quite right. Here was little more than a pile of stones—jagged walls pierced at intervals by loopholes now enlarged by wind and weather to irregular holes. Only in one corner, sturdily defiant of all that Nature and vandals could do, a square tower stood stark against the sky. In that instant I was reminded of the Lightning Struck Tower pictured on Aunt Zen's card. Was this the one she had seen, I wondered. Doom and destruction chimed well with the scene, and I shivered inwardly.

For a short space the breeze died away, and I heard nothing but the wail of the seabirds and the surge of the waves below. Then there was a slight rattle, as if a stone had been dislodged. I had seen no one as I approached the castle, but that did not mean that I had it to myself; after all, this was land over which one might roam without trespassing. I walked right round the outside walls, but saw no one. In the seaward wall a low archway gave access to a small inner courtyard, and I stooped to enter. I straightened up to find myself face to face with James Ridley.

I was so dumbfounded that I could only stare incredulously at the man I had thought to be five hundred miles away.

At last I found my voice. 'Captain Ridley! I thought you were in London.' He smiled a little ironically.

'That was the impression I wished to give,' he said. 'And I imagine that you very efficiently transmitted the information, though unwittingly.'

'Not altogether unwittingly, if you mean what I think you mean,' I said, and looked straight at him. 'You *used* me, Captain Ridley. And so did Alasdair MacRaith. He to obtain and you to pass on information—false information, so it appears.' He had the grace to colour.

'Just why are you skulking here, Captain Ridley? I hardly imagine it is to study the bird life.'

'No,' he said quietly. 'But I do ask you to believe that my reason for being here is not one for which I need be ashamed. It is important, and it is necessary, and I have to ask you now to do me a great service.'

'Why should I?' I demanded. 'If you have good reason to remain here, why don't you do so openly?'

'Unfortunately, Miss Beaton, it isn't always possible to be frank and open about one's movements. Can I ask you to trust me, and equally important, can I ask you to say nothing to anyone of having seen me here?'

I moved across to peer through one of the gaps in the wall. In the distance I could see Ishbel, standing by one of the horses. She turned to look towards the castle and I waved to her. Captain Ridley was close beside me, but out of her line of vision.

'Will she come here?' he asked. 'I saw you arrive.' He indicated the binoculars which dangled from a strap round his neck.

'So you watched me? Then why didn't you find some way of keeping out of sight until I'd gone?' I queried. He drew a deep breath.

'Will you believe me when I tell you that I very much wanted to see you again, Miss Beaton.'

'Even if it meant that your presence in these parts would be discovered? You were prepared to take that risk just for the sake of a few casual words from me? I find that extremely flattering, but a little incredible.'

He took both my hands in his and drew me away from the embrasure.

'Don't you know, Catriona, that I would come from the ends of the earth just for a minute at your side? That I would scant my duty to be with you? That I would barter my eternal soul to win you for my own?' Then his arms were round me and his lips cut short the protest that rose to mine, and in that instant I, or whoever inhabited my body, yielded completely to the surge of passion that drained all strength and resistance. The pounding of my heart all but choked me, and I could feel the responsive

142

beat of his. For a moment we clung together in fierce desperation, and the part of me that was still Katharine remembered the song that Catriona could never have known, yet which mirrored her love so clearly.

'... had we never loved sae blindly ... never met—or never parted, we had ne'er been broken hearted ...'

I drew away from him ... 'When did we love and part?' He held me close and laid his cheek to mine. 'Catriona, I don't know. I don't even understand. All I can think of is that you fill my waking thought and my dreams. I'm a soldier, a plain man, and practical. This is something beyond my experience or comprehension.'

'And mine,' I whispered. 'Hamish, I'm frightened.'

'Of me?' He took my face between his hands and kissed me, gently and without passion. 'Don't you know, my dearest, that I would never harm you?'

'But you did,' I said. 'You killed me.' I pointed out to sea, where a man-of-war seemed to ride in the bright sunlight. 'From the deck of the ship you gave the order to fire. You had your orders. You had no alternative.'

As if I had come out of a faint, I felt the invasion drain away. The cloud which had veiled the sun drifted on, and I was staring in bewilderment, at a man whom I had met casually on two occasions only and whose arms now dropped to his side. 'Captain Ridley,' I said in a low voice. 'Can you explain?'

'Forgive me, Miss Beaton, I am ashamed that I forgot myself and took an unpardonable liberty. I can offer no excuse.' I was silent, my mind still confused and unclear. 'What did I say to you, Captain Ridley? Please tell me.'

'You said—"You killed me."'

'What did I mean? Why should I say such a thing?'

He shook his head. 'We may never know, Miss Beaton.' He looked at the ruined walls, as if he saw them anew.

'Perhaps this place, these walls, are so indelibly stamped with the past.' He shrugged. 'We shall never know just how many lovers may have met here, and loved, and parted. All I know is that I had no will to do other than I did. Forgive me if you can, and I will get out of your life and never bother you again. But please believe this. I meant no insult. I don't hold you lightly, Miss Beaton, and when we both return to London—that is, if you can ever find it in your heart to renew our—acquaintance, I shall, with your permission, present myself to your guardian and seek his consent to make you my wife.'

'No! No, you must never do that! Don't ask me to explain, but please, *please*, never approach my guardian. Captain Ridley, I must ask you to promise me that you will do no such thing.' I was breathless with panic. 'I greatly appreciate the compliment you have paid me, but it is impossible. Utterly impossible. I can *never* be your wife.' *Or anyone else's wife, while I know nothing of a background which could be so discreditable that my mother had to conceal all evidence of her past life.*

'Goodbye,' I whispered. 'I am sorry. Truly sorry.' I ran from the castle ruins, and stumbled along the cliff-top, back to where Ishbel sat sunning herself at the foot of the stunted thorn tree. She opened her eyes lazily and shaded them against the sun and I was thankful that my face was in shadow and hoped that my agitation would not be too obvious.

'You look a bit windswept,' she commented. 'But it's often very gusty out on the point there. Did you see anything interesting? I'd dearly love to know what it is that Iain doesn't want us to see. I've a pretty shrewd idea, anyway, but he needn't worry that I'd give him away.'

'What should he have to hide?' I asked, grateful for a diversion.

144

'Can't you guess?' Her smile was conspiratorial and almost sly. 'Oh, well, you'll find out one day.' She held out a hand. 'Help me up, I'm stiff.' I pulled her to her feet. She laughed at my evident bewilderment. 'Don't worry, Katharine. It's nothing discreditable. Just an old Scottish pastime.'

'I'm sure that Iain would not be mixed up in anything shady,' I said. 'But I can't think of anything he'd want to keep quiet.'

'No? Never mind, then. Now let's find a sheltered place to eat our lunch. I think we'll go down the easy path— that brings us to a little bay where the river runs into the sea, below the castle cliff. You can do a bit of sketching, if you like. It's a good view from there—the ruins high above the sea, all jagged against the sky. There's some good cloud effects, too.'

We rode inland for a short way, following the course of the river. Below us the waters poured over boulders and great flat slabs worn smooth by the torrents of centuries. Gradually the ravine fell away to a gentle slope and we reached the shore where the waters finally mingled, and a little sandy, rock-strewn bay trapped the sun between two curving headlands. Wading birds probed and dabbled in the rock pools, and the sea was so calm and flat that there was hardly a ripple at the water's edge. Between the cusps of the headlands, a huge, weed-skirted rock gave standing room to an incredible number of seabirds. Ishbel said they were cormorants, and we watched, entranced, as they dived for fish, or spread their wings like marine scarecrows.

At the foot of the cliff, with a flat rock for a table and a sun-warmed boulder to lean on, we ate our picnic lunch. Conversation was desultory; on my part because I had so many confusing images to sort out; on Ishbel's, by her own admission, from sheer indolence. She pointed to the other side of the little estuary and said: 'You'll get the best view over there, if you want to sketch the castle. It's low tide now, so you can get across on Bonny; she doesn't mind getting her feet wet where the burn flows in.'

From where we sat, the cliff-top cut across our line of vision and hid the castle, but because of the morning's events, and the deep impression the place had made, I had to have a visual record.

Ishbel looked at her watch. 'You've got a good couple of hours before the tide turns, but don't leave it any later, because the water comes in pretty quickly between the headlands.'

'Oh, I shan't want all that time,' I said. 'I'll just make a rough sketch and work on it later.' All the same, I was grateful for the time alone, to ponder and puzzle, and to consider what my course should be. That was the third time I had met Captain Ridley, and each meeting had its element of mystery. Bonny carried me across the sands, plodding carefully across the shallow waters of the river. On the other side of the bay, I tethered her where she could crop contentedly, and climbed to a little grassy knoll, with an effective view of the castle, etched black against the sky.

Ishbel had said two hours. I was so utterly absorbed that the time slipped by, and when I looked at my watch, I was almost convinced that something was wrong and that it was gaining. I looked across the estuary and saw that Ishbel was waving to me. I waved back, and started to gather up my sketching things. I was pleased with my work and when I reached the foot of the knoll, where I had tethered Bonny, I slipped the drawing between the leaves of the sketching pad and put it, with the rest of the gear, in the saddle bag.

With the turn of the tide, the breeze seemed to be coming from the sea. Haze had veiled the sun, and the sea-birds had fallen silent. I mounted Bonny and as I wheeled her to ride back across the estuary, it was as though a huge mass of cloud rolled with incredible swiftness over the surface of the water, obscuring the far headland, the shore line, the place where Ishbel sat, and the whole scene before me. And even as I started to walk Bonny across the beach, that too was swallowed up, and I was alone in the world where nothing existed any more. I reined to a standstill, uncertain what to do. My best course seemed to be to return to where I had been sitting, well above the water line, and wait for the mist to clear, though how long a wait that would entail it was impossible to say. Bonny turned obediently, but somehow, even in that short interval, bewildered by the suddenness with which the mist rolled in, I had apparently lost my sense of direction, because Bonny was splashing through water that was more than just a pool in the sand. A wave broke, and soaked the hem of my skirt; I urged the horse on and she did her best, but the water was gaining, and I realised to my horror that not only was the tide gaining, but I was heading in the wrong direction entirely. The only thing to do was to let Bonny have her head. Gingerly she picked her way through the waves and would have carried me to safety but for the one odd chance that caused her to stumble and take fright—at what, I shall never know, but in one horrifying instant I was thrown from the saddle, the reins slipped through my hands, and the next wave rolled me over helplessly. Then I was fighting for my life, but because of the mist and the undertow I could make no progress, and as fast as I scrambled to my feet the dragging water tore me back, so that I was soon out of my depth.

The nightmare began. The sea played with me like a cat with a mouse, tossing me like a cork, then submerging me beneath such a weight of water that I threshed in panic. The miracle was that my saturated clothes did not drag me down beyond the point of no return, but suddenly my feet touched bottom; bruised and exhausted though I was, I was able to stand upright though the surging water still reached my waist. Cautiously I moved forward, trying to follow the direction of each incoming wave. I could barely see my hand before me, and the utter silence was unnerving. Once I thought I heard Ishbel's voice, and called desperately to her, then realised the futility of calling. I stumbled on for what seemed hours, with the water never receding; trailing weed impeded me, and more than once I fell headlong over boulders and only regained my feet with difficulty. The weed seemed to be getting thicker, and finally one treacherous swathe gave way beneath my heel and I was falling backwards, unable to maintain my balance. I felt one tremendous blow on the back of my head, and sank into blackness.

Gradually I fought my way back to consciousness, and because I was so numb and dazed, I imagined at first that I was in the grip of a nightmare which must surely recede, and I would be safely in my own bed, shaken emotionally, *but safe*. But as full consciousness returned, I knew the full horror of my situation. I was spreadeagled on the weed-clad rock; my hands were clawing desperately at the slippery weed, and as each wave broke, so my hold slithered and I was being dragged back into the water, and then, though there was no one by to hear me, I shrieked in agony. My shoulder was nearly wrenched from its socket. Something, something rough, vicelike and metallic, held my left wrist. It felt like an iron manacle. With extreme difficulty I brought my right arm over to the point where I could clasp my left wrist, which was clamped in an iron ring. That ring seemed to be attached to a heavy chain, so that each time I slithered backwards, my arm took the full weight of my body. How I came to be so manacled I would never know, but the full measure of my peril swamped me in a sea of despair deeper and more deadly than the waters that still dragged at me. Yet the instinct to survive is strong.

With my right hand I grasped the chain, to ease the pain on my shoulder, and gradually I pulled myself clear of the sea, on to the rock. At last my hand came in contact with an iron stake, embedded in the rock, and I looped my right arm round it. At least it offered a handhold to prevent my being sucked back into the sea, and I crouched shuddering with cold and terror, wondering whether this was indeed the last I would ever know of this life. Would death be early or late in coming? Would I meet it with courage? Even though no one would ever witness my last fierce struggle to hold on to life, yet I prayed that my last moments would not lack the dignity of resignation and faith that I must pass to some plane beyond. But who had done this thing to me? Why should anyone hate me so much that they would condemn me to such a barbarous end? *But then, of course, I deserved it, didn't I? I was a condemned witch, and now I had come at last to the Witches' Crag to abide by the verdict of the waters. If they received me into the eternal rest of the deep, my body would be retrieved and buried within the bounds of God's Acre, and mourned over as one whom the world had falsely accused. But if the sea flung me back with contempt, then I would be taken from the rock and burned to ashes, as a creature rejected by God, man and the elements, unworthy of life and fit only for the Company of Hell and my Master, the Devil.*

Mocking voices chanted my name and catalogued the sickening accusations that I could not deny, since terror and torture had so warped my mind that even I believed their truth. So that when my Paramour had abandoned me to the hideous justice of my accusers, my torment was less their breaking of my body, but rather the destruction of my faith. I was utterly and eternally damned in soul.

From time to time, full awareness returned to me. Darkness had fallen and the mist had cleared, but there was no moon. But perhaps, if the mist did not return, and daylight ever came, I would be seen from the shore. For I knew now where I was.

I was chained to the rock where in the old days, witches —so-called—had suffered and died, either by a merciful drowning, or later, by burning. Here, on this very rock, unlikely as it seemed. For some far memory told me that the iron stake was once much taller, and at the top had been a cage, the bottom of which would be packed tightly with brushwood. When the hapless creature had been bound to the central stake, the brushwood had been fired and her funeral pyre had become a beacon.

And now they were coming. I heard the creak of oars, and low voices. For me, there was no escape and soon the cage above me would be crammed with its deadly tinder. Would death come quick but cruel in the scorching flames of dry kindling, or in the slow but more merciful stifling of damp wood that burned sulkily with choking smoke, as if even it were reluctant to have any dealings with a witch?

The voices came nearer and a boat grated against the rock. I heard men clambering over the rock and a voice exclaimed, 'She's alive!' Hands reached to tear me from this last refuge, and I shrieked with the pain of a fresh wrench on my shoulder, and the terror of the certain knowledge of the witch's guilt.

'Don't struggle, lassie. We're here to take you ...' *Take*

me ... Take me ... whither ... to my death ... I could
endure no more, and let myself sink into nothingness. But
just before the dark curtain enveloped me, I was conscious
of arms cradling me, and a voice, low and strangled with
emotion, whispering 'My poor, bonny wee thing. Thank
God you're alive. Stay with me, my darling, stay with me.'
The voice that would have called me back from the dead;
the voice at whose bidding I would have turned back from
the dark river bank ...

The journey had been a long, weary one. I had travelled
to a far land from which I returned with reluctance, because the country held so much that was dear to me. My
mother, and someone with her whom I didn't know, but
who must have been my father, yet whom I at first mistook
for Alasdair and wept at my mistake. I had rested by the
cool, fast-flowing river, so wide that the other bank was
veiled in haze. There were other people there whom at
first I did not know, and two in particular kept me company; and I knew that the one on my left was Catriona. At
that point I began to assume that this was a peculiarly
vivid dream, and I still did not recognise the companion
to my right.

The country changed. The broad river, and cool turf,
the flowers and the birds, and above all, the sun, were
gone, and I was climbing alone up a steep ravine, with
grey, jagged rock walls on each side of me. I halted and
looked back, and my companions were behind me. One—
Catriona—was being held back by the other one, and
seemed angry that she could not still be with me. At first
I imagined that the other was a stranger, then I seemed
to know her: the eyes, grey with flecks of green; the flowing hair, like pale gold; the hands. It was the hands which
clinched the recognition. They were Aunt Zen's hands; I

had studied them so often, watching as they held, then dealt cards. I realised that what I now saw was Aunt Zen herself, the *essential* being, with the grossness and near-grotesqueness of age purged and purified. The lovely, golden girl which she had been in a far time before I knew her. Yet as I *had* known her on another plane.

The strange contest went on and I felt that I was the focus of it. For some reason, Catriona had to be prevented from reaching me before I climbed to the top of the cliff. My heart was pounding and I fought to breathe and then suddenly I was free, and walking on the open moor, and coming to meet me was Alasdair. I ran joyously towards him and he took my hand in his. 'Come, Catriona. It's time for you to come away home.'

When consciousness returns, the senses do not, so I'm told, function immediately. The first awareness is of sound. I could hear movement. Light steps, the swish of a skirt, the muted tinkle of a spoon against glass. And a voice, low and pleading. So muted that it was even less than a whisper.

'Catriona, come back to me, wherever you are. Don't wander away. Come back ... come back ... come back ...' The command was so insistent that I opened my eyes.

For a moment I had difficulty in focusing and I could not believe that I was back in my own room, in my own bed. Intensely weary, but *safe*. It had been no more than a dream. Kirsteen was standing by my bed, holding a glass. I tried to stretch out my hand.

'So thirsty, Kirsteen. So very thirsty, and I've had such a weird and horrible dream.' But of course, I remembered, she can't understand me. I tried to sit up but my body accepted no command, and then I realised that my hand was being held, as it had been in my dream, by Alasdair.

I turned my head to meet his gaze, and it told me all I needed to know about his feelings for me. He did not speak, but relinquished my hand and stood up.

He spoke to Kirsteen in Gaelic and in obedience to his command, she slid a strong arm under my shoulders, raised me slightly and held the glass to my lips. I drank greedily, and when she would have removed the glass, I tried to reach up to take it, but I had not the strength and my hand dropped limply on the coverlet; tears of weakness rolled down my cheeks as I watched Alasdair cross the room to the door and call in a low voice.

'Ishbel. Call Aunt Agnes—and Phemie.' He swung round and stood in the doorway. 'So, Katharine Beaton, you have decided not to leave us after all!' His voice was gently ironic, but his eyes still blazed with the look I had seen when I first opened my eyes to the world I had so nearly left for ever.

And as the uncontrollable tears streamed, Kirsteen cradled me and crooned soothing words I did not understand, and gently wiped my cheeks. And sighing down the centuries I heard the strange whisper: 'Witches canna greet. She was nane.' But not from Kirsteen, who had no English. Who then?

After that, everything was controlled, subdued bustle. Mrs MacRaith and Ishbel came, dressing-gowns flung hastily over their night attire. Phemie Wishart, crisp and efficient, soon shepherded them away. Together she and Kirsteen changed my bed and gently sponged the fever from my body, still bruised and aching from the battering I had undergone. My left shoulder, in particular, was so stiff that I could only move it with pain, but when I looked later at my wrist, expecting to find it chafed raw by the rasping of the iron manacle, the skin was un-broken, without even discolouration.

'There, my dear. That's better, isn't it?' I smiled weakly, and tried to thank Phemie. 'Now don't try to talk, my dear. Just rest, and get better.' She looked down at me, with a strange expression. 'You've journeyed far, have you not? But you were called back. It's not yet time for you to go.' Later I learned that the reason she was not in the room when I first regained consciousness was that she had gone down to find Murdo, to send him for Doctor Laidlaw. When I asked her why, she said: 'It was the hour when the spirit departs, and for you, it was uncertain whether you'd stay or go.' I told her about the dream, and the two women. She nodded sagely. 'I knew that something of the sort was taking place,' she said. 'You see, I have the Sight myself. You've a long hard furrow to plough, but you'll endure.'

With the resilience of youth, and with my blessedly strong constitution, I was able, now that the pneumonia crisis had passed, to regain my strength fairly rapidly, though Doctor Laidlaw was insistent that I should not overtax myself, and Phemie was a gentle martinet.

'Miss Wishart, don't you ever sleep?' I asked her.

'Call me Phemie, please,' she said, smiling. 'We're friends. Sleep? Yes, I take my rest. I need very little, and the Auld Laird is not demanding.'

'How is he?' I asked eagerly. 'I haven't seen him since the night of the ball. I wondered then whether it was all too much for him.'

'Not Duncan MacRaith,' she said drily. 'He'll make his century yet. But he was gey fashed about you, my dear. He's taken a fancy to you, I think.'

'He's a charming old man,' I said. 'Will you take him a message, please? Tell him that Catriona is still here. He'll understand.'

'I'll do that,' Phemie said. 'Maybe in a day or two, if the weather holds, Doctor Laidlaw will let you sit in the garden; it's sheltered down there, and the air will benefit you.' She helped me from the bed and into my dressing-gown. 'Now lean on me, you'll be weak at the knees, after so many days in bed.'

I struggled to my feet, and all but collapsed, but with Phemie and Kirsteen's help I was able to take a few faltering steps to the armchair which they had set in the window embrasure. I gazed with thankfulness at the sky and the trees, and the song of the birds gave form to my gratitude for being alive. Then I leaned forward to look down into Catriona's garden.

A man was sitting on one of the stone benches near the sundial, and as if drawn by my gaze, he raised his head to look towards my window. It was James Ridley. Even at that distance, I could see that his face was haggard and weary but when I smiled and raised my hand to acknowledge him, his face lit with joy, as he sprang to his feet. He did not resume his seat, but with a formal salute, he turned, and marched to the door which led to the policies.

The following day a great basket of red roses was delivered by a florist from Inverness. The attached card read 'For the fairest rose, flowering anew.' And the initials, 'J.R.' On the other side, written in a neat formal hand, 'I will call, with your permission, when you are well enough to receive visitors.'

All through my convalescence, both Ishbel and Mrs MacRaith had spent much time with me. I found it hard to express my gratitude, but Mrs MacRaith brushed my thanks aside. 'My dear, what else could we do? You are our guest, and it would have been unthinkable to despatch you to a nursing home or hospital, even had you been in a condition to endure such a journey. You must remain here until you are strong enough to travel—if you wish to do so.' Why did I then have the feeling that my enforced stay at Allt-nam-Fearna chimed very well with her plans. Though I knew she was sincere enough in her concern for my health, and would not have wanted such a drastic accomplice as the illness I had survived, I still had a conviction for which I could find no foundation, that it would not be made easy for me to leave Allt-nam-Fearna.

What puzzled me was Ishbel's subdued, unhappy demeanour. More than once she looked as if she had been crying, but I hesitated to embarrass her by asking what was the matter. She waited on me devotedly, to the point where I felt I was almost an incubus, but when I said so, she would not hear of it.

'But you're wearing yourself out,' I protested. 'You fetch and carry, and Phemie tells me that you took your full share of watching and nursing all the time I was so ill. I can never thank you enough for all you've done.'

'I could hardly do less,' she answered. 'Seeing that it was all my fault.' Her eyes filled with tears and she dropped to her knees by my side. 'Please, Katharine, I didn't do it on purpose, really I didn't. The mist came down so suddenly. One minute you were there—I saw you mount Bonny—and then you were gone, blotted out, as if you'd never existed. I called and called, and then when Bonny found her way out of the sea, I led her home, and the search started. But I *swear* to you, Katharine, that I never meant to harm you.'

'But Ishbel, who ever suggested that you were in any way to blame?'

'Aunt Agnes, for one. She has hardly spoken to me since.' She lifted a haggard face. 'And Iain.' Her voice was choked with misery. 'He *told* me not to go, and I defied him. And now I'm paying for it. I shall probably pay for it for the rest of my life.' She rested her head on my lap and I felt the wracking sobs. I was aghast at the mental suffering she was inflicting on herself, and even more appalled that Mrs MacRaith and Iain should increase her burden of imagined guilt. I put my arm round her shoulders and lifted her, cradling her head on my shoulder.

'Ishbel, dear, please, *please*! It *wasn't* your fault. How could you call down that dreadful mist—*you're* not a witch. And I know that never in all your life would you do anything to harm me. You are much too kind and gentle a person to want to hurt anyone, much less put anyone's life in danger.'

She raised her head and looked straight at me.

'How do you know, Katharine? How do any of us know what we'd do if we had to fight desperately for something?'

'But Ishbel, I can't think that I'd ever take from you anything that would drive you to those lengths.' I leaned forward and kissed her gently, then took my handkerchief and dabbed at her swollen eyes. 'Now, please, dear Ishbel, stop tormenting yourself. I'll soon be quite better, and then I'll really have to go back to London. I can't dump myself on you and Mrs MacRaith indefinitely—I mustn't turn into a sort of cuckoo!'

In spite of herself, she managed a pale little smile. 'You're very sweet, and forgiving, Katharine. I wish——' She broke off. 'Never mind.' She struggled to her feet. 'I nearly forgot, there are letters for you. I'll fetch them.' At the door she turned. 'I'm a proper hen-brain today. Your gallant captain has been waiting anxiously for news of you.' Almost crossly I said: 'He's not *my* captain.' 'No?' she queried. 'What about those?' She indicated the roses. 'Next time he calls I'll tell him you're receiving visitors!' She was gone before I could protest further.

She returned, bringing two letters, a small packet, and a picture postcard. I studied the picture with amused incredulity.

'Now who on earth would send me a picture of the Crystal Palace?'

'Turn it over and find out,' Ishbel said, with shattering logic. I did, and my bewilderment deepened as I read the message, in a small, precise script. 'Here is the view for which you asked. I hope it recalls happy memories. My sincere regards to you and to all at Allt-nam-Fearna.' The signature was 'James Ridley'.

James Ridley, with whom I had spoken—how many days ago? I did not know. But of one thing I was certain. I had made no such request, and James Ridley would be well aware of that, so he must have had some reason of his own for sending this cryptic message. I studied the postmark, which was unusually clear. The card had been posted in London on the 16th of August. Only one day before that strange encounter on the cliff-top—in 'the Lightning Struck Tower'. But how long ago had that been?

I looked up. Ishbel was still in the room, standing by the window.

'What day is it?' I asked. 'How long was I ill, Ishbel?'

'About ten days—seriously ill, that is. When they brought you back, you were unconscious, and we put you to bed immediately. By the next day you were delirious, with a raging fever, and that lasted—oh, about a week, I suppose. We were desperately worried, but at last your temperature dropped, and now Doctor Laidlaw says you'll be fine in a short time.'

'What is the date, then?'

'It's the 5th of September. Why do you ask particularly?'

'I just wondered when the letters came,' I said.

'Well, they found you in the wee sma' hours, and Murdo rode to Kyle for Doctor Laidlaw when it became obvious that you were desperately ill. He brought the mail back, so that would have been the 18th.' As Alice said, *curiouser and curiouser*! It seemed that for reasons of his own, James Ridley had wanted it assumed that he was many miles from Allt-nam-Fearna. It was a sound psychological assumption that a postcard would be read and handled by a considerable number of people, one at least of whom would let their curiosity get the better of them. After which the information would percolate till it reached its intended recipient—which was very definitely *not* Miss Katharine Beaton. It was a mystery I could not begin to unravel.

I turned to the rest of my correspondence. A letter from the trustees. A letter with an East Anglian postmark, the name and address typewritten, and the latter crossed out and readdressed by my bank. The postmark set my pulse racing with apprehension: that letter could only be from Gerald. The third letter bore a London postmark, and the handwriting was unfamiliar. I picked up the packet, which was addressed in the same handwriting. So natural curiosity made me open that letter first.

Even the address was unfamiliar. I knew no one who lived in Kennington. I turned over the folded sheet to find the signature: 'Yours respectfully, Sarah Trustcott.' Sarah—Aunt Zen's daughter, in service in one of the tall, narrow houses that sat primly watching the cricketers who played on the green oval of ground on the far side of the road.

And as I opened and read the inner pages, I knew that I had lost for ever the person who, next to my mother, was the dearest to me.

Aunt Zen was dead.

CHAPTER NINE

THROUGH A film of tears I reread the letter. It was hard to realise that never again would I watch those plump, be-ringed hands deftly setting out the cards, or hear again the deep, dramatic voice reading the message of the strange, sometimes garish mediaeval pictures. Never, too, the comfort of her compassion, the healing of her under-standing, and the warmth of her arms as she consoled a grieving child. And in my own grief, I realised my selfish-ness. Sarah, now, like myself, alone and bereft. I turned back to the letter . . .

'. . . the dear ladies have been so kind. Miss Lilian, who as you remember is such a beautiful organist, played such lovely music at the funeral that I could not keep from crying, and Miss Maud, who is so practical, helped me with all the clearing up. Which brings me, dear Miss Katharine, to your things. As you know, the house where poor dear Ma lived belongs to the old lady who bought it with what she was left by her dead hus-band, and of course, seeing that it's her mainstay, so to speak, she wanted the rooms that Ma had, so as to let them as soon as she could. She was very kind, of course, and didn't hurry me, but there was the problem of knowing what to do with your things which you had left in Ma's care when you went away, thinking, of course, that you would soon be back. So as there was an address on the letter you wrote to her, and which I'm sure gave her great pleasure, I have taken the liberty of packing your things in your big leather trunk and sending them by railway to where you are staying. I hope they will arrive safely, and shall be grateful if you will let me know as much.

'You will be happy to know that she went so sudden that she never even knew. Heart, the doctor said it was, and said that she never felt a thing. Well, Miss Katharine, she was a dear mother to me, and I know she was almost as much to you, and if it's any comfort, her last thoughts must have been of you, because she just went sitting in her chair, with the cards spread out before her, and your letter in her hand, as if she was reading a spread for you. I copied the cards on to a piece of paper because I thought you'd like to know, and as a little keepsake, I'm sending you her Tarot pack, and perhaps, holding it, you'll get a feeling that she's still with us, and I really can't believe she's gone, but wherever she is, I'm sure that it's a good place because she was a good woman and always gave help to them that needed it. Ever so many people will miss her and there was some lovely wreaths at the funeral. I am sorry I couldn't let you know in time, but I took the liberty of putting your name on the card that was on my wreath and that was the one on the coffin when they carried it into the church, so you see we was both with her and I know she would have been pleased.'

Dear Sarah, I whispered to myself. So thoughtful, and I too knew that Aunt Zen would have been pleased. I would send a little memorial to the church so that it could help someone else.

I turned the page and read on. 'So you see, dear Miss Katharine, I am now alone in the world, but my dear ladies have told me that I shall always have a home with them as long as they live, and they have said that when you come to London you are to stay here as a guest. Isn't that wonderful of them? Dear Miss Florence, who is the one with the business head, told me what to do about Ma's little bit, and the insurance and all those things. So I hope that you will come and see me, which will give me great pleasure.'

I folded the letter and returned it to its envelope, then leaned forward and placed it in the drawer of the lowboy. Tomorrow I would write to Sarah, who must surely be wondering why I had been so long answering her letter.

I turned to the rest of my correspondence. The letter from my trustees could wait, and with a quickening of my pulse, I slit the letter which I knew was from Gerald. That, too, was dated in August.

'... since your precipitate departure made it quite clear you found living under my roof intolerable and unendurable. Once again I ask your pardon for that incident, which I hope you will be able to put from your mind, and will not allow it to colour any other attachment you may form in the future. For it is my earnest hope that you *will* find love and happiness with someone else, and my only prayer is that he may be worthy of you.

'This letter is to inform you that I shall be out of the country for some considerable time, as I intend to travel extensively—not the conventional fleeing to forget my sorrow in big game hunting or foreign wars, I hasten to add!'

In spite of myself, I smiled. One of Gerald's attractions was his wry sense of humour which so often chimed with my own.

The letter continued '—revisiting many of the beautiful, civilised places I first saw in your mother's company.

It will be a kind of pilgrimage of remembrance, and I could wish, in the most platonic sense, that you might share it with me, but that is not to be. However, if you need to get in touch with me for any reason, write to me c/o my bankers. I hesitate to remind you of what to you is the distasteful fact that I am still, in law, your guardian, and that for the next eighteen months or so, should you wish to marry, my formal consent would be necessary—though I can hardly imagine that my approval and consent would weigh with you, dear head-strong little Katharine! So I will conclude with assuring you of my concern always for your happiness and welfare . . .'

In an odd way, Gerald's letter seemed to add to my isolation. Now I *was* alone, in a world where I didn't even know who I was or what place I had.

I turned my head into the cushion and wept.

'Come, now, what's all this for?' Phemie's cheerful voice roused me. 'You've no cause to greet, young lady. You're lucky to be alive, you know.'

'I'm sorry,' I gulped. 'It's just that——' And I told her about Aunt Zen.

'Oh, dear, now, I'm sorry I spoke sharpish.' Phemie was all concern. 'That is sad for you.'

I explained the full implications to her. She was silent, looking at me as if considering whether or not to say more, and then, her mind made up, she said, 'I think you will soon learn something that will have a considerable bearing on your future.' I remembered what she had said previously.

'You have the Sight, haven't you?' She nodded. I held out the packet, still unopened. 'That belonged to Aunt Zen.' She took it, and folded it in both her hands, her

163

head bowed a little as if in meditation. Then she looked up, startled. 'Oh, yes,' she whispered. 'This will tell me much. It will guide you, too. Open it,' she commanded, handing the packet back to me. 'And when you have taken off the outer wrappings, see that you let no one else handle the pack.'

'You mean you know what it is?' I challenged.

'A pack of Tarot cards.'

'Yes. Aunt Zen's. Her daughter sent them to me, as a remembrance of her mother. I will always treasure them. Can you read them?'

'I know most of the traditional meanings, yes. But a reading depends on much more than that, and in fact, you may be able to achieve a very good reading simply by letting your intuition work, even if you don't know the individual meanings.' She watched as I undid the little packet, then took the wrappings and placed them on the fire. The inner wrapping was of black silk, and I recalled how careful Aunt Zen had always been, at the conclusion of a reading, to gather up the cards, wrap them in the silk which also served as a covering on the table when she set out the cards, and to keep them in a place towards the East.

And as I held them in my hand, it was as though Aunt Zen stood near me, and told me not to weep for her, and the words came into my mind: 'May Light Eternal shine on her.'

'She was here, wasn't she?' Phemie said. I nodded, unable to speak. 'Now put the cards away,' she commanded. 'When you are stronger, you shall read them, and understand their message. But first you have to get better, really better, and you must not spend your strength.'

I did as she said, and put the cards in the drawer of the lowboy.

My next visitor was Doctor Laidlaw, and for the first

time his visit had a social as well as a professional purpose. Phemie had evidently told him of Aunt Zen's death, and his quiet sympathy, briefly expressed, brought healing of the heart.

'And you have no real home in London now?' he enquired. 'What had you in mind to do? I mean, before this happened?'

'I'd hoped to take up nursing,' I said. 'I had discussed it with Mrs MacRaith when I first met her, and it was at her suggestion that I took a holiday up here before finally making any move in the matter.'

'Well, now, and you nearly succeeded in drowning yourself, to be sure. Not a very good way of starting a career, but you're a strong, healthy lassie, and I don't doubt you'll soon be dancing "MacRaith's Rant" again.' He took my wrist and timed my pulse, then took out his stethoscope.

'All clear,' he said, folding it up and stuffing it into his pocket. 'Now I think it'll do you no harm, on a fine warm day like this, to sit in the garden for a wee while and get some good air into your lungs. The girls will help you down the stairs, and Phemie will keep a professional eye on you, just to see that you don't go exceeding your strength.'

And so, after Kirsteen had helped me to dress, I waited while she fetched Phemie, and together they would each give me an arm down the stairs. I sat by the window, and then I remembered the cards, put away in the lowboy drawer. I opened it, and took out the little silk-wrapped package. Folded in with it was the paper which Sarah had sent, and idly I sorted out the cards listed. They were right on top, just as she had gathered them up, and I spread the silk and dealt them. As I did so, I had a great sense of Aunt Zen's nearness, and I knew that as I handled each card, the message would come to me through her clear vision. Sarah had not specified, but I knew that on each occasion she had read for me, Aunt Zen had used the Celtic Cross, and so I laid out the cards. The meanings came into my mind more clearly than ever before, and I was astonished at the accuracy of the predictions. Here was the illness, and the danger from the sea. Only one puzzled me. There was still this insistence, even in the cards, of crossing a great ocean, and this I had certainly not done. Perhaps I was not reading correctly, but it seemed strange, when every other prediction, so far, had come true.

I would think about it later, these things took time, and could not be commanded at will.

The sun was warm on my face, and I must have drifted into a half sleep. Someone was calling to me, and I opened my eyes. The brightness of the sun dazzled me, but in the far corner of the garden by the laurel bush, Ishbel was standing. She smiled, and pointed.

'See what I've found.'

I got up from my chair and walked across the garden, and I was pleased at the ease with which I could move, since I had expected to be stiff and shaky after being in bed. I glided swiftly along the gravelled path, and my soft indoor shoes made no sound. At the same time, I was struck by the silence all around me. No wind rustled the trees, and no seabird wailed. The stillness was tangible and I moved as in a trance.

Ishbel, too, was a part of the overall silence. She smiled, and pulling back a concealing branch, she pointed to a door in the wall.

'You said there wasn't a door,' I challenged her. I knew the door must lead to the garden-house, and I went eagerly as to an assignation. Someone waited for me, and I knew who it was. Hamish. My heartbeat quickened with

anticipation; the few snatched minutes which were all we dare hope for made the secrecy and the waiting unendurable. But soon it would no longer be necessary to meet thus. Soon we would be together for ever ...

I stooped to pass under the twisted branches. Twigs reached out and tugged my hair and my skirt, and scratched at my bare arms, but I cared little. I was grateful for the concealment they gave, and I knew that there would be warning should anyone approach. Who would think that Ishbel's lighthearted singing in the garden would carry a warning to me to hurry back?

I grasped the iron handle, turned it and dragged open the heavy oak door. One step, and I would be held in his arms ...

I took a step forward, and realised, with incredulous horror, that one more step would take me over the edge of the cliff that dropped sheer to the hungry sea hundreds of feet below. The sky went black before my eyes, and a great clap of thunder stunned me. And as I swayed and fell, I heard Ishbel's mocking laugh ...

I was falling, falling, twisting helplessly like a puppet hurled from a great height. Soon I must endure the agony as my body smashed on to the rocks which the swaying sea bared ready to take me in their unrelenting arms ...

And as my heart lurched, I opened my eyes ... I was sitting in the armchair in my room. Ishbel stood by the lowboy, examining curiously the spread of cards. Still with her back to me, she asked, 'Do you believe in all this, Katharine?' When I did not answer, she turned casually and said, 'Are you ready? I'll ring for Kirsteen.' She stretched out her hand to the bell-pull, then paused, staring at me closely.

'Are you all right, Katharine? You look as if you'd seen a ghost.'

'What happened?' I whispered. 'How did I get back here?' I looked at my hands, and my dress. There was neither scratch nor even a torn skirt, and I felt no bruising from the fall. And the sea—how did I escape the sea? Incredulously I took a handful of my dress.

'But it's dry,' I exclaimed. 'Completely dry. I don't undestand.'

'Neither do I. What did you think had happened?'

'When you came in, was I asleep?' I asked.

'You were leaning back in the chair with your eyes closed,' Ishbel answered. 'Why? Did you doze off? I wasn't away more than five minutes. Nothing could have happened to you in that time.'

'Then I must have dreamed . . .' I shuddered. 'You were there, and I went through the door in the wall. To meet my lover. But he wasn't there. Only the sea, and the cliff, and I was falling . . .'

'You were dreaming,' she laughed, and her laughter had an echo of the sound I had heard. 'Did you really think you'd fallen over a cliff? You do sometimes get that sensation of falling and then you wake up with a jump—it's quite frightening sometimes. Anyway, how on earth could I have got you up here?'

'It was so real,' I said. I stood up and took a few steps to the window. 'Down there, in the garden, and I opened the door in the wall . . .'

'But there is no door. You've seen for yourself.'

'But there was once, wasn't there? That was the way Catriona went—the way I was going, to meet my lover, as if I were her, or she was me.' I swung round and grasped her arm. 'Ishbel, what does it all mean? What's happening to me? I come here to stay, to a place where I've never been before, and where I could have no possible connec-

168

tion. And I *know* it. And sometimes I'm almost someone else. It frightens me, Ishbel.'

She took me gently by the elbows and eased me down into the armchair.

'You've been very ill, you know. It does bring strange fancies. You mustn't worry. And Katharine,' she dropped to her knees at my side, 'you *must* believe that no one here would harm you.'

'But there's danger,' I said in a low voice. 'You were looking at the cards. That was the spread Aunt Zen laid out for me the night she——' Tears of weakness blurred my eyes, and I shook my head angrily. I must not weep. Aunt Zen would be unhappy at my grief. But yet I could not help it; it was hard to realise that I would never see her again.

'And what do the cards tell you?' Ishbel's question brought me back to the present. She stood up, and moved the table towards me. I looked again at the cards.

'Ishbel, have you touched these at all?'

'No, of course not. Why should I? I was simply looking at them, from curiosity, I suppose,' she said defensively.

'I'm sorry,' I placated her. 'I may be wrong, but they don't look quite the same as when I laid them out—some of them are reversed.'

'Does that make any difference?'

'Sometimes, yes.' I pointed. 'Look, that's the Four of Swords. It can mean several things; an enforced rest, an illness, say. According to the spread, that's behind me. But above me, overshadowing everything, is the Nine of Swords. When I laid out the cards, it was upright, meaning a new life out of suffering. But reversed, as it is now, it can mean slander and malice, and utter desertion.'

'As you were deserted on the rock,' Ishbel said soberly. 'It's strange, isn't it. Is there more?'

'The Tower—always the Tower,' I said. 'Some kind of catastrophe one can't avoid—something cataclysmic, in fact, like a war.'

'Oh, but that's nonsense,' Ishbel exclaimed. 'Wars don't happen here any more. We've done our share of fighting, but on the whole, we're fairly peaceable now.'

I shrugged. 'Well, it can mean other things, emotional rather than physical. But one thing Aunt Zen did say. Something that *hasn't* come true, even though everything else has. She warned me that there was danger if I crossed the ocean, and of course, I haven't done that, and I don't intend to.'

Every vestige of colour drained from Ishbel's face.

'Oh, *no*,' she whispered. 'That can't—it *mustn't*—be true.' The fear in her eyes was unmistakable. 'Don't you know that you *have* crossed the ocean, Katharine? But then, how could you know? It just looks like an ordinary bridge——'

'Over the gorge where we saw the Maiden's Tresses?' I asked. She shook her head. 'That's spectacular, and of course, there's legend enough and to spare. But what you don't know is that Allt-nam-Fearna is an island, and there's a stone bridge connecting it to the mainland—it's known as the bridge over the Atlantic. You probably didn't even notice it as anything special, just like crossing a river. The Devil hacked off a piece of land and gave it to Calum Dubh in return for his soul, and now it's said that there's danger when a MacRaith crosses it. You can't get some horses over it.'

'I'm not a MacRaith,' I said slowly. 'Why should there be danger to me?' Ishbel shrugged evasively. 'How should I know. You don't have to believe it, do you?'

She crossed to the bell-pull and this time tugged it purposefully.

'Come away now, and we'll sit in the sun and forget all these fancies. I'll be in trouble from Aunt Agnes if I upset you. She had quite enough to say when I had to come home without you.' And again I sensed the tension of her supposed guilt. 'Katharine, you do believe that there really is no danger; I'm not your enemy, whatever it may appear.'

Her insistence puzzled me. Did she protest too much? Was I a potential rival? If so, I could not think in which direction, since she had never talked of a possible fiancé.

'Tell me something,' I said quietly. 'Tell me honestly, Ishbel—have you any reason for wishing me away from Allt-nam-Fearna? Because if so, I'll go, and the sooner the better. I like you too much to want to bring you any un-happiness.' Again the untenable thought passed through my mind, and now I had to know.

'Is it Iain?' I asked. 'Are you afraid he'll fall in love with me? You needn't worry. I like him very much, but I would never marry him. But Ishbel, my dear, you'll have to let him go some time, won't you? If it's not me, it will be someone else—that's only natural, isn't it?' She left that question unanswered, and said instead, 'You're reckoning without Aunt Agnes. She usually gets her own way.'

'Not with me,' I said decisively. 'No one dictates to me whom I marry, and anyway, she has no rights whatever over me.'

Ishbel tilted her head a little to one side and regarded me almost slyly. 'Are you quite sure of that?' she asked.

'What on earth do you mean?' I demanded.

She smiled. 'Simply that you should be sure of your facts before you make sweeping statements. Oh, and by the way, Captain Ridley has called several times, and it's quite possible that he will join us in the garden for tea, if you're feeling up to it.'

The *non sequitur* left me speechless, and then no fur-

171

ther conversation was possible.

'Come in,' I called, in answer to Kirsteen's knock. The door opened, and it was not Kirsteen who entered, but Alasdair.

He strode across the room and taking me by the wrists pulled me, not ungently, to my feet. Then in one swift movement, before I could protest, he picked me up as if I were a child, and carried me from the room. To steady myself, and because it somehow seemed utterly natural, I let my arm lie across his shoulders. With the utmost care, stepping slowly on to each stair, he manoeuvred his way down the steep, twisting staircase and through the arch-way into the gallery, to the head of the broad flight down into the great hall.

'I can manage the rest,' I protested, and he paid not the slightest heed.

The next stage of the excursion was almost like a royal progress. In the hall were gathered Phemie, Mrs Mac-Raith, and Iain. Ishbel had followed close behind us, and when we reached the foot of the stairs, the others fell in and completed the entourage which accompanied me across the hall, through the salon on to the terrace, and through the door in the wall to Catriona's garden. A large square of drugget had been spread on the turf, under-neath a wicker chaise-longue, and thither Alasdair carried me, setting me down with the care and gentleness of a woman settling a baby in a bassinet. He straightened up, and almost before my rather breathless 'Thank you' was said, swung away and marched from the garden.

From then on all was fuss and flurry. Mrs MacRaith directed operations. 'Ishbel—that knee-shawl, now.' Obed-iently Ishbel spread a small tartan blanket over my knees.

'Iain, put that Shetland shawl round Katharine's shoul-ders.'

'Yes, Aunt Agnes.' Iain spread the shawl across my shoulders, and I leaned forward so that it could drape down over the hollow between my shoulder blades, where cold always seemed to find its home. And was it mere imagination that his hand lightly smoothed the delicate folds in a tentative caress? And for all that, I knew that had it been Alasdair's hand, my heart would have leapt. But why think about that? To him I was no more than a rather tiresome bird of passage that had had the stupidity to break a wing.

And now I might have been holding court. Kirsteen carried out a laden tray which she set on a wicker table brought by Murdo from the terrace, and Mrs MacRaith dispensed tea. Kirsteen had whispered a message before returning to the house and Mrs MacRaith had said something to her in Gaelic, the drift of which became plain when the girl returned with another cup, saucer and plate. Behind her, carrying a great armful of bronze chrysanthemums, came James Ridley.

'Miss Beaton, I cannot tell you how pleased I am to see you looking so nearly your old self again.' He laid the flowers in my lap.

'Oh, how beautiful,' I exclaimed. 'You must have guessed that these are my very favourite colour. Thank you very, very much.'

'You will take tea, Captain Ridley?' Mrs MacRaith's interruption was quite deliberate, and because the only available chair was beside her, he was forced, out of politeness, to move away from me and take that place, leaving Iain still sitting next to me. It was quite a manoeuvre, since Iain had stood up as if to reliquish his seat, and had been forestalled by Mrs MacRaith.

Nevertheless, James Ridley played the social game gracefully and the conversational ball was kept bouncing adroitly, until Mrs MacRaith decreed that I had stayed long enough in the garden and must run no risks. Ridley stood up, came over to me and took my hand.

'May I come again, Miss Beaton? Perhaps, when you are feeling stronger, we might ride together?'

'It will be quite a long time before Katharine is strong enough to go riding again, Captain Ridley. We must not tax her strength. But call, by all means—to make enquiries.' I felt a sudden surge of resentment that Mrs MacRaith should answer for me, as if I were a child not able to decide for herself.

'I shall be delighted to ride with you, Captain Ridley. Not for a few days, of course, but I will ask Doctor Laidlaw. You must forgive Mrs MacRaith's anxiety that I should do nothing that might cause a relapse, though I hardly think that very likely—I'm much stronger than I look, you know.' I was reluctant to let him depart, and I was determined that despite Mrs MacRaith's ukase, I would contrive to meet James soon—and *alone*.

'You must not overtax yourself, Miss Beaton,' Ridley said. 'I'm sure Mrs MacRaith is only anxious for your well-being. All the same, I shall look forward to riding with you some time not too far distant.'

'I *must* see you,' I whispered. 'No matter what she says. I'll think of some way.' Aloud I said lightly. 'I'll do as I'm told—I'm a good patient, am I not, Phemie? And I know it's all for my own good, and I can never be sufficiently grateful to Mrs MacRaith and all of you. What a nuisance of a guest I've been, and I've been cared for as if I had been one of the family.'

The tiny silence which followed was almost conspiratorial, a kind of 'I-know-something-you-don't-know!'

'My dear, you have *not* been a nuisance.' Mrs MacRaith's tone was warm and sincere. 'What else could we have done?' She looked across at James. 'Perhaps you will dine with us again soon, Captain Ridley. That is, if you plan to stay long in these parts?'

'As long as it takes me to conclude my business—satisfactorily,' he said smoothly, and turned back to me. 'Au revoir, Miss Beaton, and make haste to get well.' My fingers curled and closed on his, and I felt the responding pressure. My hand still lay captive when Alasdair came through the garden door. He reached my side in a few swinging strides.

'Enough for today, Katharine Beaton,' he said, and stooped and picked me up as he had done before. This time I was less acquiescent.

'Put me down, please,' I said imperiously. 'I want to see whether I can still walk.'

'Very well,' he said, and set me on my feet. 'But you'll take my arm——'

'——and mine.' *Hamish was at my side, and I took each of them by the arm. Slowly we walked towards the house, and I felt the current of antagonism that flowed between the two men. At the door to the terrace Alasdair halted.*

'Thank you, Ridley.' That was all, but Hamish had no option but to accept dismissal.

I walked across the hall, still holding to Alasdair's arm, though I did my utmost not to lean heavily, and determinedly I forced myself to climb the stairs. Each step was a laborious drag, clinging to the bannister rail with one hand, and every stair demanding Alasdair's support, try as I would to dispense with it.

'You're a stubborn besom, Katharine Beaton,' he said, and I lacked breath to reply.

At the half-landing I was forced to rest, and he seized the opportunity. This time I did not resist, but allowed him to swing me off my feet. I hoped desperately that he could not hear the beating of my heart, and I turned my head away so that he should not read the betrayal in my eyes. I would not be bested, though.

'I'll be walking down these stairs, and up again, without your help, before the week's out!' I flashed.

'Is that a challenge?' He laughed, and it was the first time I had ever heard him laugh. 'Well, Katharine Beaton, you're game, I'll say that for you. We will see what a week will bring.'

At Phemie's insistence, I rested on my bed until dinner time; Kirsteen helped me to tidy myself, then brought my dinner on a tray. Behind her, Ishbel came, also carrying a tray.

'You'll not be minding?' she asked.

'Of course not,' I answered. 'I'm delighted to have your company, though you must be sick of spending so much time in this room.'

'Don't be daft,' she said, and when the door had closed behind Kirsteen, continued: '——besides, we can chat now we're alone.'

'What about?' I said cautiously. 'Anything in particular?'

'Captain Ridley?' She regarded me quizzically. 'What did I tell you? I'm willing to wager that he'll be proposing to you before he returns to London.'

'Oh, rubbish,' I protested. 'He was only doing the gallant. Anyway, you say before *he* returns to London. What makes you think that I shan't be returning to London myself very soon, as soon as I'm able to travel. I just can't stay here indefinitely.'

'How do you propose to make the journey?' she asked. She leaned forward and stared intently into my face. 'Tell me, Katharine, just how you'd set about it. I don't think you'd find it so easy to leave Allt-nam-Fearna.'

'What do you mean? Who'd want to keep me here against my will, and for what reason?'

'I didn't say it would be against your will.' She looked mysterious. 'As for reasons, well, wait and see.'

And that was all I could get out of her that night. We finished dinner, and after Kirsteen had removed the trays, Phemie bustled in.

'Come, lassie, there's been enough excitement for one day. Away to your bed, now.'

'Yes, ma'am!' I laughed, with mock meekness. 'I'll be a good patient.'

'Och, you've been that all along,' she said. 'You don't know how pleased we all are that you're well again. Just be patient a wee bit longer, and then you can go galloping over the moors again.'

I lay in bed, watching the light fade. Though I was weary in body with the effort of the day, my mind was a maëlstrom of confusing and contradictory thought. How was it, I asked myself, that I swung dizzily between Alasdair and James, like a demented compass unable to find true North. The real Katharine, I was convinced, was not fickle. She would set her heart on one fixed course, and would not swerve. Who, then, was this other creature at whose instigation I flirted outrageously with Captain Ridley, and whom he obviously found more than a little attractive. Certainly it was gratifying to find myself with rival admirers, but the emotional dichotomy could become a strain, and whatever I might dream about, it was Captain Ridley whose approach was the more overt. Alasdair would not betray himself. But his love would be worth the winning. And yet, was I deceiving myself that the tenuous flame burned at all? Was I following a will o' the wisp that would lure me into the marshes of despair?

On an impulse, I flung back the bed-clothes and stole

across to the lowboy. I had remembered Catriona's diary. Perhaps that would give me a clue, though what it might be, I couldn't imagine, since I could not read it. I took it from the drawer and leafed through it. The last film of light was draining from the translucent sky, and the faded writing merged with the yellowing paper, so that I could read nothing. Except that one word, a name, seemed to glow from the page. *Hamish*. Did that explain why, in my mind, I thought now of Captain James Ridley, and now of *Hamish*, as if I saw through the eyes of a woman long dead?

I shivered a little as I replaced the diary in the drawer and crept back to bed. Maybe I would know one day. I knew now where my hopes lay, but were they destined to be fulfilled? I must 'dree my ain weird'. Alasdair had said that. So must he, then. Did our paths run parallel, side by side but never meeting? Or did they converge, becoming one highway into the future?

I had at last admitted to myself the thing which skulked in the attic of my mind. I loved Alasdair MacRaith. I, who had thrust away, with sick revulsion, the very thought of marriage. I, who was—nobody. What had I to offer, save love. I turned my head into the pillow, and wept for my lost dream.

I had slept at last, the deep sleep of utter weariness, but it had at least 'knitted up the ravell'd sleeve' and I was ready to face the world again, head high and defiant of Fate. True to my boast, within a week I was walking unaided and unwearied up the stairs to my room. Permission to ride came later, from Doctor Laidlaw, and so I slid gradually back to the *status quo* which existed before the day of the Witches' Crag.

Afterwards I was to wonder whether Ishbel's excuse of a

twisted ankle was contrived and obvious. Did she want to prove something? It seemed so, from what transpired.

'Where will you go?' she asked. 'Not that I'm over-curious, but we do like to know in which direction people are riding, just in case——'

'Don't remind me! I'm not going far, only as far as the Tower, to look at the seabirds.'

Did that other self, as I rode along the cliff-top, cherish the hope he would be there? I had had no opportunity to make any assignation, and I hadn't wanted to. Not since I had allowed the beacon of my love for Alasdair to burn freely. And yet I felt the impulse, stronger now, as I neared the old castle ruin. But that was absurd. How could he know I would ride that way.

In the event, I never reached the Tower. My horse shied and I had some ado to control her as a man emerged from the bracken and stood in my path.

'You'll not be passing this way, young leddy,' he said, and reached up to take the bridle.

'Whyever not?' I demanded.

'Because the Young Laird would not wish it,' he said.

'The Young Laird?' I said uncertainly. Was I then trespassing on ground which belonged to a neighbouring laird.

'That was what I said. The Young Laird, Mr Alasdair.'

'Oh. Oh well, I suppose I must respect his wishes. He probably has his reasons.'

'Aye, he does that,' the man said ironically.

'Good morning,' I said shortly, and wheeled my horse. I did not turn, yet I knew that he watched me out of sight. I could, of course, return by the more roundabout route which Ishbel and I had taken, but somehow I knew it would lead to the same dead end—the Young Laird's wishes. This was the first time I had heard Alasdair so named. I had still not sorted out the family ramifications, but it seemed obvious that he might succeed that Auld Laird.

I rode down the glen and came at last to a stone bridge. Was this the 'bridge over the Atlantic'? Well, I had crossed it once, and Fate had done its worst. The bridge looked innocuous enough. Would it be tempting providence to cross it once more? Perhaps crossing it in the other direction would wipe out the danger?

A movement on the far bank caught my attention. A man was riding down the steep path. James Ridley. I urged my horse to a trot, but she tossed her head irritably and would not respond, so I tapped her lightly on the flank with my crop, pulling on the rein to turn her towards the bridge. Reluctantly she walked towards it, but at the last minute, as if an invisible bar stretched between the grey, moss-encrusted stonework, she stopped so suddenly that I was nearly unseated. Nothing I could do would induce her to set foot on the bridge. James Ridley had ridden to the far end; to my utter amazement, his horse behaved in exactly the same way.

'Wait,' I called, and dismounted. 'I'll come to you.'

'Oh no, you'll not, Katharine Beaton.' I swung round, to face Alasdair.

'How did you get here?' I exploded.

'The same way as you did.' He indicated with his crop the horse which grazed, all but out of sight behind one of the alders which grew along the bank. 'And along the same path.'

'You followed me! You were spying on me! Why?' I demanded.

'You'll not believe, of course, that I had only your well-being in mind?' He raised an eyebrow quizzically.

'I will not,' I retorted. 'Tell me, Mr MacRaith, what you have against me. Since the first day I came here I've been aware of your animosity, and I know no reason for it. Believe me, I won't trouble you much longer. I shall be sorry to leave Allt-nam-Fearna, where I've been treated with such kindness. But I don't think you'll be sorry to see the back of me.'

The deep hurt in my heart stung me to lash out at him, and his air of amused tolerance was all the more infuriating.

'Now, why should you think that, Katharine Beaton? You could be wrong, you know.' He turned his head at the sound of footsteps on the bridge. James Ridley had dismounted, and was striding towards us.

Before he could reach the near end of the bridge, Alasdair moved so that the other man's way was blocked and he had no option but to halt.

'Good afternoon, Miss Beaton.' James Ridley raised his voice, and I acknowledged his greeting. He turned to Alasdair. 'Good afternoon, MacRaith.'

'Good afternoon.' Alasdair's tone was cool and he made no move to let him pass. 'We'll not detain you, Ridley. I will escort Miss Beaton. I assure you I will see that she comes to no harm.' I had moved nearer to where they stood, face to face, like two angry animals boiling up to a combat.

'Good afternoon, Captain Ridley,' I said. 'How pleasant to meet you, and what a beautiful day. As you see, I'm out and about again; possibly we shall meet again soon, if you are riding this way?' Inwardly I was fuming, but a scene would be distasteful and embarrassing.

Captain Ridley took his cue. 'I shall look forward to it, Miss Beaton. Good afternoon, then.' He raised his hand in salute, turned, and strode back across the bridge.

Alasdair linked his hands to make a step for me, and I remounted. His horse came at his whistle, and he mounted and wheeled to fall in beside me. In silence we rode back to Allt-nam-Fearna. But all the way I was aware of the quiet half-whistle under his breath; the sound that one makes almost without being aware of it, when thoughts are engaged elsewhere. And if the airs were any clue to his thoughts, they were of me, for I recognised the song he had sung. And so the confusion in my mind grew; would it ever be resolved, I wondered.

'I'll take your nag,' he said, when we had dismounted in the courtyard. He led the mare away, and left me to make my own way into the house.

'Ah, Katharine, my dear. You enjoyed your ride?' Mrs MacRaith was sitting in the window embrasure in the Guardroom.

'Thank you, yes. It's lovely to be able to ride again, though I'm sorry Ishbel was unable to join me. I hope her ankle's not too painful?'

'No, just a little swollen. Nothing to worry about and she'll be able to hobble down to dinner tonight.'

She stood up and came slowly towards me, putting her arms round my shoulders.

'Dear Katharine,' she said. 'I wish you had been my daughter.'

Impulsively I kissed her cheek. 'Thank you, Mrs Mac-Raith. You've been more than kind to a stranger in your midst. For the rest of my life I'll be grateful, and I'll never forget you, and Ishbel, and all the dear people here. I could wish that they really were "my ain folk".'

'You'd be happy, then?' she asked. 'It could happen, you know.'

'What do you mean?' I asked. Her answer was no surprise.

'My dear, haven't you noticed? Surely you must know how Iain feels about you.' She took my hand in hers. 'It would make us all very happy if you could return his affection. Think about it, my dear.'

I dressed for dinner with Kirsteen's help, and I was a little surprised that she had laid out my white evening dress, and the tartan sash. Were there guests tonight? Mrs MacRaith had said nothing to that effect.

But I understood when I reached the gallery staircase. Below me in the hall, with Iain, Ishbel, Alasdair and Mrs MacRaith the Auld Laird waited. I came down the stairs almost in a trance, and he moved slowly to meet me, extending his arm as I reached the last step.

'My Catriona,' he said.

And when we had dined, he signalled for the glasses to be filled. He rose to his feet, as did Iain, Alasdair and Mrs MacRaith. A little tardily, because of her damaged ankle, Ishbel struggled to stand up. I sat uncertain what to do. It was not my birthday, and I was aware of no reason why I should be so honoured.

The Auld Laird raised his glass.

'I give you Catriona,' he said. 'She is home again.'

I sat silent and bewildered, but for no reason that I could name, a great surge of happiness seemed to lift me on a wave of exaltation.

CHAPTER TEN

I<small>T IS</small> an extraordinary experience to start the days as one person, and end up as somebody completely different. I was Katharine Beaton, nineteen years of age; I had received a careful education in a secluded boarding school in Sussex; my mother had died in a boating accident. And that, as I knew it, summed up my life. Until tonight.

Again, I had the feeling of taking part in a play. The stage—the hall. Enter, from up Right, the Auld Laird, leading Katharine Beaton and followed by Agnes Mac-Raith, Alasdair, Ishbel, and Iain.

I took my seat beside Mrs MacRaith on the leather-covered chesterfield which stood at an angle to the great canopied fireplace with its carved coat of arms, flanked by crossed claymores. At the other side of the wide hearth, the Auld Laird sat upright in a heavily carved chair of black oak upholstered in dark red leather, and Alasdair stood behind the chair, his elbow resting on the back. Ishbel and Iain sat on another settee, she with downcast eyes, idly examining her hands; he with a distant, almost resigned watchfulness.

Mrs MacRaith took my hand. 'My dear, you must be wondering what this is all about. We think the time has come to tell you just why you are here.'

'Because you invited me. Nothing more,' I said. 'I had no motive in coming here.'

'But I had a reason for asking you,' she said. 'Do you remember the day we first met?'

'I shan't forget it in a hurry,' I laughed. 'What a mess I

must have looked!' I turned to the others. 'Did Mrs Mac-Raith ever tell you? I tripped over the dog's lead, fell flat on my face, and she picked me up and later sent me home in a cab.' Mrs MacRaith smiled at the understatement.

'Do you remember the man who followed you, though?'

I stiffened. 'Yes, of course. I thought he was—oh, well, never mind. It doesn't matter now.'

'You shall tell us later what you thought, my dear. In fact, he was an enquiry agent—in my employ.' I stared at her in amazement, speechless.

'To find you,' she said. I still could not speak, and the little silence was disturbed by a sigh.

'Three sons.' The Auld Laird's voice was barely audible. 'Three fine sons. They all marched away, and they all lie in foreign lands.' I looked across at the old man, and the urge to try to comfort him was strong. I moved swiftly to kneel at his side and clasp my hands over his, and then I turned slightly to sit curled at his feet, my arm resting on his knee, his arm round my shoulder. Mrs MacRaith smiled across at me. 'That is where you should be, my child. The toast was true: Catriona is home again.'

She was watching, I swear. That other Catriona from long ago. She was half hidden in the shadows, but she was there, waiting. She knew, and I knew, that I must stay. But what did she want of me? Fear brushed me like a moth from a dark place.

At last I found my voice. 'You mean that I'm—a member of this family? That I really am—that I've really got a *name*?' I shook my head, dazed and unbelieving. 'How can you be so sure?' Mrs MacRaith answered with a question. 'What do you remember of your early life, Katharine?'

'I remember moving around a lot. Living in lodgings when I was very small, then, when I was about eight, being sent to a boarding school, and coming home for holidays in many different places—I mean, home in the sense that my mother was there, and Aunt Zen. And latterly, when Aunt Zen didn't tour the halls, staying with her in London and my mother would stay there too when she wasn't touring. But of course, you wouldn't know, would you? She was an actress, a singer. Mostly she played in light opera. She was Katharine Beaton, too.'

'And then? When you were older?' Mrs MacRaith prompted. I felt the hot colour mount to my cheeks. How could I tell them the rest of the story? I must find some way round the unpalatable, unacceptable truth.

'She became quite famous,' I said. 'And we weren't poor any more. I think she had devoted most of her earnings to keeping me at boarding school, but later on she was able to afford a house in the country, and I used to spend the school holidays there.' That at least was true. It was because she rented the cottage at Fordingham that she met Gerald, who owned the estate. He had been so infatuated with her that he had followed her all over Europe, taking a box for every performance wherever she appeared, and finally he had persuaded her to—*I must not remember.* The deep shame flooded back, and I was grateful that Mrs MacRaith took up the story and the moment of danger was past.

'It was a great loss, my dear, and very tragic. I'm sorry this has brought back recollection. Now tell me, do you remember your father?'

I shook my head. 'I think he died abroad, but I don't know where. I asked Aunt Zen and she didn't know. My mother never spoke of him; I think her grief was so deep that she hid away everything that would remind her. After she died, I had to go through her things, and there was simply nothing——'

'—except your brooch,' Ishbel interjected.

'Why, yes, I did find that, tucked away at the bottom of her jewel box. I never knew where it came from. I never remember her wearing it, either.'

'It was part of a cap badge,' Ishbel said. 'The shanks had been taken off and a pin attached.'

I twisted round to look up into the Auld Laird's face. 'Was my father one of the sons who marched away? Are you my grandfather?'

'Aye, lassie,' he said softly. My eyes filled with tears and my throat tightened. His hand closed on mine, and I lifted it to my cheek. 'I'm so happy,' I whispered. 'So happy— and so very proud.' I felt his hand rest lightly on my hair, stroking it gently. 'Such bonny locks. You're your father's daughter.'

'Tell me, please,' I begged. 'I can't take it all in, it's like a fairy tale, almost.'

Mrs MacRaith took a small packet from her bag, and sorted through it. She held out a photograph, which Iain passed to me.

'Why, that's my mother,' I exclaimed. 'The baby she's holding, that must be me. And the soldier—my father?' I looked at the written inscription.

'My darling wife and my Bonny Wee Thing.' I felt again the tightening in my throat, and I remembered the song which Alasdair had sung.

'How did you—I mean, where did this come from?'

'It was sent back to us by a fellow officer, after Malcolm died of heat stroke in India. All his effects were returned to us.'

I felt the Auld Laird's hand tremble in mine, and his voice shook.

'We parted in anger. I never saw him more. I'd have given my right hand to recall him and ask his pardon.'

'Please, Grandfather. Don't grieve. Whatever it was that

parted you, he understands now, and he and my mother are together, for always.' Was that, I wondered, the cause of the quarrel?

'Headstrong,' said the Auld Laird. 'Always headstrong, like me. And I was a pig-headed tyrant. He wanted his Katharine, so they ran away. Who can blame them—I'd have done the same.'

But the grief. To know that one you loved had died amongst strangers, a world away. Dimly I understood, because my mother's death had left me bereft.

'So then we had to try to find you,' Mrs MacRaith said. 'This was the first we knew of Malcolm's marriage, and it seemed that even his commanding officer had not been informed, otherwise his effects would have been sent to your mother.' *And you would never have known, and I should not now be here.* What strange tricks fate plays. What path, then, would my life have taken?

There was a pause, and I sensed a reluctance on Mrs MacRaith's part to go on. Did she know that part of the story which had caused me such heartburning?

'Mrs MacRaith?' I said. 'No, that's wrong, isn't it. I mean, now you are—Aunt Agnes?'

'Yes, my dear. But what were you about to say?'

'Something I hardly know how to put into words.' I said. 'When my mother was drowned, nothing was ever found when her body was—was washed up later. I mean, the yacht was a total loss, so that any private papers which she might have had with her—well, you see, she always carried a large handbag, and I believe it held papers and things which she wouldn't want to leave lying around. So I've nothing, no marriage certificate, no birth certificate. How can you be so sure I'm who you say I am. I simply don't know. Legally I don't even *exist*.' And I told them how I had searched at Somerset House.

'Under what name, Katharine Beaton?' Alasdair spoke for the first time.

'Why, under that name, of course. It was the only one I'd ever known.'

'Spelled?'

'B-E-A-T-O-N. How else should I have spelled it. That was how my mother spelled it, and she was billed under that name.'

'Of course.' He moved across to where Aunt Agnes sat, and picked up the packet of papers. 'Here, you ignorant little Sassenach——' He tossed a paper at me. I unfolded it. It was a birth certificate. Or rather, a certification that a birth had been registered. It gave no more than the bare fact that the birth of Katharine Bethune had been registered on the 7th January 1893. None of the details of parents, and so on, normally found on such a certificate.

'But this isn't mine,' I protested. 'And anyway, it's not a complete certificate, is it? It proves nothing.'

'It's the shortened form,' Aunt Agnes explained. 'It was with Malcolm's papers. We later sent to Somerset House for a full certificate.'

'But the name,' I persisted. Silently she handed another paper to me. It was a full birth certificate, and one entry burned into my brain.

Name and Maiden Name of Mother:	Name of Father	Rank or Profession of Father
BETHUNE KATHARINE		

The second and third columns were blank.

I took a deep breath. I had to *know*. 'Please tell me,' I said. 'Is that really *my* birth certificate? I don't understand the different name, and—the blanks,' I finished lamely.

'B-E-T-H-U-N-E is pronounced Beaton,' Alasdair said. 'At least, in this part of the world. As for the blanks,' he shrugged. 'Never fash.'

I looked down at the paper in my hand. That vital piece of paper, which told me who I was—yet snatched away my birthright. I looked up at Alasdair to see whether he mocked, but his expression told me nothing.

'You say "don't worry",' I said. 'But these blanks— what do they make me? Now I wonder whether it would not have been better to remain the nobody I am.'

'No, my child.' The Auld Laird's voice was gentle, comforting. 'You are my Catriona, *my* bonny wee thing, as you were to your father. And you must understand that since you are Scottish born, you have a very different status.'

Scottish born. I had not appreciated that point, nor did I know that it was important. Again I examined my birth certificate. 'Place of Birth ... Inverness'.

'So you see, my dear, the blank spaces carry no stigma,' Aunt Agnes took up the threads of the strange tale. 'By Scottish law, "consent makes marriage", and even though no ceremony has taken place, such a marriage is still valid. This' —she pointed to the photograph, —'is an open acknowledgement, and no doubt Malcolm would have referred to his wife in the presence of his brother officers, even if he had never made a formal statement to his Commanding Officer. I think, though this is only surmise, that no application was made to the registrar of the parish, because your father was posted overseas at very short notice. But that does not make you illegitimate.'

I don't know what made me look at Ishbel just at that moment, but I was surprised to see that her face was white and set. Our eyes met, and I was shocked at the hatred in them, the more so because I had thought we were friends, and I had become very fond of her. The fact that we were cousins drew me closer. She was the sister I had never had, and Iain—almost my brother, and that was indeed the only feeling I had for him. Whatever Aunt Agnes' wishes were, it was for me to choose my husband. I knew where my heart lay, though whether that dream would come true was problematical. Again, I thrust the thing away from me, and deliberately brought myself back to a practical plane.

'How did you find me?' I asked curiously. 'It seems too much of a coincidence that we should meet, Aunt Agnes and me, by blind chance.'

'It was no blind chance.' Aunt Agnes said. 'The day you tripped over the dog's lead was the end of a long and tortuous trail. Right at the beginning, when we learned that Malcolm had indeed married his Katharine, we advertised for her. But she never made any contact with us, possibly because of the old feud—you'll learn of that later——'

'She was afraid you'd take me away,' I broke in. 'Aunt Zen told me that, when I was trying to find out more about my background. They met in a theatre dressing-room, so she said, when I was only eighteen months old. Aunt Zen didn't know about the changed spelling, either. She'd have told me, when I couldn't find the entry in the records. But that may have been because it made an easier stage name. I mean, why she adopted that spelling.'

'That's more than likely. Anyway, it did confuse the trail at first, but your mother soon made a name for herself and of course, it was inevitable that she should be photographed.' Aunt Agnes sorted through the packet again and passed me a picture postcard.

'Oh, I remember this one,' I exclaimed. 'It was one of the best she ever had taken.' My eyes filled with tears, seeing her dear face again. 'She never changed, she was always beautiful.'

'You are very like her, you know.'

'Oh, no,' I exclaimed. 'I could never be as lovely as she was. But please go on. I'm sorry I interrupted.'

'We followed her career, and we *were* concerned about your upbringing, my dear. After all,' Aunt Agnes shrugged, 'the theatrical profession can be a little dubious. But we found that you were, in fact, being suitably educated, so we were content to leave things as they were—always hoping, of course, for some sort of reconciliation. Then, of course, that tragic accident was reported, and we knew you must be completely bereft. So we took steps to get in touch with you, only to find that you had left Fordingham and no one knew where you were. We had to start looking again.'

'How?' I asked bluntly. 'The man who followed me?'

'Yes, my dear.' Aunt Agnes looked a little embarrassed. 'I'm more than sorry that you were distressed, but it was the only way.'

'But why didn't you tell me before? When you invited me to stay here, for instance?'

'We needed to be absolutely certain. It could have been no more than coincidence that you so closely resembled Katharine Beaton. I see now that it was really not a very good idea, but I hope everything will turn out for the best.'

'Then why are you so sure now? I have no papers, no proof. I could be an impostor, willing to accept your relationship merely for what I could get out of it.'

'You will probably find it hard to accept this,' Aunt Agnes said quietly. 'The things which finally convinced us are not such as would be accepted in a court of law, but to us, they have more force. For one thing, you are left-handed. That is a dominant and persistent family characteristic. You have the same eyes and hair, and the same cast of features. And do you remember the egg-shell?'

192

'Why, yes,' I laughed. 'That seemed such a childish thing.'

'A family habit, too,' she said. 'Then the bairn greeting, and the water that tastes of blood. Only the MacRaiths hear, or taste.'

'So, Katharine MacRaith, how does it feel to acquire a completely new family?' Alasdair's sardonic voice was like icy water thrown in my face. I took up the gage.

'How does it feel,' I riposted, 'to acquire a new cousin? For that, I assume, is our relationship?'

'Touché. As to how it feels, I'll tell you some other time.'

A clock struck, and I counted. 'Twelve o'clock. A new day, a new life.' I stood up, and looked at each of 'my ain folk' in turn. My heart was too full to say more. All I could do was to drop a kiss on the cheek of the Auld Laird, and bid good night to the others. I took my lamp from the table, and walked slowly up the broad staircase. I had come down them as Katharine Beaton, a nobody with no known background. I ascended them as Katharine Mac-Raith, and the portraits that lined the walls seemed to smile their approval.

I lay in bed, watching the dying glow of the embers, thinking, thinking, thinking, my mind seething. I supposed there would be practical considerations to be sorted out. Where did I stand, for instance, with regard to Gerald's guardianship? I imagined that his rights must yield to those of the Auld Laird, and I was thankful that his hold on me was broken for ever.

As to my future, that needed consideration. I could not see myself settling down to a routine of assistant to Aunt Agnes, much as I liked and respected her. I wanted to *do* something with my life, and although I was so very happy to have found this new world in which I had a definite place, at the same time I felt trapped. I could not stay in this remote corner and let life pass by.

But then, I was going to marry my Hamish. How could I have forgotten that. I went to the lowboy and took out my diary and read the last entry.

I did not remember getting out of bed. I was standing by the window, the diary in my hands, open at the last written page. I was very cold; colder even than the dead hour before dawn; the ashes were grey and dead in the grate, and somewhere out on the moor a whaup cried forlornly.

And on the other side of the panelling—the soft whisper of a skirt.

With the morning sun, the fears of the night vanished. The days that followed were filled with a gentle happiness and contentment, and if they seemed too lovely to continue, then at least the stored recollection would bring solace when the heart was sore. I didn't know why I should have this feeling of foreboding, but the message of the Tarot cards still haunted me, particularly the Tower. But for the time being I accepted gratefully the golden beauty of the days as they passed. I rode less, because the Auld Laird had taken to spending much of his time in Catriona's garden, and often I sat with him in preference to joining the others when they went riding. Ishbel's attitude still mystified me, swinging as it did between affection which I could not truly regard as false, and a kind of envy, for which I could find no reason. So I put it down to my own fancy, and let my mind relax and enjoy the present.

Iain's attitude was far more straightforward. Although he had said little on that memorable evening, he slipped naturally into the role of an indulgent brother. It was he who had performed the service of lighting my lamp, which he had handed to me, saying: 'Cousin Katharine, welcome. Here is your lamp, and you bring a more lasting light by your presence here.' His kiss was gentle and without passion, and I was happy that he would make no demands on me, yet would be a friend and companion. I knew intuitively that his deep affections centred elsewhere, and I hoped for his sake that they would be returned.

The garden sessions were by no means solitary. Captain Ridley was a frequent visitor, but opportunities for private conversation were limited. Ishbel still insisted that I was the attraction, but that I could not believe. There must be some more important reason for his remaining so persistently in the neighbourhood. Alasdair's dislike of him was barely veiled, yet he seemed at times to be relieved that Ridley was, in fact, under his eye. As for Iain, he took a perverse pleasure in trailing a coat when James Ridley was around.

'How is your—business—progressing, Ridley?'

'Well enough.' The reply was short and gave nothing away.

'You're very mysterious. No one quite knows what your business really is.' Iain was watching Ridley's reaction. 'Now, when are you coming out with the guns?'

'When I'm specifically invited.'

'Ah, well, we must attend to that. You must excuse me now. I have—business to attend to.'

Afterwards I asked Ishbel: 'Why does Iain bait Captain Ridley?'

'Don't you know?'

'Well, I wouldn't ask, would I?'

'I wondered whether he'd told you anything of his reasons for staying. Don't misunderstand me, Katharine, but there's more in it than just a desire to see you.'

'You mean he's using me as an excuse?'

'Something like that. Oh, I know he's keen on you. Very keen. But he does have other things to do.'

'Such as?' I burned with resentment at her implication, and at the same time I was hurt at her apparent malice, though if I were really being used as cover, better to know than to dwell in an illusory world.

'Such as looking for stills and smugglers. We've heard that he's hand in glove with the Customs Officers at Kyle.' She watched me carefully, noting my reaction. Outwardly I was cool.

'Then why bother to be secretive about it? It doesn't concern me, anyway,' I said casually.

'It might,' she said darkly. 'You're part of Allt-nam-Fearna now, whether you like it or not. He's not to know how far you're involved.'

'Involved? What in, for goodness sake?'

'Smuggling.'

I burst out laughing. 'Now I know you're pulling my leg. Me a smuggler? That's just nonsense.'

'Is it? I've pulled an oar on many a run, when they've been short of men. How do you think you got rescued from the Witches' Crag? They weren't expecting to find you on the end of that chain, Katharine. They were getting the still up. The still for making whisky.'

I sat dumbfounded, unable to believe such a fantastic story. But odd unexplained snippets rattled in my mind. I remembered how impatient James Ridley had been on the evening of the dinner party, and how, after a certain point in time, he had relaxed, as if something had passed beyond his control. Again, what had he been doing near the Tower, and above all, why had Iain forbidden Ishbel to take that direction. I began to understand.

'Was there a run, as you call it, the night of the dinner

party?' Ishbel smiled. 'You're learning! Why else do you think the gallant captain was invited? And why did Alasdair tell you to keep him busy?'

Once again I burned at the way in which I had apparently been used. 'Keep the captain entertained so that he won't go prying into what's none of his affair!'

'And the day we went to the Tower?' I asked. 'Was there something round there that we weren't supposed to see?'

'Something that *you* weren't supposed to see,' she corrected.

'And now it doesn't matter?' I challenged. 'Now I'm to be tarred with the same brush?'

'No, Katharine,' she protested. 'It's not quite like that. It's done with. Alasdair put a stop to it. He found out that Iain was mixed up in it, just for the thrill, I suppose, and so he went out with Iain in the boat to pick up the still, and found you instead.'

I shivered at the recollection. 'I suppose I must consider myself very lucky, then?' Or was it more than luck? Fate, perhaps. And the question still remained—how did I come to be manacled to the iron stanchion, and why did my wrist show no marks?

'All the same,' I said, 'I can't see why he should be concerned with the odd bit of smuggling in a remote part of Scotland. He's a soldier, isn't he?'

'Is he? What's his regiment? He's never in uniform. Is he on leave, or what? The fact is, dear Katharine, your captain is a bit of a mystery.'

The golden days of September drifted into the blazing colours of October. The leaves on the rowan burned red, and the birches turned to a delicate golden brown before scattering in the rising winds. Soon it would be Hallowe'en, and because that was Alasdair's birthday a party was planned—a double celebration.

'What do we do?' I asked Ishbel. 'All the usual Hallowe'en things?'

'All the usual Hallowe'en things,' she agreed. 'And a few more, which are peculiar to Allt-nam-Fearna. You'll see.' She would tell me no more.

I dressed for the party with breathless anticipation. For some reason that I could not explain, I knew that this evening was a turning point in my life. Even the indignation I had felt at apparently being exploited, now dwindled to an amused irritation, as if Alasdair and Ridley were schoolboys playing Cowboys and Indians. I shrugged it off, and took extra care with my toilette.

The great hall was a kaleidoscope of colour and movement, and I was keyed up to an unbelievable pitch of exhilaration. *Tonight, I knew, he would ask me to marry him, and I would give him the only possible answer, even though it must be our secret till the time was ripe to disclose it. I waited at the top of the stairs, knowing he would come to me.*

'My Catriona.' I swung round, and melted into his arms. 'My lovely girl. It has been so long, but now the long waiting is nearly over.' His kiss was warm on my lips, and I in my turn allowed passion to take us along on its heady flood. At last we drew apart, dazed and shaken. 'When, my darling? When?'

'Soon,' I whispered. 'As soon as I can escape.'

He took my hand and peeled off my glove. 'Wear this for me,' he whispered, and a ring slid on to my finger. I eased my glove on again, and though it could not be seen, I could feel the ring under the fine kid. The ring that bound me for ever, for eternity.

'Come,' he said. 'We shall be missed. I will take the other stair, then it won't be so obvious that we've been together.' I felt him leave my side and drift into the darkness, and then I rejoined the company in the hall. There were so many people, many of whom I did not know, that it did not seem possible that my absence had been noted. I had counted without Ishbel's sharp eyes.

'Well?' she whispered, as we took hands in a grand chain. I felt her fingers linger as she took my left hand, and next time we passed, she said 'You'll not need to burn chestnuts or peel apples tonight!' I must remember to remove and hide the ring, but I would wear it next to my heart, hidden, warm with my love.

Where was he? I searched the hall with my eyes, but he was not there. But when the great door opened, there he was, his coat silvered with light rain. He crossed the hall to where the Auld Laird sat in his great carved chair.

'My apologies, sir, for my lateness. I had urgent business.' He turned to me. 'Miss Beaton, is it too much to hope that you might have saved me just one dance?'

Mechanically I handed him my card. 'Yes, Captain Ridley, I think just one remains—the last waltz.' He pencilled in his initials and then moved away to speak to Aunt Agnes.

'Ah, Captain Ridley, you're just in time. Perhaps you don't know of our family charade. It is always performed on this night. Come, girls,' she motioned to me and to Ishbel. Slowly I followed them along the dark corridor to the Guardroom. What was happening to me? Had I dreamed the incident of the gallery? The hard metal circle beneath my glove gave the lie to that.

'Now, Katharine, my dear.' Aunt Agnes's voice brought me back to the present. 'You shall be the Bride of Alderburn—— '

'Aunt Agnes, you promised me!' Ishbel's tone was sharp with disappointment. 'It's always been my part; besides, Katharine won't know her place——'

'Then you must instruct her,' Aunt Agnes said with quiet firmness. 'You must be courteous, child, and yield your place to your cousin.'

'And more than my place, if you get your way.' Ishbel's angry whisper reached me, and I hope no one else had caught it.

'Now, Katharine, this is one of our family legends.' She beckoned to Ishbel. 'Help Katharine with her cloak. The rest of you know your parts from last year.'

'But I shan't know what to say,' I objected.

'You say very little,' she assured me. 'The words will come by instinct, you'll see.'

And she was right. Something seemed to take control of my mind, and I knew where to move, when to speak, and the macabre little drama was played out.

When we returned to the great hall, the transformation was eerie. The candles of the wrought iron chandelier had been extinguished, and the lamps turned out. The acrid smell of the candles and of the lamp wicks would remain for ever with me, recalling the dim expanse of the hall, lit only by the flames from the burning logs, that left the corners as dark caves of menace.

The Auld Laird's chair had been carried to the half-landing so that he sat in an improvised royal box; a glimmer of faces watched from gallery and stairs. As I waited to make my entrance, the commonplace intruded in the form of Ishbel's practical assurance that I need have no fear of tripping over the rugs, which had all been removed for the dancing.

The past took over, and I moved to the centre of the hall, led on each hand by Ishbel and another girl whose name I did not know. With hands outstretched, Iain waited, and as we came face to face, each of us placed our raised hands together, and knelt, while Iain, in a low voice, intoned the traditional lines:

'Hand-fast we ha'e been for a year and a day;
'Then tell me, my love, will you go, will you stay;
'Gin ye'll bide neath my plaidie, my sweet cushie-doo,
'I'll take ye to wife and rest leal and true.'

Then our fingers twined and closed, so that our hands were clasped, and I repeated the lines which Ishbel had taught me, so grudgingly and hurriedly, yet it seemed that I had known them all my life.

'Hand-fast we have been for a year and a day;
'My heart will be sore, gin ye send me away;
'I'll come in my sark to thy bed, my dear lord;
'I take thee as husband and pledge thee my word.'

Hands still locked together, we stood up, and Iain drew me to him as if to kiss me, but before he could take me in his arms the double doors at the end of the hall were flung open and about half a dozen men, led by Alasdair, stormed into the hall, brandishing flaming pine torches. Alasdair tossed his torch to one of the men, and seized me, and because I was so taken by surprise, my scream echoed to the rafters. Two of the men held the struggling Iain, while Alasdair spoke his lines:

'Hand-fast ye may be, but I'll take her this night;
'I'll bed her, my brother, and e'en in thy sight;
'Gin she carry a bairn, then mayhap we will wed;
'Until there's a fairer to take to my bed.'

The charade took on the character of a ritual; those of Alasdair's retinue, who were not holding Iain now formed themselves into a circle. Each man unfastened his plaid and held it, arms extended so that he touched the hands of his neighbours, thus forming a curtained enclave.

'Never fear, Katharine. All I'll take from you this night is one kiss.' The irony of the tone was belied by the passion of that kiss, and I held my breath in an effort to subdue the pounding of my heart. But I could not control the response of my betraying lips.

'Oh, Katharine. My bonny wee thing.' The whispered endearment was so faint that only I could possibly have heard it, and even I was left wondering if I had imagined it.

The curtain of plaids swirled away as each man swung his own round his shoulders. Alasdair held me imprisoned, one hand clamped round my wrists, while he spoke his final lines.

'Hand-fast are we now, for the rest of our days;
'Gin ye love, gin ye hate, 'tis the lassie that pays;
'Thy pain is my pleasure, thy loss all my gain;
'Nine moons shall bring proof that with thee I
    have lain.'

It was my turn to speak, and again, the words came with a strange familiarity.

'Hand-fasted to thee, and in enmity ta'en,
'Let the wife thou has won bring thee naught but
    thy bane:
'Let the sons thou shalt get take in hatred thy life;
'In Hell, rue the taking of thy brother's wife.'

To Iain fell the last lines of all, and the bitterness of so long ago tinged the present with unaccountable relevance.

> 'The evil that springs from this Hallowe'en rite
> 'Be held in remembrance on each Samhuinn night:
> 'The Bane of MacRaith strike each branch of the tree
> 'Till the Rose from the South bear my pardon to thee.'

Then, as Alasdair carried me to the Guardroom door, Iain was dragged away to the main door and thrust out into the night, and the door slammed and barred. And although he could have put me down as soon as we were out of sight of the audience, Alasdair did not set me on my feet until we were back in the Guardroom. 'That was well acted,' he said. 'I wish it were in my power to make——' He broke off. 'Don't heed my blether. Put it down to the whisky I've taken.' He swung away from me, leaving me hurt and bewildered by his sudden changes of mood which swung between tenderness and downright dislike.

The others now came swarming in, laughing, teasing, and the rest of the evening was spent in the traditional Hallowe'en manner. The girls, myself included, peeled apples, and tossed the long strand to learn the initial of the future lover. There was giggling and teasing, and disclaimers, and when it came to my turn, the resultant squiggle of peel seemed to mean nothing.

'It looks like a "J" to me,' Ishbel declared.

'It's an "I".' Aunt Agnes spoke decisively. 'It has to be an "I", doesn't it?' There was an undercurrent of seriousness, and she watched me carefully. 'I wonder whether he'll hold you to your declaration?'

'Who?' I asked. 'You mean Iain? But that was only a charade.'

'Maybe,' she laughed. 'But in law, it was a marriage.' My utter astonishment left me dumb. I had not thought that she would make such a public declaration of her wish for a marriage between Iain and me. And in the taut silence which followed, I looked from Ishbel to Iain, and then to Alasdair, and from each I sensed anger. I was grateful when one of the girls broke the tension with a nervous giggle.

'Well mine's a "D", plain enough, 'And if that stands for Dougal, well, maybe I'd better be seeking him to take me home—who knows, anything could happen on Hallowe'en!'

At last the party was over, and as a final concession to the old rites, Ishbel and I walked upstairs backwards. I did not see which direction she took, but as I reached the half-landing and looked across at the gallery, two shadowy figures stood close together, and I wondered.

Because it was Hallowe'en, we mounted the stairs by candlelight, and as I reached the door of my room a sudden draught killed the flame. I opened my door, expecting the lamp to have been lit by Kirsteen, as usual, but the room was in darkness, except for a shaft of moonlight through the window.

Then I realised I was not in my own room. I was in Catriona's.

As if impelled by some other will, I moved towards the dressing table, and in the dim light I saw myself reflected, pale as the dress I wore. A cloud covered the moon and took what faint light there was, so that I saw myself veiled like the portrait. And over my shoulder I saw my lover.

Slowly I turned and held out my arms to empty space.

Shaken and suddenly afraid, I moved carefully across the room and out into the corridor, at the end of which was a window. Outlined against the lesser blackness a figure moved away and was gone.

I was still trembling when I reached the door of my room, and opened it into a blessed lightness. The fire glowed and crackled, and the lamp shone bright and steady. Outside, the wind could tear the ragged clouds; the witches could ride; I was safe. On my pillow lay a sprig of rowan, tied with a red thread. Who had put it there? Ishbel? Kirsteen? Phemie?

One reality remained. When I peeled off my glove, the ring still glowed on my finger. Reluctantly I took it off, and crossing to the lowboy, hid it in the folds of the black silk which wrapped the Tarot cards.

Soon I would tell him who I was, and he would make a formal request to Grandfather. Soon. Let it be soon, my heart besought.

CHAPTER ELEVEN

WITH THE winds of that Hallowe'en night went the last
of the leaves and the last of the golden days of autumn.
Now the jealous, shrouding mists closed in, keeping us
close to the house and barring the outside world from us.
Inevitably much of my time was spent with Ishbel, but
there were days when I sat with Grandfather. More and
more I sought his company, as if storing up a treasure so
long withheld from me, and soon to be snatched away
again.

'How is he today?' I asked Phemie. She drew me into
the little ante-room and closed the communicating door.

'Sleeping now, but it will warm his heart if he wakes
to find you at his side.' She took my hand in both hers.
'You *know*, don't you, Katharine?'

'Yes,' I said. 'I don't know *when*, but soon. I shall miss
him.'

'We all shall,' she said sadly. 'He is a wonderful man.
Even his faults had a taste of greatness. May he travel
safely to Tir-nan-Og.'

He lay in the huge fourposter bed that was so wide as
to dwarf even as fine a man as Duncan MacRaith, and as I
gently took the hand that lay inert on the smooth sheet,
the waxen face came alive and he opened his eyes. He
smiled, and his fingers, still with the strength of a young
man, closed on mine.

'Catriona. My Catriona. You give me so much of your
time, my child. You should be out leading the young men
a dance.' His clasp tightened. 'Give me your promise,

Catriona, that you will never wed unless your heart tells you clearly—*there* is your man.'

'I promise,' I said. 'And I could wish that he may be like you, Grandfather.' He smiled again. 'Maybe he will,' he said. And I wondered which of them he had in mind, Iain or Alasdair. I knew where my heart lay, but I was still being quietly manoeuvred towards Iain, though I did not know why. I could manoeuvre, too, I thought; nor would I be deflected from my chosen path, even though I must walk it alone.

Grandfather's voice brought me back to the present.

'I have a charge for you, Catriona. Take care of Ishbel. She will need all you can give her of love, and she will need your help in the face of all their contriving. She's a good lassie, for all that——' He broke off, as Ishbel herself came into the room. She crossed to take Grandfather's other hand, and leaned over to kiss him.

'My two bonny lassies,' he said. 'I'm a fortunate man, for all that my three sons marched away. Now off with you both. Young lassies should be away spinning webs to catch young callants.' I leaned over to kiss his cheek, and caught his whispered 'remember' and I nodded.

He turned to Ishbel and looked at her searchingly. 'What is it?' he asked quietly. 'Nothing, Grandfather. I'm well.'

'Well enough in body, no doubt. But sick at heart. Believe me, child, I *know*.' He brought over his other hand to clasp hers and underline what he said. 'Do as your heart bids you. Katharine will help you and stand by you —I have her word for it and she'll not renege.'

For the first time, there was hope in Ishbel's eyes.

'Thank you, Grandfather. You give me courage.'

'No, child, I don't *give* you courage. It was there, already, but it needed to be wakened.'

'What did Grandfather mean?' Ishbel asked. We sat in my room before the fire, drinking our morning coffee, and munching oatcakes.

'He told me to take care of you. Not in a material sense —at least, that was how I translated it. But emotionally. A shoulder to weep on, if you like, though I hope there'll be no need for tears.'

She stirred her coffee and crumbled an oatcake, pushing round the small fragments absentmindedly. 'There could be,' she said. 'Oh, yes, there could be.'

'Tell me?' I asked. 'That is, if you want to, I'm not just curious. I really do want to help, if you need it.'

'You may *want* to. The point is—*can* you?'

I gathered cups, plates, and the coffee jug, and put them on the tray, which I set on the little console table outside the door.

'We shan't be interrupted now,' I said. 'And there's a lot I need to know.'

'There's a lot you ought to know,' Ishbel said. 'Some of it I should not be telling you, I suppose, but Grandfather was right—I have to screw my courage to the sticking place.' She leaned forward, searching my face. 'Are you in love with Iain?'

'No. I like him very much, and now I realise he *is* my cousin, it puts him in the place of a brother, and that makes me very happy. But love, in the way you mean—no. I think that Aunt Agnes very much wants me to marry him, and I don't know why. Anyway,' I shrugged, 'I wouldn't give much for a husband who would have his bride chosen for him.'

'She wants you to marry him because that will fulfil the prophesy and destroy the Bane of MacRaith for good.'

'The Rose from the South?'

Ishbel nodded. 'It fits in so well,' she said, 'and there's a deal more than the apparently superstitious killing of a curse.' I nodded, remembering Aunt Zen's philosophy: every curse had its 'escape clause' however improbable it might be.

'When Grandfather dies,' Ishbel continued, 'you and Iain will probably stand jointly in his will, because your father and his were twins. If you did marry, it would avoid splitting the estate.'

'That's a cold-blooded reason for marrying,' I said bitterly. Ishbel's smile held a touch of malice. 'There's more to it than that. You remember the twin sons of Alasdair Dubh? The two lines have been at enmity ever since. The other line intermarried with the Bethunes and between them they got some of the lands that were confiscated after The Fifteen, and you'll inherit your mother's share. You can imagine the hullabaloo when your father actually wanted to marry a Bethune!'

'The classic "Us and Them" conflict,' I said. 'All down the ages, from Romeo and Juliet to Malcolm and Katharine. Now I begin to understand. But I tell you, Ishbel, I'm not going to marry Iain to please anyone, or to join up any estate. I'd rather renounce the whole lot.'

'I really believe you would,' Ishbel's look changed to one of reluctant admiration. 'You're a very determined person, Katharine.'

'I'm a MacRaith, aren't I? That's enough to make me dig my toes in. But what I don't understand is where you come in. I mean, surely you and Iain take equal shares?'

She flushed crimson. 'You mean you don't know? Who do you think I am?'

'I suppose I jumped to the conclusion that you were Iain's sister. That's why your——' I fumbled for a word which would not wound her, but she herself voiced it bluntly.

'——my jealousy.'

'Yes,' I admitted. 'I couldn't understand it. It seemed unnatural, somehow.'

'It would have been, wouldn't it? Though with a family like ours, anything could happen: you've found yourself a strange haven, Katharine.' She stared into the heart of the fire, and I waited.

'So—who am I?' Her voice was low and bitter. 'I'll tell you who I am. I'm nobody—haven't you guessed? A nothing, a come-by-chance. Sheltered like a stray cat. Tolerated because of a family obligation. But with no position, no rights, no *hope*.' She raised her head and my heart was wrung at the misery in her eyes, because I too had known what it was to be—nobody.

'What have I to look forward to, Katharine? Fetching and carrying for Aunt Agnes. Shut in these walls like prison, to the end of my days, like the poor creature in the Tower room, only she lacked the wits to know and to suffer.'

'Surely,' I said gently, 'it can't be as bad as that. Things loom when we're young, but it can't be all black. You're young, and pretty, and you'll meet someone——'

'I don't care *who* I meet,' Ishbel interrupted fiercely. 'It's Iain I want. I shall never want another.'

'Then get him,' I said firmly. 'What's to stop you. What can Aunt Agnes do? Shut you in a dungeon on bread and water?'

'You don't know her. She might even do that. Anyway,' Ishbel shrugged, 'she's been kinder to me than you'd expect, in all the circumstances.' Again I waited. 'She could have hated me, and I couldn't have blamed her. All this'—she waved an all-embracing arm—'could have been hers, if things had been different. She married the eldest of the Auld Laird's three sons—your father's brother. Her baby was still-born, and the doctors told her she could never have another child.'

'So you're adopted?' I asked. Ishbel's laugh was harsh and derisive.

'I'm a MacRaith,' she said. 'We're cousins all right— only my mother was the daughter of one of the gillies. I was born about six months afterwards, and my mother died when I was two days old. Work it out for yourself.' For answer, I moved across to sit on the arm of the chair and take Ishbel in my arms. I was bereft of speech, for what could I say? What comfort was there for this burden that she must bear to her grave. And Aunt Agnes? What a canker of bitterness must have bred within her over the years? That serene, elegant woman, living her life with the daily reminder of betrayal, yet great enough in mind to raise the child of that betrayal.

'She was good to me. She never let it show; in fact, she never even told me. For a long time I thought Iain was my brother. It would have been better, perhaps, if I'd gone on thinking that, then I wouldn't have got myself into this muddle. But someone with a grudge made it their business to tell me just who I was.' My arms tightened round her, and I ached to bring her some kind of solace. 'Ishbel,' I said. 'You *can* marry Iain, you know. It's just come to me—this is Scotland, not England. If you make a declaration, that is a marriage, isn't it? You're both of age, aren't you?'

'I'm over twenty-one, yes. Isn't it odd, I'm older than you, but you seem the one to take the lead. And Iain— he's twenty-two. His father was killed at Ladysmith, and Aunt Agnes brought us up. He's almost like her own son, that's why she's so ambitious for him. It would set the seal on her achievements if she could see him as the Laird of Allt-nam-Fearna.'

'She may yet see that,' I said. 'Oh, Ishbel, dear Ishbel. I'm so glad we've got this thing sorted out. You know, at one time I almost felt afraid that I was in real danger. *Physical* danger.'

Her hand clasped mine. 'I'd never have harmed you, Katharine. I didn't know who you were, or why you were here, but I loved you from the start.'

'Bless you.' I said. 'Now, what are we going to do? We've got to work things out very carefully. The marriage part is easy enough—you and Iain simply make a declaration which I will witness. But it has to be registered, doesn't it. Where?'

'Inverness. I suppose we shall have to think up an excuse to go there.'

Remembering my journey, I said: 'Can't we go on the train?'

'We'd have to get to Kyle,' Ishbel objected. 'We can't ask Murdo to drive us there—he'd have to ask the Young Laird first.'

'Alasdair?'

'Himself—and behaves as though he's Lord of the Isles.'

Again—*Alasdair*. Making decisions, issuing orders, imposing bans—just why, I wondered, did he have the right to exercise this authority? Where did he stand in the hierarchy of Allt-nam-Fearna? I remembered that he had addressed the Auld Laird as 'Grandfather'. Why, then did he not stand to inherit in the same degree as Iain and myself? But Ishbel and I had other, more important matters to pursue, and I pushed away the thoughts that flashed unbidden in my brain. Nor was this the most tactful moment to question Ishbel, in view of her own so recent revelations.

'Never mind about him,' I said impatiently. 'Who else would help us?' And because my glance rested on the lowboy and I remembered the ring in the drawer, my train of thought led inevitably to James Ridley. 'Captain Ridley,' I said. 'He has a motor car. He'll help us. I know he will.'

'He'll do anything for *you*.' Ishbel said.

'So—if *I* ask him to help *you,* he'll do it to please me?'

She nodded.

The rattle of the tray being collected by Kirsteen brought us both back to the everyday world. Hurriedly I said, 'We'll talk about it later, after lunch. We've got to get in touch with Captain Ridley somehow.'

Ishbel stood up, and I marvelled at the transformation. Her eyes were bright with hope, and excitement had brought colour to her cheeks. She came to me and flung her arms round me.

'Dear Katharine. Thank you. I'm so happy I could explode.'

'You'd better not explode in front of Aunt Agnes,' I said. 'And this is going to take a bit of time. Don't be too impatient.'

'I've waited so long, and without hope,' she said quietly. 'I can bide a little longer.'

We went down to lunch together, and it almost seemed as though Fate took a hand. Standing by the fireplace in the Guardroom, where luncheon was set for six persons, was Captain Ridley, with Iain and Alasdair.

When Aunt Agnes joined us, we took our seats, and I was thankful to be placed between Iain and Captain Ridley.

Under the cover of the slight rattle of plates between courses, I whispered, 'I have to see you. There are things to discuss.' He nodded imperceptibly, and carried on with the usual table talk. Passing me the sugar, he whispered; 'When, and where?'

'In the walled garden, after lunch. This mist helps, I don't want us to be seen.'

'I'll wait. A lifetime, if need be.' He looked across at the window. Mist still made a white curtain, masking everything.

'Well, Ridley, it doesn't look as if we'll get any shooting today.' Alasdair followed Ridley's glance. 'Damned mist. Sorry to drag you over here on a wild goose chase.'

'Not your fault. Some other time, perhaps, but if you don't mind, I'll be on my way.'

The garden in the mist was full of ghosts. They whispered and jostled and tried to deflect me and then, when I challenged, they sighed away like fallen leaves, or stiffened into bushes. But I knew I would find Hamish and I made my way unfalteringly towards the laurel bush. And because of the veil of mist, he came boldly, not waiting until I slipped under the tangled branches to the hidden door.

He took me in his arms, and his lips were urgent and demanding. I had to remind myself of the business in hand. When I had explained, he was silent, turning over in his mind the tactics to be adopted.

'Wait till the mist clears. It may be days, but I'm inclined to think we shall have a St Martin's Summer. Ride to the Tower, all three of you. When they have made their declaration, with you and me as witnesses, then I will motor you to the Sheriff's office, to make the declaration.'

'How will I get in touch with you?'

'Let Iain ride over to my lodgings, he knows where. You and Ishbel ride to the Tower, and we'll join you there.'

Still the mist would not release us. I felt Ishbel's impatience mounting, and to distract her I told her about the diary I had found.

'Let me see it,' she said excitedly. 'I've got enough Gaelic to make something out of it.'

I went to the lowboy, took the diary from the drawer, and placed it in Ishbel's hands. She stroked the dry, flaking leather almost reverently, and looked up, her eyes shining.

'Oh, Katharine,' she said. 'What a wonderful discovery. A whole missing slice of family history—another section of the picture, like piecing together a jig-saw puzzle ...'

And as we pored over the faded lines on the yellowing paper, the whole scene came alive to me, and I lived over again the last days that Catriona had spent at Allt-nam-Fearna ...

'... the English are come. They are courteous enough, but to see them sitting at my father's table while he rots in a bleak cell makes me burn inside and I have much ado not to poison their viands, though it is not they, but their masters, who treat us so ...

'... I can fight no longer, and I must give this love its rein. A month ago I would have scorned to admit that I would ever speak civilly to one of them. Now I tremble if he so much as glances towards me and I know that his passion for me is deep and true ...

'... at first he would not so dishonour me, and I had much ado to make him understand that in this barbarous land we made our own laws! Tonight he will come to me, and Kirsteen will witness our pledge ...

'... I am torn in my loyalty and yet my duty is to my husband, to follow him to the ends of the earth, if need be. I grieve that I will never see my father more. There is talk of amnesty and I must be gone ere he return, lest he discover what to him will seem treachery to our ancient lineage. Hamish has taken passage for me on a boat bound for the West Indies, where I will await him. Mayhap when the king enjoys his own again, we will return to Allt-nam-

*Fearna, and the child will take his rightful place among
the chieftains ...'*

'The child that cried in the night,' I said.

Ishbel looked up and nodded. 'That was how I knew,'
she said. 'Only a MacRaith hears that.'

'Is there more?' I asked. 'I wonder what happened in
the end.' Ishbel turned the page. 'They went to France,'
she said. 'It's here—at least, all that led up to it.'

*'... and I am to take the bairn, and go by the cliff steps
to the boat that waits ...'*

'I wonder why the plan miscarried,' I said.

'How do you know that?' Ishbel demanded. 'Or are you
just imagining the end of the story?'

'No.' I shook my head slowly. 'Something happened.
What it was, I don't know. But she went suddenly, and she
left her book, and her sampler, as if she had been sum-
moned.'

'What sampler?'

I nodded towards the adjacent room. 'The one that still
stands in the window,' I said. 'I mistook my way and
found myself in there one evening, I didn't mean to pry.
Why, what have I said?' For Ishbel was staring at me in
horror. 'You *couldn't*,' she whispered. 'That *was* Catriona's room, yes. But it was destroyed when the English
shelled the castle, and it wasn't rebuilt when the castle was
restored, because of the cliff fall. Katharine, there is no
room the other side of that wall.'

'Very well,' I said quietly. 'I accept that I must have
dreamed it. We can't explain these things, can we?' I
was too stunned to argue. I needed time to think. I must
find my own way in this strange half-world that seemed
to be closing round me. But I still had to know what
happened to Catriona.

Ishbel closed the book. 'That's all,' she said. 'She must

have gone abroad somewhere with her English captain. Maybe somewhere we have distant cousins descended from the bairn that cried in the night. We shall never know.'

'What happened to Allt-nam-Fearna—after the shelling, I mean?'

'There was a brother. After their father died, he came back and scraped along as best he might. The castle was a ruin and the estate confiscated. Some of the land was bought back later, but it's only a fraction of what it was.'

I began to see some light, but I didn't like what I saw. 'Alasdair,' I said. 'Tell me where he fits into the picture. Why is he referred to as the Young Laird? Why doesn't *he* stand to inherit Allt-nam-Fearna?'

'Because he's not in the direct male line. His mother was your father's sister. She married a MacRaith cousin, so that's how he retains the name. But you must not think too hardly of him, Katharine. He has run Allt-nam-Fearna ever since the Auld Laird could no longer get about. It's his whole life, and it was always his dream that the old lands would have come back. So you see, it would have meant much to him to see Iain and you, and your children ...' She tailed off lamely, and dropped her eyes at the fury which must surely blaze from mine.

'So *that* was it! I was to be thrown to the lions to further his ambition. Iain and Katharine, the puppet king and queen, and Alasdair the *Eminence Grise*. Well, I won't play his game. I'll see you married, and I'll leave Allt-nam-Fearna ...'

'Katharine—*no. Please*, Katharine. I shouldn't have told you. Please, please don't go away.' She was nearly distraught, and I took her by the shoulders and shook her gently. 'Ishbel, hush,' I said. 'It's not the end of the world, and I'll come back, I promise. And forgive me, I shouldn't spoil your joy. Come, now, and think how happy you and Iain will be. Look——' I pointed to the window. 'The mist is clearing. Perhaps tomorrow or the next day ...'

But for most of the night I lay dry-eyed, willing tears not to drench my pillow, sick with misery that he cared so little that he would exploit me so. I dared not weep. Once I allowed myself to give way, I would sink into a morass of misery; nor would tears be any relief, but a tearing shattering storm that would buffet me into insensibility. So for Ishbel's sake I must not weep. And for my own pride, I must not weaken, even though for the rest of my life my heart would mourn the murder of my love.

In the morning the sun shone. Rowan and birch dropped their few remaining leaves as a tribute to this strange bridal, as we rode out together.

There had been a moment of panic at breakfast.

'Such a beautiful day,' Aunt Agnes had said. 'Maybe I'll ride with you. We'll all be penned up here soon enough.'

I caught the alarm signal which flashed between Ishbel and Iain, then I breathed again when Iain said, 'But Aunt Agnes, you said last night that Alasdair was driving you to Kyle to visit old Morag. She'll be sad if you don't go—you know how she scrubs and bakes before one of your visits.'

'Ah, yes. Thank you for reminding me. Well, another day, maybe.'

So that removed the two principal obstacles.

When we reached the Tower, Iain and Captain Ridley waited. The little homespun ceremony had a moving dignity that brought a lump to my throat. *But soon, I told myself, it would be my turn. Hamish and I could not wait much longer to bring our love to fruition.* I dared

218

not meet his eyes, and I moved quickly to stand at his side. Hand in hand, Iain and Ishbel faced us, like partners in a set dance.

Iain spoke first. 'Cousin Katharine, Captain Ridley, be witness that I, Iain MacRaith, do take Ishbel MacRaith for my wife, and I swear to her that I will take no other while she shall live.'

Ishbel's words were a psalm of joy. 'Cousin Katharine, Captain Ridley, be witness that I, Ishbel MacRaith, will be a loving and faithful wife so long as I draw breath, and as I have known no man, so shall I know none but thee.'

She turned to Iain and he took her in his arms. *With no word between us, Hamish and I turned and passed through the broken archway and out on to the cliff. 'I could wish,' he said quietly, 'that we could have made like promises.'*

'When the time is right,' I said. 'Don't ask me why, because I can't tell you. But I will come to you, my dear, when Fate decrees.'

'Then let it be soon, my love. I have waited an eternity.'

And as we turned to walk towards the Tower, the wind carried the wail of the pipes. The sound brought Ishbel and Iain running, and I saw that the sound must have a significance for them.

'The Lament,' Iain said. 'We must go back.'

'Grandfather?' He nodded. And the tears I had refused to shed for my love now streamed down my face, mourning the passing of a man I had known for so short a time, but who had given me so much of love.

'Don't greet, lassie,' Phemie said gently. 'He was very old, and tired, and now he's away to the Land o' the Leal, we mustn't wish him back.'

We sat in the great hall, Aunt Agnes, Ishbel, Phemie, and myself, with Kirsteen, red-eyed, moving silently about her duties. We sat together and alone, each one with her own thoughts, waiting till the men came home. The tall, grave men, led by Alasdair and Iain, who had borne the Auld Laird on their shoulders to the burial ground on the hillside. Tomorrow, or the next day, I would go alone, to kneel and tell him my coronach, before I returned to the everyday world and its duties and mysteries.

I had the feeling that soon, very soon, I would be caught up and sent spinning away into a new orbit. The death of the Auld Laird had brought matters to a climax, and the waiting was done. Alone in my room, the previous night, I had spread out the cards; I had felt very near to Aunt Zen and her message seemed clear.

Always, the Tower, with its message of an impending cataclysm which would change my life, though I was powerless to do anything about it. Then the Lovers, the card of choice—not necessarily between two people, but between two paths. Again, if it were to signify Iain and Ishbel and Aunt Agnes, they too were at a crossroads. And coming last, an indication of the future, the Chariot, the card of movement and of achievement through one's own effort, rather than through inheritance. I knew now what I had to do.

The men were returning, and we moved towards the dining-room. Later, when the guests had left, we took our places in the hall, for the reading of the Auld Laird's will.

CHAPTER TWELVE

THE SWAYING of the train and the rhythm of wheels drew me gradually into a trance of recollection. Recollection of the evening and the night following the Auld Laird's funeral, when I had learned that jointly with Iain, Allt-nam-Fearna was now mine. Whether I would or no, I was shackled, as firmly as on the night I lay manacled on the Witches' Crag. I had the macabre fancy that on that dreadful night I could have regained my freedom by severing my arm from my body. Symbolically, I had done that very thing. By renouncing my right and leaving Allt-nam-Fearna, I had cut myself free at the cost of my love for Alasdair. Had he given the least hint, by word or look, that he wished me to stay, I would have done so. But he had raised an impenetrable barrier between us, a wall wherein there was no postern gate through which I might gain access to his heart.

The scene had been conventional enough, the gathering to hear of the disposal of the estate. The joint inheritance was no great surprise in view of Ishbel's revelations, though I was surprised that the division did not include Alasdair. But the expressed wish that Iain and I should unite the estate by our marriage came as a shock to me, until I realised that this will must have been made before I even came to Allt-nam-Fearna. In those brief days, Grandfather had realised where my heart lay, and his injunction had more force than any written directive. Had he guessed, I wondered, how things were between Ishbel and Iain?

I had waited for Iain to speak, but before he could do so, Alasdair addressed me.

'Well, Cousin Katharine, will you take this man . . .?'

'No.'

'Well, that at least is plain and to the point. Iain, what have you to say?' For answer, Iain crossed to Ishbel's side.

'Here is my allegiance,' he said.

I had expected furious reaction from Aunt Agnes, but she sat quiet and unprotesting, and I pitied her air of defeat. I came to sit beside her.

'Aunt Agnes, I'm sorry, really I am, but I could never marry where I did not love, nor could I take love that belonged to another.'

She smiled wanly, and pressed my hand. 'Dear child, don't distress yourself. I should not have tried to manipulate other people's lives.' She turned to where Ishbel sat, her hand clasped in Iain's as if seeking support and reassurance. 'Ishbel, my dear, I do wish you happiness, truly I do.'

Alasdair's interruption was brusque almost to the point of brutality.

'Where does that leave us, then? May one be permitted to know your plans, Cousin Katharine?'

'I must leave the legal formalities to you,' I said. 'But I wish to renounce my share of the estate. All I want is that I may still regard this as my home. As to income, I have enough for my needs, and I suppose the rents from my mother's estate. But what should I do with that——' I spread my hands helplessly. 'I know nothing of estate management. So I'm quite happy to leave it in your hands, as it has always been. Only—let me always come back when I need to.'

'You speak as if you planned to be away.' If only I could have read the thought behind Alasdair's words.

'I had originally planned to take up nursing. When I return to London, that is what I will do.'

We were still discussing the practicalities when Kirsteen ushered in James Ridley. Under cover of the serving of drinks to the men, I studied the two between whom I seemed to swing like a pendulum. Decisively, I now crossed my Rubicon. Unnoticed, I slipped away to my room. From the drawer where it had lain since Hallowe'en, I took the ring which Hamish had given Catriona, and slipped it on to my heart finger.

If my departure had passed without comment, my return down the main staircase did not. Alasdair saw me first, as I came down the first flight to the half-landing, where I paused as he raised his glass and said:

'To Katharine MacRaith, Lady of Allt-nam-Fearna.' The irony of his voice burned. 'For all your renunciation, dear cousin, you cannot alter that.'

'I've no wish to,' I said quietly. 'I am proud to be called thus and I give you my word that I will never disgrace the name.' And as I came down the last few stairs, James came forward and took me by the hand—the left hand, on which I wore his ring. His face lighted as he saw it and he led me forward.

'Miss MacRaith has done me the honour of consenting to be my wife.'

If there was a momentary flicker of pain across Alasdair's face, it was gone in the instant and his congratulation had a ring of sincerity. What the mask hid, I would never know.

It had been a strange day, perhaps one of the strangest in the history of Allt-nam-Fearna; a burial, a betrothal, and a marriage revealed.

Something had called me back from sleep, and I had sat

up, staring into the darkness. I had drawn back the curtains and opened the shutters before I went to bed, and now the moon probed with pale fingers. But I had become aware of another light in the far corner of the room. A vertical pencil that widened and spilled on to the floor, as from an open door. I told myself it was not possible. There was no door; there was no longer a room. Nevertheless I stood in the doorway, and stepped over the threshold, bridging nearly two hundred years.

Catriona looked up from her tapestry. 'You must help me,' she said.

'How can I?' I asked. 'You're a dream. This is not real.'

'No?' She stabbed the needle into the margin of the canvas and came to stand by my side, taking my hand in hers. I had expected that it would be chill, but it was warm and substantial as my own. She led me back to the doorway.

'Look,' she commanded. I saw my room, contained like a stage set within the framework of the doorway. The dying fire glowed in the grate; the moonlight had veered so that a long strand of light lay across the bed. The bed was not empty. A woman slept there. Myself.

'No!' I whispered. 'I won't believe it, I won't!'

'You've no choice. This time, you may return. But when your body journeys southward, you must yield it to me. I must find him, my Hamish. He went away, beyond the Border, and I'm weary of waiting for his return.'

The train swayed and chattered over points and I opened my eyes.

'You've been asleep,' James said gently. 'Pleasant dreams?' I shook my head. 'Well, never mind, my darling. Come back from wherever you were and we'll talk of happier things. We know so little of each other, really. And we've had so little time together.'

'Dear James.' I leaned across the space between us and took his hand. 'You've been so good to me, so helpful. I'd never have managed this journey without you.'

'Oh, yes, you would,' he said. 'You're not the clinging vine type. You've more strength of purpose than most women. Now,' he took out his watch. 'Lunch is being served, and you must be needing it.' Life shifted back on to its normal, prosaic plane.

Outside the window, the fields and trees and hedges hurried past, and in our own closed world we talked.

'Where are we, exactly?' I asked. 'We're over the Border, aren't we?'

'About five minutes ago.' He looked at me closely. 'Any regrets?'

'Not regrets,' I said slowly. 'Only a kind of sadness, as if I've left a part of myself behind.'

'Then you'll return,' he said. 'Some day. You can't ever escape, you know.'

'What do you mean?' I said, startled. How could he know of the despairing cry which still echoed in my mind, as if Catriona were calling me back. And how could he know that all last night I had not dared to sleep, fearing that if I did, Catriona would usurp my body and leave me in darkness. But James restored normality. 'It's just that once Scotland has captured your heart, you *must* go back, from time to time. I know I must.'

'Why were you there in the first place?' I asked. 'Is your business done? Or are you just on leave, as it were?'

'My official business—yes, that is concluded. One of these days I may be able to tell you about it. It had nothing to do with smuggling whisky. But that was only part of my reason for coming to Allt-nam-Fearna. That was in effect a pilgrimage. And now that I have met you, a fulfilment.'

He looked at me searchingly, as if assessing my possible reaction to his words. 'I've never told anyone my real reason for coming to Allt-nam-Fearna. I've hardly admitted it to myself. My—assignment—that was genuine enough, but it could have been done by anyone. I—well, I engineered the appointment, because I had to see the place.'

'To see whether it matched up with your mental picture?'

'You understand, then?'

'A little. The masquerade, when you wore the uniform of the English captain——'

'And you were Catriona——'

'I think we stepped back into the past. I know now what my own connection is, but yours?'

'There was a Captain James Ridley. One of the officers when the castle housed an English garrison. He was an ancestor. After the castle was bombarded—he was on board the ship in the Sound, and had to give the orders—he shot himself. Among his effects, which are still in the possession of my family, there was a miniature, for which you might have been the sitter, and a drawing of a castle. When I read in a guide-book about the restoration of a castle which has been destroyed by the English, I compared that drawing with the photograph, and I knew then that I had to go there, to find out what had happened. Because for as long as I could remember, I had been in love with the girl in the miniature. I'll show it to you, when we visit my people.'

'Was that why you—fell in love with me?' I asked.

'A little, at first. But now I know I love you, and you love me.'

'Yes, James,' I said. And I believed it. 'I wonder, though, why the captain shot himself. I mean, he had every reason to want to live: Catriona was waiting for him, with his son——'

'Where?' he demanded sharply. 'What do you know?'

'I found Catriona's diary, in a drawer—a secret drawer in my writing table. I slept in her room, and we walked in her garden, you and I.' But I did not tell him of the room next door. The room where I had talked with Catriona. The room which was never there.

'The diary was in Gaelic. I couldn't read it, but Ishbel had enough of the Gaelic to translate. Catriona and the English captain were secretly married—by declaration only, but that was valid in Scotland. She had a son, and she and the captain were planning to go away together. She was to take passage for the Indies. The diary ends there.'

'But the captain had an English wife,' James said. 'Was that the reason he shot himself? Poor Catriona, I wonder what happened to her in the end.'

'We shall never know,' I said. 'She disappeared completely after the castle was destroyed. But they say she will return.' I told him about the portrait.

'Two hundred years? Nineteen-nineteen? Perhaps we shall go back and see whether time has erased the veil. An artist will tell you that the original painting will always show through what has been superimposed.'

'We shall have to wait, then,' I said. And we went on to talk of other things, and our plans for the future.

Yet try as I would, I could not shake off the feeling of having left a part of myself at Allt-nam-Fearna. Oh, I knew I would return, but now I felt a desolation, as if I had been torn in two. And the irony of the dichotomy was that I had left behind the part of me which yearned for

Hamish, and the Katharine I now was, the real Katharine of the twentieth century, was pledged to the man for whom a sad, earthbound being pined and waited for all eternity.

But James loved me, and I would keep my side of the bargain. He must never know.

Nor must he ever know of that last shattering scene with Alasdair, when I had finally made plain my unalterable decision to leave Allt-nam-Fearna, and my renunciation of my rights in Iain's favour.

A scene all the more devastating to me in that it occurred in the garden I had come to love so much. Catriona's garden. My garden.

I had slipped away to make my own secret farewell to a beloved place, and because it was for me such a private thing, I wanted no one, not Ishbel, not Iain or James, and above all, not Alasdair himself.

But he was there. Watching, in the gathering dusk, half hidden by the laurel bush; watching as I made my pilgrimage of memory, collecting in my mind the things I would take away with me. And so, when I came to that corner of the garden, I was startled by the shadowy figure that detached itself and came towards me. I stood silent, almost defiant, and for a space we faced each other without speaking.

'So,' he said at last, 'you're running away, Katharine.'

'If you say so. I'm not prepared either to argue or give reasons. I am going away.'

'You say "I am going" rather than "I want to go".'

'Is there a distinction?'

'I rather think so, in your case. I feel there is a deeper reason for your going.'

'In that case,' I flashed, 'it's none of your affair, is it— *Cousin?*'

I sensed rather than saw the ironic twist of his lips at the deliberate emphasis. *Cousin*, no more, and don't you forget it, I thought.

'Very well, *Cousin* Katharine. I have no rights. That is what you are trying to say. But this marriage you contemplate—have you considered it fully?'

'Yes,' I said steadily, 'and I intend to go through with it.' He caught my wrist and the grasp was near agony as rough as that of the Night of the Rock.

'Do you *love* him?' The words were spoken in a low voice, with a slow deliberate emphasis of each word.

'Why else would I have accepted his offer of marriage?' I wrenched my wrist from Alasdair's grasp. 'What concern is it of yours, may I ask?'

'The natural concern of any man for someone as near in—well, as close a relation, and as young, who is taking a step so vital and far-reaching.'

I stopped my slow pacing and so did he, and we turned to face each other. In that moment, the future balanced on a pinhead and a breath would have caused a swing that would have changed three lives. Had he given me even the shadow of an indication that he wanted me to stay . . .

I waited, desperate with hope. I did not dare to speak, lest I should betray myself utterly. Alasdair looked down at me, and because it was so nearly dark, I could not read his face. He drew in his breath sharply, then swung away from me, almost in anger.

'If you are so determined, Cousin Katharine, then there's nothing I can say which would carry any weight with you.'

Nothing? Oh, Alasdair, did you but know. My heart wept, but I kept my voice steady. 'Are you trying to tell me that you have something against James Ridley? Something which might influence my decision? Something discreditable?' I asked bluntly. 'If so, why not have the decency to meet him face to face and tax him with it.'

Alasdair sighed. 'Oh, Katharine, what a spitfire you are! No, I don't know anything to his detriment. So far as I know he's a thoroughly decent man, and a good soldier. But you know so little about him. For that matter, we none of us know his background. It's all very hush-hush, whatever his reason is for being here at all. Will you believe me, my dear, when I say that my only concern is for your happiness?'

'Yes, Alasdair, I believe you.' I shivered a little, as if a wraith had brushed me. 'Let's go in now. I'm cold.' Cold and desolate in my heart, but you will never know ...

So here I was, rushing southwards with the same urgency as I had come to the north, so few weeks ago, and the very speed of the train imparted a new impetus to my life, for my arrival in London seemed like plunging into a maëlstrom of people and traffic and bustle, so unlike the slow quietness of Allt-nam-Fearna that I was left breathless and half scared. I was grateful for James's quiet organisation of taxi-cabs, porters, luggage, and all the business of travel.

I was grateful, too, for the quiet welcome to the tall house in Kennington, where Sarah and her 'dear ladies' made for me the only home I would know during the arduous months which followed.

CHAPTER THIRTEEN

'INTERREGNUM' WAS a word which puzzled me greatly when I was a child; but that was how I came to regard the time which elapsed between my leaving and my return to Allt-nam-Fearna. I would not have believed it possible to be so homesick for a place where I had lived for so short a time, yet every night or day, when I came off duty, in the half-conscious gap between sleep and waking, I wandered in the rooms and corridors of Allt-nam-Fearna, or in the policies, or out on the windswept cliff top to Calum's Tower. There were times when I was tempted to throw in my hand altogether, but pride would not let me do that and I set my teeth and got on with the task I had set myself. My training followed such conventional lines that the narration would be tedious, and my life settled into a routine at times arduous and exhausting, so that my social life was all but non-existent. I lived in a limbo, neither happy nor unhappy. Waiting.

I saw comparatively little of James, since he had to re-join his unit, and his duties were still something of a mystery to me. I reproached myself that I did not miss him more acutely, but I strove to keep my letters free from any such implication.

Letters from Ishbel and Aunt Agnes were a tenuous life-line still linking me with Allt-nam-Fearna, but I would not trust myself even to return for a holiday, and I forced myself to endure a self-imposed exile.

And then ... 'the lamps are going out all over Europe ...' No one believed it at first. It just wasn't possible. 'Can't afford a war ... all over by Christmas ...' And they went off, singing the music hall songs and the marching songs, and behind all the singing and the joking lay the grim reality of a life-and-death struggle.

James refused to let me go to the terminus to see him off, and for that I was grateful. We said goodbye in the prim seldom-used room on the first floor known as 'Mama's Drawing-room'. Outside, the hot sun burned the smooth turf; but they had exchanged their whites for khaki, and it would be the crack of a rifle, not the bat, which might be the last thing they heard, those players of the long summer days.

'Goodbye, my Catriona.' James kissed me gently, passionately, and I knew that my kiss returned no ardour. 'When this is all over, my darling ...'

'Yes, my dear,' I said. 'God go with you. Come back safely.' And beneath the sincerity of my words, I sensed the mockery. In England, in France, in Germany, and Austria, women in towns and villages were saying the same words that would not, could not, be true for all of them.

Once again, it was Hallowe'en, and in spirit I was back at Allt-nam-Fearna, remembering. Where were they all, the men who had joined in the charade and the traditional games? There had been no party for me this year. I had come off duty and dropped exhausted into bed, and slept.

I don't know what time it was when I woke. But I *was* awake. Wide awake; and I was sitting up in bed, which was alongside the window. I drew back the heavy curtain and stared out into the darkness. The clouds parted, and the sky glowed with a clear, white light that sent a broad shaft downwards like a pathway. Men were marching, men in kilts, and I heard the distant wail of the pipes. They marched away into the darkness, all except two. One lay on the ground, and I saw that it was Iain. The one who knelt by him was Alasdair, who turned his face towards me. But Iain's eyes were closed.

The light faded, and I was left weeping in the darkness.

I stood outside the door to Matron's office, the telegram clutched in my hand, and my heart jumping with apprehension. It was going to be difficult to explain, I thought. The telegram was from Ishbel and bore but two words: 'Please come.' But I *knew*.

Matron looked at me keenly. 'You wish to return home, MacRaith?'

'Please,' I said. 'I have some leave due to me, and if I might take it now.' She inclined her head. 'You may. I hope it is not serious trouble.'

'I think it is. But thank you for letting me go.'

And so, for the second time, I came to Allt-nam-Fearna.

Everything was grey. The skies, the stones of Allt-nam-Fearna, the fear in my mind, and Ishbel's face when she greeted me. She didn't speak, but as I took her in my arms, she bowed her head on my shoulder and I felt the wracking sobs which shook her. I knew, then, that I had dreamed truly.

A slight sound drew my attention and I looked up, to see Aunt Agnes enter the Guardroom. Over Ishbel's head our eyes met, and I read the pity and anguish in hers. She did not weep, but the compression of her lips showed the inner struggle for self-control. At last she spoke.

'Thank you for coming, Katharine dear. How long can you stay?'

'I've two weeks' leave of absence,' I said. 'I was granted an extra week on compassionate grounds.' Aunt Agnes looked at me searchingly.

'How did you know?' she asked. 'We only heard two days ago.'

'I just—*knew*,' I said simply. 'I *saw* them.' And I told her about the Hallowe'en vision. But the question I wanted to put stuck in my throat. I had to know, but I did not dare to ask. Aunt Agnes's next question gave me the answer.

'You said "*them*", Katharine. Who else—Alasdair? But we've no news of him at all. No letters, not even a field postcard.'

'He's alive,' I said. 'Don't ask me how I know. But he is *alive*.'

Ishbel stirred in my arms. 'I'm sorry, Katharine. This is no welcome for you.' She sat up, and fumbled for a handkerchief. 'But I can't believe it yet. He's gone, and I'll never see him again.'

'Ishbel, dear, you must go back to bed, you know Doctor Laidlaw said you were to rest.' I glanced at Aunt Agnes and she nodded imperceptibly.

'Come, darling,' I said firmly. 'Nurse MacRaith says back to bed for you.'

Ishbel stood up, a little shakily, and managed a tremulous smile. 'Don't bully the patient. I'll go quietly.'

'I'll call Kirsteen,' Aunt Agnes said quickly. 'You've had a long and tiring journey, Katharine. You'll be needing a meal.'

When we were alone, after I'd worked my way through a truly lavish Scottish tea, we talked. Aunt Agnes wasted no words but came to the point.

'Katharine, will you come home? You're needed here now, and there will be work you can do—I'll tell you of that later. What are your immediate plans?' She leaned over and took my hand. 'Forgive me, child. I should have remembered that you have your own anxieties. What news of Captain Ridley?'

'Very little. Just a field postcard that he's well, but of course, I've absolutely no idea where he is. I've left word with Sarah to forward letters.'

'Poor child,' she said. 'I wonder how long it will be now to your wedding day?'

Unwillingly, my gaze was drawn to the stiff figure of the Redcoat, still on guard in that dark recess. And was it only the mist of the November day seeping into the castle, or did Catriona stand at his side, waiting . . . waiting? I shook myself free of the fantasy.

'I think we must wait now until the war ends,' I said. 'Naturally we both hope it will not go on for long; in London they were hopeful at first, but I'm not so sure.' I shrugged in resignation. 'All we can do is wait, the lot of all women in time of war.'

'We need not wait with our hands in our laps,' Aunt Agnes said. 'Of course, now that Iain——' For a moment her composure all but crumpled, but only the slightest wavering in her voice betrayed her emotion. 'Now Allt-nam-Fearna is yours, Katharine, whether you will or no, and I do not think you will shirk your responsibilities.'

'I won't let you down, Aunt Agnes,' I said quietly. 'What do you wish me to do?' She sat up straighter, and began to explain her plan.

'Here we are, two—now three—women alone in this great place. We could, with a little expenditure and some co-operation in the right quarters, turn it into a convalescent home. There will be men, shattered in mind if not in body, who will need care, and rest, and quiet. We can give them those things. And you, with your training, will be doing as great a service as if you were emulating

Florence Nightingale on the battlefield. Think about it, Katharine.'

'I don't need to,' I said. 'I cannot see any finer use for Allt-nam-Fearna.'

That night I slept once more in my old room. I say 'slept' but it was short enough rest, for shortly after midnight Aunt Agnes came to me.

'I'm sorry to disturb you, Katharine, but I think you should come to Ishbel.'

'I'll come at once,' I said. 'I'm used to being called at all hours. Is it possible to send for Doctor Laidlaw? I think it's better we should—and Phemie, if she's available.'

But in spite of all we could do, Ishbel miscarried.

In normal circumstances, her recovery would have been rapid, since she was of a strong constitution, and the pregnancy barely three months. But she had no will to live, and though her body clung tenaciously to life, her spirit died. It was heartbreaking to see the gay, lively girl transformed into a creeping shadow.

'Oh, Katharine,' she whispered. 'There's nothing left of him. Even my baby—it never even stirred.' And because there was no comfort in words, all I could do was hold her close and let her weep out her grief.

And then they came, the tired, broken men. In ones and twos, sometimes as many as a dozen in a contingent. Some of them would never return to the Front; some would limp for the rest of their days; some would never be sure of what went on in the world around them, but would wake in the darkness shaking and calling to comrades who would never hear.

We worked like slaves, Phemie, Doctor Laidlaw, Aunt Agnes, Kirsteen—and many more, drawn from the crofts, and others, grateful for a respite from the air raids now beginning to terrify the people of the south. 'Over by Christmas' was an unfilled dream, and gritting our teeth we settled down to endure.

Then, after long months, there was news of Alasdair. He had been taken prisoner, and had escaped and rejoined his regiment. He was coming home on leave—and two days later I received a telegram from James, arriving in London for three brief days; might he visit me at Kennington?

So as I travelled southwards, Alasdair returned to Allt-nam-Fearna. At what point on the journey did the trains pass each other? Was I thankful that I would be spared the tension of a meeting that would highlight my divided loyalty?

Nevertheless, a brief respite from Allt-nam-Fearna was welcome. There was still the sense of invasion. Catriona was not yet at rest, and the strange half-dreams persisted. As it had on that other night before I had left Allt-nam-Fearna, the door that did not exist had opened, and again Catriona beckoned.

'See,' she said, 'the English have returned. I knew they would.' And then, though I knew I was asleep in my bed, she and I together moved between the rows of iron beds in the dormitories created in the spacious rooms of the castle.

She seemed to be searching. 'He's not here,' she said. 'But he *will* come back. He must. And then——' she turned to me, '—then, it will be time for you to go.'

Once again, James and I sat in 'Mama's Drawing-room' and talked. Of everything, and nothing, avoiding always the war and all it had done to all of us.

'Bad show about MacRaith,' James said. 'What about Mrs MacRaith—will she remarry, do you think?' I shook my head.

'There was never anyone but Iain. There never will be. But she helps me, and the men like her. She sits with them, and reads to them, or writes letters for them. But all the time, she's just *killing* time.'

'Poor girl. She was so gay and pretty.' He took me in his arms, then, and said, 'But I have you, my Catriona, and for that I'm eternally thankful. You go with me always, and when this sickening business is over——'

'I'll be waiting for you, my darling. James,' I took his hand, and held it in both of mine. 'I know you can't tell me where you're going or what you do, but there's danger, isn't there? I mean more than just the ordinary everlasting danger in war. Something special.'

'Yes, my darling. More than ordinary. But it's my job. I've been doing it for years; even in peace time, there's a war going on. This had been looming for a long time. When I was at Allt-nam-Fearna, it wasn't just idle curiosity about smuggling that took me out with the Customs men. There are deep waters in many of the sea lochs, hidden, secret places where submarines could lurk, or men come ashore in the mist. And now there is other work for me— the gathering of information in strange places——'

'You mean behind the enemy lines?' I whispered. And in my mind I could see the card in Aunt Zen's spread. The Hermit. Alone, seeking, always seeking. 'There is always danger, isn't there, James?'

He bowed his head in acknowledgement, then reached into his inner pocket.

'I have an amulet,' he said. In the palm of his hand lay the miniature of Catriona—or Katharine. The colouring, the hair, even the dress which I had worn to the ball. And once again I said: 'God go with you.'

With an abrupt change of subject, James asked, 'When do you return to Allt-nam-Fearna, Katharine?'

238

'Whenever I choose,' I answered. 'I know I can stay here with Sarah and the Newmans for as long as I wish, but of course, Allt-nam-Fearna is now my real home. Why do you ask?'

'I have a favour to ask.'

'Of course. It's granted.'

'Before you even know what it is, my trusting Katharine?'

'I know you would ask nothing dishonourable of me. Tell me.'

'May I come once more to Allt-nam-Fearna, please? It has been so much a part of me, for so long, even though I did not know where it was. I would like to take one more photograph, and one more mental image.'

'When shall we travel?' I asked.

And so we returned to Allt-nam-Fearna, James and I; we were greeted by Aunt Agnes and Ishbel—and Alasdair. My surprise must have been manifest because, after the initial meeting and exchange of the usual gambits, he said, 'Well, Cousin Katharine? So you returned, after all. Do you regret it?'

'Why should I regret returning home?' I challenged. 'This is where I belong. This is my home—and *yours*, Cousin Alasdair.'

'That remains to be seen,' he said, and turned to leave the Guardroom. And for the first time I saw the stout walking stick he used, and the limp.

When the door had closed behind him, I said, 'I didn't know Alasdair had been wounded.'

'He mentions it as little as possible,' Aunt Agnes said. 'But he has to face the fact that he will not return to the firing line.'

'What will he do?'

'Oh, he won't be thrown on the scrap heap yet, thank the Lord. I doubt if we could endure having him hirpling around angrily—he doesn't take kindly to any limitation. No, he'll be away to Strathpeffer soon, as an instructor, training officers.'

But afterwards, I thought. When all this mess is cleared up, and we all start the business of rebuilding our lives? But the mists obscuring the future would not clear, and I must wait. I was almost thankful when James's leave came to an end, because there was no lessening of the tension between him and Alasdair.

The days, the months, and the years dragged on. This incredible war, which they said could not last, endured, and so did we, Aunt Agnes, Phemie, Ishbel, and all the other women who waited, and hoped. And I had the unseen enemy, who watched and waited. There was no personal animosity. Catriona was with me more and more, biding her time, until I would, in effect, leave the door open so that she could slip back on to another plane, and use my body as a means of reuniting herself with her captain. For a time I was able to hold her invasion at bay by undertaking night duty, until Phemie put her foot down.

'Katharine, my dear, you're wearing yourself out. You haven't slept properly for months now. You really must not drive yourself like this.'

We were drinking coffee in my room, and although I had dozed through the day, I was still dazed with fatigue, and would gladly have let Phemie or one of the other nurses work my duty through the long hours of the night. Phemie was studying me keenly.

'Tell me,' she commanded. 'There is some reason, is there not?'

'Yes,' I said. And told her the whole story. She was thoughtful for a space, then she said, 'This must be settled,

Katharine, once and for all. I will help you all I can, but you have to face a great danger—alone.'

'You do understand, then? You see, at first I thought the danger was physical, particularly when I was nearly drowned. I really thought I had an enemy who wanted to drive me from Allt-nam-Fearna. But afterwards, when the door opened into the room that no longer exists, I was really afraid. That was why I ran away, to London.'

Phemie's next question hit me as surely as if she had struck me physically. 'Why did you become engaged to Captain Ridley when it is Alasdair you really love?'

'You *know*?' I whispered. She nodded.

'Does anyone else—I mean, is it obvious? I thought I'd concealed it, but it's true. I shall always love him.'

'But you will marry Captain Ridley?'

'I've given my word. And Alasdair does not love me.'

'Oh, but he does, lassie. He pines for you. That is why he stays away so much. But he has his code of honour, as you do. He will not take away the betrothed from another man.'

Fatigue undermined my self-control, and I could fight the tears no longer.

'What can I do, Phemie? I'm torn in two. You must believe me when I say that I do truly love James—*when I am Catriona*. Can you understand that? Yes, of course you do. And you know what I must do, don't you?'

'Yes, my dear. I will help you all I can on this plane, and you will be helped on your journey——'

'Aunt Zen? She knew about the danger. Yes, she will take care of me.'

Phemie nodded. 'You see,' she said, 'Catriona must be released, but first she must be convinced that she will never find her captain on this plane. You say that the earlier Captain Ridley took his own life.' I nodded. 'Poor

241

soul,' she said. 'Had he but waited, he would have been reunited with his Catriona.'

A new fear gripped me. 'Phemie, does she wait now for —James?'

'I think she does,' Phemie said.

'For how long?' I asked.

Phemie's expression was guarded. 'That I cannot tell you, lassie.' She stood up and collected cups and plates. The little activity was commonplace enough but I knew she was planning. She took the tray to the table in the corridor, then returned, closing the door behind her.

'Now,' she commanded, 'You go to your bed. And *sleep*.'

Sleep. The one thing for which I longed so desperately. Even the coffee I had just drunk had barely touched the fringe of the fatigue that was always with me.

'Sleep,' Phemie repeated, and her firmness gave me courage. I knew she would not leave me defenceless.

'I will give orders that you must on no account be disturbed, and I will keep watch myself. Because you're so desperately tired, you will move quite easily to the other plane. Take careful note of all you see, and above all, hold in your mind a picture of the way back. Remember that, Katharine. *The way back ... the way back ... the way back ...*' Her voice was receding and I was drifting into sleep ...

I moved about the room purposefully, collecting the small belongings I would take with me. 'As little as possible,' Hamish had said. 'Nothing that anyone will notice. The clothes you are wearing, no more, and I will see that there is all you need waiting for you on board—it shall be the best, my sweet, to make up to you for all you are giving up for my sake.'

'It will be worth it,' I answered. 'Don't you know,

242

Hamish, that I would walk barefoot through the world to be with you.'

'It will be a long, hard road,' he said soberly. 'We shall have to live in poverty, in obscure places, and maybe never return to these shores.'

'I care not, so long as I'm with you—and the bairn.' I rocked the cradle gently with my foot. 'My little English Hamish.'

'My little Scottish James,' Hamish teased me. 'Now listen, carefully, my darling, because the timing is important. The bombardment is timed for noon, two days hence. I should not be telling you this, but for you I'd betray any trust, God forgive me.'

'But surely they'll not be so barbarous as to destroy the castle with living souls in it?' I stared round at the possessions I had loved so much, soon to be blown away like chaff on a winnowing floor. 'Must it be done?' I said, 'Alltnam-Fearna has stood for centuries, a fortress, a stronghold——'

'It's just because it is so strong and so defensible that it must be destroyed,' he said. 'Forgive me, my darling, but I serve the Hanoverian, and we must keep the Stuarts from regaining control of Scotland, else an invasion of England would certainly follow.'

'And why not?' I flashed. 'We're as good as you are, bad as we are! But I'll not argue, because I've gone over to the enemy already. Tell me what I must do.'

'Tomorrow, at noon, because the tide is right, go to the garden-house as usual—you've done it so often that nobody will question you. But slip out of the far door, on the cliff path, and down the Fisherwomen's Stairs to the little landing-stage. There will be a skiff there to take you to the fishing boat in the loch beyond the headland. The master will take you across to Dublin and I'll join you

there. I've booked passage to the Indies and there we'll take a boat to America. It's a country where there is room for all. There, my darling, we will make a new life for ourselves ...'

... it lacked but ten minutes to noon. I sat at my little table, and wrote in my diary for the last time. I debated whether I should take it with me, then, reluctantly, I returned it to its secret place in the table. I would have no time from now on for keeping a diary. And for the last time, I looked out on my little garden that I had loved so much, and where, secretly, I had kept tryst with Hamish. I looked at the garden-house, where we had made our vows in Kirsteen's presence, and where we had loved ...

She was there now, struggling with one of the Redcoats. He seemed to be telling her something, rather than indulging in the usual amorous attempt. But he might as well have saved his breath, because Kirsteen had no English. She wrenched herself free and started to run towards the house, but he caught her again, and roughly bundled her ahead of him, through the door in the wall leading to the policies. I could hear her screaming, but I knew she could deal with any Redcoat, and now I must think only of Hamish and my escape. Tomorrow would be too late.

I slipped like a ghost down the winding stairs, to the Guardroom; to my surprise, it was empty, and no sounds of accoutrements rattling, bugles, voices, or military hubbub to which I had become accustomed, echoed from the outer courtyard. Silence brooded over the whole of Alltnam-Fearna. I might have been the only person alive within its walls. I and the bairn.

I stole across the walled garden, bent aside the branches of the laurel bush and dragged open the door to the garden-house. In the darkness I felt my way to the outer door, out into the sunlight on the cliff path, and started the slow, careful descent of the steep, narrow steps, cut in the rock face, over three hundred of them, up which the women carried the loaded creels.

I saw the first flash, and took it for the sun's reflection from a burnished surface on board the ship anchored in the Sound. The thunder that followed came out of a clear sky which had not promised a storm; the hail of stones and small boulders had me crouching in alarm close to the cliff face, wondering what had been the cause of the landslip. The next flash blinded me, and the last thing I saw was the whole earth erupting in one gigantic explosion ...

... I was falling ... falling ... helpless and unable to grasp at anything in the misty void ... then I heard Phemie's voice ... '... the way back. Remember that, Katharine. The way back ...'

But something—no, *someone*, barred my way. I stood on the threshhold of my room, helpless, unable to move, while Catriona glided ahead of me towards the bed where I lay. Phemie sat by my bed, and I saw her stretch out her hand and take my wrist, as if she felt for my pulse. I sensed her alarm, and I shared it. For I knew that if the entity which drifted like a cloud across the room could seep into my living body, I was lost in eternity, to wander in the outer darkness.

I watched in fascinated horror as Catriona struggled to take over completely. She seemed to melt away, and the form on the bed stirred uneasily, as if it would move and become a living person. It half sat up, then fell back on the pillow as if the effort had been beyond its strength. Phemie turned her head, and I saw her lips move. But her voice was so far away that I could not catch the words. Yet they must have carried beyond the walls of the room, for the door opened and Kirsteen came in. She stared in terror at the bed, then ran from the room, to return with Aunt Agnes and Doctor Laidlaw. All this time Phemie held my wrist, nor did she ever relinquish her hold in the hours which followed, though how long that was I had no means of knowing, for time as I knew it had ceased to be. I could move freely enough, but only in the part of Allt-nam-Fearna which no longer had any existence in the present. The open door was an impassable barrier, framing a scene where people moved and talked and consulted, and Catriona's spirit strove to move the body she inhabited. Strove in vain. Once she managed to raise herself and look across the room at me. Her lips moved, and in some strange way the message became clear in my mind.

'Help me ... help me ... Hamish, tell Hamish he must come to me.' Her face seemed to change, to take on an expression of malevolence. 'Go away, Katharine ... Go away ... go away ... go away ...'

The scene dimmed as the light faded. I saw Kirsteen enter with a lamp, and still Phemie sat holding my wrist, as if it made a kind of lifeline. And then the door opened again, and Alasdair entered. He limped across the room, and stood looking down at me. Then he stooped, and took my hand, the one which lay limp and flaccid on the counterpane.

'Come back, Katharine.' His voice reached me, clear and commanding. 'Do you hear me, Katharine? Come back.' And I had to obey. But how was I to displace Catriona?

... I was walking along the bank of a wide river. The same river where I had once walked. And with me walked Aunt Zen—and Catriona. There was no malice now, only a look of great sadness and resignation. I turned to her and took her hand. 'He will come to you, Catriona. I don't know when, but he will return to you. He loves you for all eternity. Be patient a little longer.' She smiled, and was gone.

'It's time to return, Katharine.' Aunt Zen, the young, ever-lovely girl she had once been, guided me gently towards the light that shone so blindingly that I could see nothing, only hear Alasdair's voice. 'Come back, Katharine.'

I opened my eyes.

'Katharine. My bonny wee thing. Thank God.' He held my hand, then leaned over and gently kissed my cheek. 'The war is over, my dear. Your war, and the war outside. Your James will come to claim you soon.'

But the days dragged slowly by, and still he did not come. Only a buff form, with the sinister, indefinite statement, '... missing ...' forwarded by his elder sister, named as next of kin. Her letter to me was kind and understanding. I strove with words, but I knew that there was no comfort, though I did sincerely offer her my love and sympathy in her loss. It was, did she but know it, greater than mine.

I lived now in a limbo of uncertainty and divided loyalty, tormented by guilt. My love for Alasdair seemed an unforgivable betrayal of a man for whom I had the deepest respect and admiration—but not that unpredictable vital flame which was, for me, the very essence of love. And trapped by my need to stay loyal to James, I wronged Alasdair by the denial of that love. Yet I knew he would not have it otherwise, because to him, loyalty and integrity mattered above all, and I would not offer him a tarnished love.

'He may come back, Katharine.' Aunt Agnes tried to solace my misery. 'Even now, after all these months, men are making their way back by devious paths, after being lost in the hinterland of war.'

'If only I *knew*, Aunt Agnes. If only I knew. All I can do is wait. And I may never know.'

'What will you do?' The straight, uncompromising question pulled me up with a jerk. What *would* I do. It was a difficult question to answer.

'I don't know, Aunt Agnes. I have the feeling that I must wait, that there is nothing I *can* do. Whatever it is, it will come to me. When I was—well, when I took that journey, that again was something I *had* to do. Part of my destiny, if you like. What the next step is'—I shrugged my shoulders—'I simply don't know. I suppose I must learn patience.'

I spent much time alone. I went riding, sometimes taking my sketchbook, at other times, just sitting, studying the everlasting, ever-changing landscape. Sometimes Alasdair rode with me, and always we avoided the subject of what the future would be. Nor did I speculate upon how Alasdair would plan his life. The whole situation was anything but simple. With the death of Iain, Allt-nam-Fearna had of necessity reverted to me, but it was obvious that I needed guidance, since I knew nothing of the running of the estate.

It was a strange, cloistered existence. Just the four of us, Ishbel, Alasdair, Aunt Agnes, and myself, with Kirsteen in the background, and the occasional visit from Phemie and Doctor Laidlaw. They in particular watched me closely, not because they had any doubts as to my sanity, but from a natural concern for my health and well-being.

Winter passed, and spring, and the outside world was filled with rejoicing and celebration. Decorations and processions brought colour and pageantry to the cities ... but in the background, some wept for those who would never return; some waited for those who *might* return ...

'Murdo's away to Kyle,' Ishbel said. 'Will there be any messages, Katharine?' I shook my head. 'There's little enough that I want—or need,' I said. She smiled understandingly, and because the day was fine and warm, we sat in Catriona's garden.

The garden had not altered at all. Only our lives had changed. Ishbel must have read my thoughts for she said, 'It seems only yesterday that we first walked and talked here, Katharine, yet nothing will ever be the same again. Tell me, what really happened when you—when you were gone away from us? Did you know, you lay like a marble statue for days? You were breathing, and part of the time your eyes were open, but you simply *weren't there*. It was utterly uncanny.'

'I wasn't there. And yet I saw it all,' I said. 'I think if it hadn't been for Phemie's vigilance, I might have given up, and Catriona would have taken over completely, and because her spirit was not strong enough to animate my body, I would have died. And even then she wouldn't have been at rest, because somehow it was only when she took possession of me that I really *wanted* to marry James. But I must still wait. He may come back.'

Ishbel looked at me shrewdly. 'What will you do then? Will you marry him, Katharine?'

I bowed my head as the tears welled into my eyes. 'I daren't think,' I whispered. 'I can't *wish* him dead, I can't wish him *here*. I'm trapped.'

'Do you—dream, I suppose you'd call it?'

'No,' I said. 'I sleep so deeply that when I wake I simply don't know whether my other self has wandered. But I *shall* be guided, somehow, some time and, I hope, soon, because life must go on, and I must be part of it. I must wait for the mist to clear.' My words might almost have been prophetic. Murdo came through the main door to the garden carrying a packet of letters, and for the first time for many months one was for me.

A thick letter, in a large envelope, with a German stamp.

And because I have a pernickity objection to a carelessly ripped envelope, I searched for scissors in my work bag, and disciplined myself to slit the envelope tidily. It contained two more sealed envelopes. One, addressed to Miss Katharine MacRaith, was in an unfamiliar handwriting. The other, with simply the name 'Katharine', was in James's writing. I held one in each hand, uncertain as to which I should open first.

Carefully, slowly, I slit the letter from James ...

'My Darling Girl,

When and if you receive this, I shall have reached my destination.

First, my dearest one, I take with me, for all eternity, the remembrance of your sweet companionship and the peace you brought to a troubled and bewildered soul. I know now that I shall not return to Allt-nam-Fearna, either in body or spirit, and that the destiny of two uneasy spirits will be fulfilled at last. I know, too, that for you there will be a temporary drawing aside of the veil, and that you will understand. Because I think you know, as I do, that we were not destined for each other on the plane on which we met, but that somehow your destiny and mine were bound up, and through you, Catriona and the James Ridley of two hundred years ago will be united. There were times, my love, when you *were* Catriona, and then we truly loved each other. But now is the parting of the ways, and you go to your real love, and I to mine. Each of us is grateful for the encounter on this plane; each of us is grateful to have found fulfilment.

The love I take with me into the shadows is sweet and gentle; the love I send you is pure and true. May the rest of your life bring you happiness.

James'

Folded into the letter was the miniature of Catriona.

Through a film of tears, I reread the letter, then folded it, and slid it back into its envelope. I opened the other letter. It was dated July 1919, so it had taken some weeks to reach me. The address was 'Schloss Grülenberg', and the signature, 'Amelia von Grülenberg'.

'Dear Miss MacRaith,

I am only now able to send you the enclosed letter entrusted to me by Captain James Ridley, and I feel some explanation is necessary.

I am an Englishwoman, the widow of a German land-owner; until the outbreak of war, I had maintained a correspondence with the Ridley family, friends of long standing. The war, naturally enough, was doubly distressing to me, since it threw up a divided loyalty, but I continued to live quietly and unmolested in my home near Cologne . . .

'. . . some weeks before the Armistice was signed, word was brought to me by one of my servants that there was an Englishman hiding in the woods, and that he was badly wounded. The girl led me deep into the forest, and there, in a rough shelter, I found James Ridley. He had managed to reach Grülenberg with considerable difficulty. All he wanted was the chance to rest till he was well, but was desperately anxious not to cause me any embarrassment, though he trusted me not to give away his whereabouts. Naturally, I insisted that he be brought to the Schloss, which was big enough to hide a regiment. At first he was very reluctant, but at last I overcame his scruples.

'It was not difficult to conceal his presence, but I soon realised that he was dying. I nursed him for about a month, and when there was talk of an end to the war, I hoped it would be possible to get him repatriated, but he died on All Souls Day, nine days before the Armistice was signed.

'. . . there were times when he imagined he was back at Allt-nam-Fearna, which must be rather similar to Grülenberg. He called often for Catriona, and sometimes for Katharine. I think he knew he was dying, and he gave me the letter, which he had written sometime previously. I promised him that when the war ended, I would send it to you as soon as communications were restored.

'. . . I send you my sympathy, and I hope that when it is again possible and even desirable to travel to Germany, you will visit me. The captain rests in our private vault, and later I will have a memorial tablet placed on the chapel wall, in memory of a brave Englishman. I do not know how much you knew of his work, but he took the most fantastic risks to obtain information which might be of use to the Allies. May he rest in peace . . .'

I looked up. I was alone in Catriona's garden. I had not been aware of Ishbel's silent, tactful withdrawal, but I was grateful for the solitude. I went through the gate in the wall, and walked carefully by the cliff path to the head of the old steps, now securely fenced off, with a small platform and a seat. I watched the setting sun dip towards the calm sea, and the lines of a poem sang in my mind.

'Sunset and evening star, and one clear call for
   me ...
'... may there be no sadness of farewell, when I
   embark ...'

'Goodbye, dear James,' I whispered. And symbolically,
the little fishing boat rounding the headland carried into
the sunset the two restless spirits, now at rest.

I turned and went back to the castle, to look for Alasdair.

I found him at last, in Catriona's Gallery. He was standing in the window embrasure, gazing at the sunset. The
very last rays shone red, through the window, to bring
Catriona's portrait to startling life. We turned, and stared
at her face.

The veil had gone. And in the background stood the
shadowy figure of the Redcoat ... And I remembered that
it was once again Hallowe'en ...

Wordlessly, we turned to each other, and Alasdair held
out his arms to me.

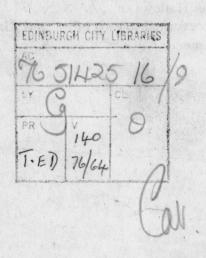

EDINBURGH CITY LIBRARIES

AC 76 51425 16 /9

LY G   CL

PR   V 140   θ

T. ED   76/64

Cat.